Book 2 of the Pawns Series

Fallout

by doc mike

Can't Put it Down
BOOKS

Book 2 of the Pawns Series
Fallout
Copyright 2020 by Mike Michael

ISBN: 978-0-9994623-6-2

Published by
Can't Put It Down Books
An imprint of
Open Door Publications
2113 Stackhouse Dr.
Yardley, PA 19067

Cover Design by Eric Labacz,labaczdesign.com

This novel is dedicated to my wife

Forward

September 11, 2001

American life changed forever on the morning of September 11, 2001. The terrorists hijacked four commercial jetliners, crashing two into the World Trade Center towers in New York City. Overall more than 3,000 people died in the terrorist attacks September 11, 2001.

America was suddenly at war. The government shut down all air traffic for two days as fighter jets patrolled the skies. National Guard troops were deployed on the streets in New York City and Washington, D.C. The major stock exchanges were closed.

The event traumatized the nation. As the 21st century began, most Americans had thought their country virtually unassailable. With the Cold War long over, America's status as the world's lone superpower seemed secure. But as millions watched the catastrophe unfold on television, it was clear that the country was vulnerable in ways that most people never imagined.

I want to tell you a story of what happened after the 9/11 attacks. What if, unknown to the general public, the crash foiled a massive financial coup on the USA? Remember, this story is a fictional supposition, supported by no known facts.

Of course, you can decide for yourself if any of it really happened.

Chapter 1

Four days after September 11, 2001
Franklin Lakes

As usual the five-foot, ten-inch redheaded man, known to his colleagues as Red, was the first to arrive. He proceeded to the library and found someone new. The young, blond-haired man with steel-blue eyes, was the son of his former boss. Red shook hands with the young man but didn't know what to say to him about the loss of his father, so he silently headed to the bar to prepare himself a drink.

A short time later Red's associates, Max and Numbers joined them in the library. Last to arrive was the small but wiry Cyn. Unlike the others, he did more than just silently shake the young man's hand.

"I'm so sorry to hear of the death of your father and one of the finest men I have ever known," he told him, patting him on the back before heading to the bar to get his own drink.

When they all held drinks in their hands, Cyn said, "Let's raise our glasses to one of the most brilliant minds in the criminal world."

"Hear, hear," was the unanimous response. But a memorial service was not the real reason for the meeting, and Cap would have been disappointed in them all if they had not quickly gotten down to business. His son knew that, and wasted no time taking over the conversation.

"We set up one of the biggest coup ever, and we were interrupted by some covert operation of Osama bin Nadel, the man we had built up to gather the followers of the Ali Ki," he said, summing up the fiasco that the world was already coming to call "9/11." The date would always have a different meaning for these five men.

"We made a critical mistake," the young man continued, and while an observer might have been surprised that this man, who was not yet 30, could speak to the other, older and more experienced men in this way, such was the respect they had held for his father, that it seemed only natural that he should be their new leader. There would be no questioning of his decisions, no juggling for power.

"We will not make that mistake again," he continued, looking around and catching each one's eye. "Our intelligence gathering was woefully missing. This will not happen again. In about ten minutes, you will meet someone who will not let that happen ever again. The identity of this man must be kept secret at all cost. Whenever we meet, no one will mention our real names even here in the library."

"Do we really need to do this?" ask Cyn.

"Yes, we do. Our guest, John Harrison requires it. That brings me to a must-be-understood point. We need to do just what he says and ask no questions. He does not know anything about our operations, and he needs to know nothing. He is simply our security man and intelligence source. There will be no social talk with him. Everything is strictly security with respect to him. When he is with any of us, it is strictly him doing the talking. We say nothing unless he makes a request.

"Gentleman, what I have just stated is imperative. Anyone having any problems with these arrangements, please speak up now." He again glanced around the room as everyone murmured their agreement.

"What do we call you?" asked Max.

"How about Cisco, the name of your horse," Red, who had often ridden with his father, suggested.

"I like that," said the young man, with a smile.

At that moment there was a knock at the door and Johnson stepped into the library. "Your visitor is here, sir."

"Please show him in."

John Harrison, a short man wearing a bespoke suit, entered the library. He, too, wasted no time as he quickly glanced around the room, sizing up the occupants, and began to explain to them his requirements.

"Gentlemen, I have your private mobile phone numbers. If I need to contact you, you will address me as John Harrison, and I will address you with the name that has been given to me. I do not need to know who you really are, nor what you do. None of you are to contact me directly except you." He nodded at the young man.

"You can refer to me as Cisco."

Harrison nodded again. "I doubt that I will need to contact you, but in the case that I do, please follow the protocol. Also, any contact will be short, no longer than 35 seconds. As of now, Osama bin Nedal is in Afghanistan. He is moving from one cave location to another. He has dozens of couriers who he uses to send orders and requests to his key personnel—who literally are stationed throughout the globe. All communication to and from him is through the couriers.

"Over the next six months, the NATO countries in a cooperative intelligence effort will track down approximately ten of Nedal's key personnel. Most likely they will initiate missions to capture those men. The probability that they can capture at least half is about seventy-five percent. We will gain a great deal of intelligence from these covert missions. The information that I send you will not have a source identified. All of you must resist the temptation to inquire from where or by whom this information has been acquired."

All responded that they understood, and Harrison continued.

"The reason that I am here personally is to assure you that I do exist, and that the information that I deliver has an extremely high probability of being correct. This is the last time any of you will see me. I leave you with one major thought that is part of my agreement. None of you shall take any actions to circumvent or interfere with any actions of the NATO coalition. If that happens, our arrangement will become null and void. I will leave now. Good day."

John Harrison turned and silently left the room as Cisco took over the conversation.

"Gentlemen, what is the status of our ability to reinstate the Big Kill?" he asked, referring to the operation that had failed on September 11.

Red gave a status report. "Anu Ladin, who was known in this country as Tom Rowe, implanted his information into the ActSof predictive accounting software works, so even though he died in the Towers, we can easily continue. I ran the test exercise just before I left this morning. We already have a second location set and ready to go, except for one thing. In order to activate the entire system, we need the password key. We don't have it. Anu Ladin was the only person who did. This means that we need to implant a new person into ActSof and find the password key that Anu Ladin set up."

"Red, are you telling us that we are dead in the water without this password key?"

"That is right, Cisco. However, when we set up Anu, we already had a backup person ready to go in case Anu did not complete his work. ActSof is aware of our backup as a person with similar skills to the man they knew as Tom Rowe. They have already contacted him. He should be working at ActSof within a week at the latest."

"Red, who is this new man, and how does ActSof know that Tom Rowe is deceased?"

"As Tom Rowe, Anu told them that he was going to see an old colleague in the Twin Towers that day. When Tom did not return to ActSof they tried to find him and came to the obvious conclusion, as we have, that he was one of the casualties of 9/11.

"Our new man's name is Pat Sherman. His credentials are impeccable. We have been grooming him for the last four years. He is single, he lives in the Hoboken area, and has the expertise needed to take over for Tom Rowe."

"That is well done, Red," said Cisco. "Now, Numbers we need to ensure that the FBI cannot trace the demised office at the Towers to us."

The prim and proper man with steel rimmed glasses responded. "I can say with certainty that the FBI nor anybody else can trace that office to any of us or to the group."

"I am glad to hear that, Numbers. Max, we need to get more implants into the NYPD. As usual, these implants are for information gathering only, and only when we contact them. They have to be very much below the radar. No patterns must be seen. No connections must be made by personal contact."

"That will be done within the next two weeks. We will have all of New York City covered along with Northern New Jersey."

"Cyn, you need to reestablish the implants we have with Ali Ki. We need to find means to have contacts not only in Iraq but also in Pakistan and Afghanistan. We also need to beef up your contacts in Munich—the ones with connection to Interpol."

"I agree, Cisco. It is going to take some time to make all these arrangements, but I know they will pay dividends down the road."

"Max, find out who or what uncovered Abu Ladin, our FBI plant who was masquerading as Sauly Omara."

"Consider it done."

"All right, gentlemen. The Big Kill is back on the table and once again at center stage. We have too much invested to let it slip through our fingers. We will meet again in a week."

After the men had left, an attractive well-dressed woman, joined her son in the library.

"Were you able to hear everything, Mom?" asked Cisco.

"Yes, it went very well. Your Mr. Harrison made quite an impression. You might have been a little too quick when you asked Max to get more implants into the NYPD since that really is more of Cyn's domain. Likewise, even though Cyn is tightly connected to the Mideast and the Ali Ki, it's Max who usually carries out the operation. Don't worry, you'll pick it up as you go along. Even so, they know what to do because they communicate with each other when carrying out operations."

September 18, 2001
NYC FBI Headquarters

Bob Hollis was head of the Special Task Force that had been investigating a suspected financial coup. They had been warned by the CIA that the coup would occur in Manhattan on Sept. 11. It hadn't happened. Had it been connected to the attack on the Twin Towers? Or had one terrorist group accidentally thwarted another terrorist group's plans? These were the questions Bob pondered as he assembled his team in a conference room in their New York office to go through all the reports and come up with some conclusions.

"After a lot of work and following of leads, we actually have very little to tell us about the financial coup on Manhattan," he told his task force members. "Our investigation into whoever rented the office space on the 87th floor of the North Tower is still underway. Our people performed an extensive but unsuccessful search to unearth who rented the office. What they have found is one paper company after another finally ending in Luxemburg. It's a dead end.

"Discussions with officials in Luxemburg have been initiated. However, the possibility of discovering anything is extremely low. The CIA have not been able to give us any more intelligence on the financial coup. The disappearance of Sauly Omara has been also investigated and it is believed that he vanished in the office on the 87th floor when the commercial airliner crashed into the North Tower. How he had been able to obtain employment in the FBI is still under investigation. Preliminary findings indicate that a very clever and well executed plan had altered necessary information.

"Some information points to a possible conclusion that the man we thought was Sauly Omara was really Abu Ladin, the son of Mohamed Ladin, the suspected leader of an antigovernment group based in Cairo, Egypt."

Bob paused and raised his hands to quell the astonished mutterings that accompanied his announcement that the man they had all thought of as a colleague had turned out to be a plant.

"It is also believed that Abu Ladin had undergone surgical procedures to look like the true Sauly Omara. What part of the financial coup Abu Ladin had is unknown at this time. One speculation is that Abu Ladin was a deep mole placed to keep his benefactors informed of the FBI's and to some extent the CIA's knowledge of the planned financial coup.

"Our friends at the NYPD have not been able to give us any information about a possible financial coup in Manhattan. All in all, we just have very little information to go on right now."

"Bob, what does Horton think about all of this?" asked John Thompson, one of two key men reporting to Hollis.

"He is as frustrated and in the dark as we are. Even though he is our boss and has privy to many more things than we have access to, his upper management is at a loss."

"That's not a good sign. It seems there is an unknown somebody who is pulling all the strings and watching us as we jump through the hoops."

"You know, John, that is an interesting thought. If somebody is planning a major financial coup right here in Manhattan, they just might be close by."

"Right, and their financial attack is probably with software, not a hardware shutdown," added John's partner, Cory Carlson. Cory, unlike the more thoughtful John, was known as a bit of an eager beaver to the task force. He was often willing to jump to conclusions while the rest of the group was still doing research. His intuition, Bob knew, sometimes led him to the right conclusions long before the others.

"What makes you think so, Cory?"

"Think about what has been happening over the last couple of years. Let's say they are the ones responsible for putting Abu Ladin as a mole inside our group. Maybe, just maybe, they have been the ones responsible for some if not all of the recent terrorist attacks planned on Manhattan." Also, they could have planted other talented people in other places like a software company whose products are used by the companies in the financial world."

"That is a lot of ifs and maybes, Cory," Bob said skeptically.

"John, what do you think about Cory's ideas?"

"I believe that Cory is onto something. We need to find some patterns in all the things that have been happening in the last couple of years. I suggest that we turn this task over to our software people to see if they can find some patterns in the information that we just haven't been looking for in the past."

"Excellent idea, John. I will get with Horton and pass this by him." Bob began to gather his papers as he added, "Well, gentlemen we have some new avenues to pursue. Let's get to work."

Bob headed to see his boss, Jeff Horton, the head of the Division and inform him of the task force's new ideas.

"Jeff, I have just had an enlightening discussion with John and Cory," he said as he entered his boss's office. They believe that we have been looking in the wrong places to uncover the financial coup on Manhattan."

"This I would like to hear since just about everything we have done seems to have totally missed," Horton said, looking up from his paperwork.

"The guys believe that there exists a powerful group that has been maneuvering and manipulating things over the last couple of years to setup their plan to perform this financial coup on Manhattan. Why Manhattan? There are many financial centers in the U.S. not to mention around the globe? So maybe, they are nearby. Maybe even under our very noses."

"Wow, that is an interesting idea. The CIA told us that they stumbled onto the information about the financial coup while eavesdropping on the Ali Ki. So are you telling me that this group must have some tight connection to the Ali Ki and that maybe they have been manipulating the Ali Ki?"

"Right, I know it sounds a little wild, but it is another avenue that we have not even considered in the past. We think it's a good idea to look for patterns in the information we have collected over the past few years."

"You know, Bob, that is sounding more feasible all the time. I'll set up a meeting with my software man, Fred Newman."

"Thanks, Jeff. Oh, one more thing. Since we lost Sauly Omara, I need to get another Mideast expert."

"I'm ahead of you on that one. We hired one of the people that you interviewed when you selected Sauly Omara. I'm getting her transferred to your group. Her name is Janet Orr."

"Great news. When can I expect to see her?"

"That's what I am working on."

Back in his office, Bob called Cory. "You have the go ahead, Horton will set up a meeting with his software people."

"All right, I would like to have Thompson in that meeting. Actually, he thought up the idea and talked to me about it two days ago."

"No problem. I'll get back to you as soon as I hear from Horton."

September 22, 2001
Bronx, NY

"Well Sister, my wedding day has finally arrived." Shelly turned slowly in her wedding gown so her sister could see her.

"You are a beautiful bride, Shelly. You've chosen a very good man. You two have so much in common. So now, let's get ready to meet your man at the Church."

"I love Damian very much, but I am a little nervous."

"It's to be expected."

At that moment Shelly's brother-in-law walked in the bedroom door. "Well girls, we need to get a move on. Damian is very patient, so let's not tempt him to walk."

"Oh Bob Hollis, sometimes you make me so mad. We will go when we are ready. Mother should be here any minute. Then we can proceed so as not to worry Damian," his wife and Shelly's sister Louane said.

"That's my girl. I just heard a car pull into the driveway. I will check to see who it is. Who knows, it maybe somebody who came all the way from Paris, France," Bob laughed and pretended to be mysterious.

"Go!"

Bob was heading to the front door when it opened and his mother-in-law, Margo Nasser, appeared.

"Hello Mom, you are looking as radiate as ever," he said, giving her a hug.

"Flattery will get you anything. Now where are my daughters,"

"They are anxiously awaiting your arrival."

"Well, that can be taken care of easily enough. Please let me go so I can join them."

"Why all the hurry?" Bob teased.

"We don't want to keep that young man waiting too long. A little wait is good enough." As Margo hurried up the stairs, she called, "Louane, I am anxious to see my soon to be bride Shelly."

"Come up and see the radiant bride-to-be."

"Oh my goodness, you are truly radiant. So let us go meet your husband to be."

As the wedding party arrived at the church, a large crowd awaited them, smiles on their faces on this overly cool September day. As Shelly walked down the aisle, her father, VJ Nasser, was at her side. VJ had postponed a very lucrative business meeting in order to be in New York for his daughter's wedding, of which he'd paid for in its entirety.

After the ceremony, they all went directly to the reception. Nearly all of ActSof, the company where Shelly and Damian worked, were there, along with some of Damian's schoolmates. Also in attendance were the Cigar Team and about a dozen NYC FBI personnel. Unknown to most of the attendees was a heavyset man named Kachen Mihad, a terrorist with connections to the Franklin Lakes Group.

"Damian, I heard you are having a variety of food."

"That's right, Warren," Damian told the Cigar Team member and boss of an energy management crew. "We actually have two different sets of serving tables set up. One for Italian food and one for Mediterranean food."

"That sounds delicious. Did your mom and dad have anything to do with the Italian food?"

"Absolutely. Can you imagine me having Italian food at my wedding without consulting my parents?"

"Actually, no I could not see that happening. It looks like you are being summoned. I'll catch you later."

Damian turned to see his new sister-in-law, Louane, a very attractive Middle Eastern woman, calling him.

"Damian, we need to take the pictures now. Everybody else is there."

Yes, everybody was there including VJ Nasser, who rarely had his picture taken. However, this was a situation that he could not avoid. In the past, he had strongly protected his anonymity. The fact that he was allowing his picture to be taken was a major break in his stringent protocol.

Kachen sat quietly in a corner, observing. Cory noticed the guest sitting by himself and approached, holding out his hand. "Hello, my name is Cory Carlson. I work with Shelly's brother-in-law, Bob Hollis. I know many of the guests but I have never seen you before. Are you a friend of Damian?"

"I only met Damian once. I know Shelly. She has helped my cousin with his accounting for his bookstore. She is very smart and one of the most cordial young persons I have ever had the pleasure to meet," Kachen spoke in a formal manner that showed English was not his first language, despite his lack of a noticeable accent.

Cory's antenna suddenly started to hum at the mention of the bookstore. "What bookstore is that?"

"It's in Brooklyn and deals mostly with different cultural history. My cousin could not attend the wedding today and wanted me to be here for Shelly. He thinks the world of her. She has helped him to straighten his accounting books and to stay out of trouble with the IRS."

"Well, that sounds like Shelly. Bob says she is as a very giving person."

"My cousin can vouch for that. By the way, have you tried the Mediterranean food?"

"Yes, Bob has talked about Mediterranean food and how much he enjoys his wife's cooking. You know she was born in Egypt."

"Was Shelly also born in Egypt?"

"I believe so."

"Do you know where in Egypt?"

"She and her family lived in Cairo."

"Is that where her father is from?"

"Yes, VJ Nasser was born and raised in Cairo."

Kachen was well aware that VJ Nasser was born and raised in Cairo. He also knew that VJ was a very cunning businessman who used his Merchant stores as a front for his many business dealings that had nothing to do with his stores. What Kachen had not realized that the girl who had been such a help in his cousin's bookstore was VJ's daughter.

"It has been great talking to you, Cory, I am going to try some more of this fine Mediterranean food," he said, standing up.

"Enjoy yourself, Kachen." Cory said and quickly headed to find John Thompson.

As Kachen was partaking of the baklava, Pat Sherman approached him. "I see you like the baklava. I'm here for my second helping."

"Young man, you need to be careful, baklava is a very rich dessert."

"I know, a friend of mine named Tom Rowe already alerted me."

"He sounds like a good friend. What else has he told you?"

"Many things."

"Maybe someday we will need to get together and talk about Tom Rowe."

"I would like that, Kachen."

Kachen was very surprised to hear that this young man knew his name. "How do you know my name, Mr. Sherman?"

"A man who knows the Benefactor told me your name and said that you would be here."

"Yes, indeed we need to get together. Now I believe that I will need some hot coffee to help me enjoy my first serving of baklava. This is my card, please give me a call soon."

"I look forward to it."

On the other side of the room, Cory found John Thompson. "John, I just met a man named Kachen who knows Shelly because Shelly helped his cousin with his accounting at a bookstore in Brooklyn."

"Well, we need to have a conversation with our boss about Kachen and his bookstore cousin. Let's be patient and catch him at work. That will be a better place to talk."

"Good point, John."

Moving to the coffee table, Kachen overheard an older man telling Bob about a meeting "to discuss patterns" that was set up for next Tuesday. Obviously, this man was also from the FBI, maybe Bob Hollis' boss. What Kachen didn't understand was the reference to patterns, although it obviously meant something because Hollis looked happy about the meeting. *I wonder if this young man Pat Sherman may know something about patterns. It appears that Shelly's brother-in-law could be very high up in the FBI. Hm, could it be that Shelly has been a mole at my cousin's bookstore? Maybe I could give her some bogus information and see if the FBI comes to investigate.*

Kachen started to move away from the coffee table as Shelly and Damian approached him. "I am so happy to see you have been able to be here," Shelly said.

"I would not miss such an event for someone so deserving as you. It is good to see you, Mr. Narpati."

"Please call me Damian."

"Yes, I will. I have not seen your friend Mr. Rowe. Is he not here?"

"Unfortunately, we believe Tom may have been in one of the Towers when the planes hit. We have heard nothing from him since that time."

"Oh, I am so sorry to hear that. You know he came back to the store for some other books. We talked for awhile. He really loved his mother. He said he told her everything. There were no secrets between them."

"Wow, that is good to hear of such love. Do you know where he was living with his mother?"

"I do not know. I believe he said that his mother had returned to England some time ago, so he was probably living by himself. He said he would get a little nervous because he had some sensitive information at his mother's house."

"Did he say what it was?"

"No, he just seemed to be a little nervous about it—I believe I see someone who wants to get your attention."

"Oh, that's my dad. He wants Shelly's sister to meet the guys in our Cigar Team."

"Cigar Team?"

"Just a group of us who get together about once a month to chat and smoke a cigar."

"Well, I think your dad is becoming more anxious for Shelly to meet his friends."

"Yes, it has been so good talking to you. Shelly and I need to get over there before my dad has a heart attack." Damian laughed.

"I wish you both the best. Now go see your dad."

As Damian and Shelly left him, Kachen had a smile on his face as he pondered if the FBI was searching for Tom Rowe's mother and the house in which Tom had sensitive information stored away. Kachen knew where Tom lived; he would have some of his people stake out the house to see if the FBI showed.

Damian reached his dad. "Shelly is getting her sister and her husband to meet the Cigar Team."

"Oh, that is a great idea."

"Really, Dad. You have been bending my ear for weeks to have the Cigar Team meet Louane and her husband."

"Has it really been that long? Oh, here they are. Louane and Bob, this is the Cigar Team."

"Pleased to meet you. My name is Warren Baron," a tall lanky man with a bald head and athletic build. "Roy has been telling us for months about you and your family."

"I am also pleased to meet you. I'm Reuben Steinber," a stocky man about 5 feet 10 inches with short arms and legs held out his hand. "My job is to keep Warren from shaking anybody's hand too long."

A third man moved up. "Hello, I have been looking forward to meet the two of you. Damian has told us that you two are some of the nicest people he has ever met. Oh, I'm John Lipton," an energy manager with a nationwide hotel consortium.

"I second John's comment. I'm Cosmo and pleased to make your acquaintance."

"I'm doc mike," one of the older members of the Cigar Team who usually did the most kidding around. "As you can see, we are all very fond and proud of Damian. We know he would only choose a very special person as his bride. We have had the pleasure of meeting with Shelly several times. Now it is heartwarming to meet Shelly's family. You have a beautiful and a very caring sister."

Louane blushed, and her voice choked as she replied. "You are such wonderful people. Shelly has told us how much fun she has had with all of you. She often talks about the relationships among all of you and how wherever you go, so many people know you and enjoy seeing you." Tears start to form in Louane's eyes. Pardon me, I am overwhelmed."

Bob hugged Louane. "All of you have touched my wife's heart. When we met Damian, we knew that Shelly had found someone wonderful. As time went on, she told us more and more about the Cigar Team. We have wondered who all of you are. A group of people who had made a lasting impression on Shelly. It is our honor to meet all of you."

"There is one member of the group that we have noticed is not here at the reception," mentioned Warren.

Bob responded, "Who's not here?"

"Tom Rowe, a fellow worker with Damian."

"Damian, did we not invite Tom Rowe?"

"Sir, after the attacks on the Twin Towers, we have not heard from Tom Rowe. He was on vacation on that day and said he was meeting an old friend in the Twin Towers. We tried to contact him to no avail. We believed that he died in the Twin Tower attacks."

"Really Damian, why didn't you tell us?" stated Warren with a quizzical look on his face.

"Warren, we really weren't sure. We didn't want to say something without really knowing what happened, so we decided to say nothing."

"Wow, I really liked Tom. He seemed so interested in our energy work."

Bob's FBI training kicked in. "What were the things that interested Tom Rowe the most?"

"He spent most of his time with Warren."

"That's right, Tom spent most of his time with me. We talked about cooling systems for the computer centers for large buildings. There are many subsystems that perform the cooling. Tom was interested in the large chillers. He couldn't believe they didn't work as simply as an on-off switch."

"Louane, I see your mother is signaling to you," Bob said, interrupting Warren..

"Yes, she wants Damian, Shelly and myself to talk with my dad. Come on you two, that time has arrived."

"You three go ahead, I'll be here talking with the Cigar Team. Was Tom interested in other items?" Bob asked, turning back to Warren.

"We talked about the other parts of the cooling system including what kind of information was being sent to the maintenance control center."

"Did that really interest him?"

"Actually, he seemed more interested in the information that was not sent to the control room. Damian said that Tom was their network expert and could connect many things together so that all could work together instead of colliding with each other."

"Did Tom spend much time with the people in the control room?"

"Actually, Damian spent the most time in the control rooms. At times, Tom and Damian would get into some conversations. However, it meant little or no sense to me."

"I'm with you on that count," Bob smiled. "The software world is an enigma to me. Actually, I would like to talk to all of you more, but I know that Louane will be expecting me to show up any minute. I would like to join you sometime when you meet."

"We would enjoy that. Damian can cue you in when we will

meet."

"Sounds like a plan. Now I need to go do my duties."

Kachen had moved to a table next to the Cigar Team. He heard the conversation between Hollis and the team. *What did I just hear? It sounded like Hollis did not know about Tom Rowe. I just told Shelly about Tom. She had no time to talk to Hollis. So maybe they really didn't know about Tom. There is too much here. Somehow, I need to find out what they know. The Benefactor needs to be told.*

"Well doc, what do you think about my new in-laws?" Damian's dad asked.

"Roy, you hit the jackpot."

"Right, Nancy and I are very proud of Damian."

"Now you have two in your family who can help you with your computer problems."

"Yes, and I hope there will be more on their way."

"By the way, where are they going on their honeymoon?"

"Shelly's mom has a chalet outside of Paris. She has set up everything for them to stay there for the next two weeks."

"Is Shelly's mom going to be there with them?"

"No, she is going to visit Shelly's dad in Egypt. Apparently, they get together for a couple of weeks about twice a year."

"How long have they been separated?"

"Many years, I don't know how long. Even so, they stay somewhat connected."

"That's a little unusual."

"Yes, there is a lot more there than meets the eye, but I get the sense that it has to do with his businesses."

"What about his businesses?"

"I don't know. It may be the type of people that he deals with."

"I hope this is not a fairytale with a bad ending!"

"You're not the only one."

Kachen also heard the conversation between doc mike and Roy Narparti. *Things are starting to get a little sticky. What do they know about VJ Nasser? I must get to the Benefactor.*

"Bob, did you have a good time with the Cigar Team."

"Yes, I had a great time with the guys, Shelly. They're an interesting group and I intend to meet with them. Damian will be my link to the Cigar Team."

"Is that right, Damian?"

"Yes, it is, dear. In fact, I believe I have another soon-to-be Cigar Team member. Bob, I'd like you to meet Pat Sherman. He is replacing Tom Rowe at ActSof."

"I'm pleased to meet you, Mr. Hollis."

"Please, Pat, call me Bob, and please do not try to explain to me what you do at Actsof because I wouldn't understand a thing you said."

"Don't worry, Bob, ActSof wouldn't let me. I have some big shoes to fill but I do understand good cigars as taught to me by my dad. As far as you not understanding what I do, it is really simple, I connect the different accounting locations of a company so that all the changes and updates to each system appear as if they are happening in real time."

"Wow, now that is what I would call a simple and straightforward answer. I assume that is very important to a company that has many locations."

"Absolutely, it saves them valuable time and therefore in the long run a great deal of money by having a more efficient and effective accounting system across their company."

"I can tell from the tone of your voice that you truly enjoy what you are doing."

"I do. Your sister-in-law, along with Damian, can then project and forecast the company's ledger sheets so they know the financial health of the company."

"That's impressive. What if somebody hacks into your system or network or whatever you call it? What could happen then?"

"That's the danger. Somebody could truly foul up everything and put the accounting system far off track."

"I see; that is scary. How do you stop that from happening?"

"Actually, that is out of my expertise. We have security people who handle that end of the business. We count on them to keep things safe."

"Sounds like a lot of pressure lands on their shoulders."

"It is; we are constantly looking for threats to the system."

"Bob, I need you over here," called his wife.

"Excuse me, Louane has something else I am supposed to be doing. I have enjoyed our conversation. Thank you for simplifying things for me."

Still quietly observing everything, Kachen was ready to hit Pat alongside the head. *What do you think you are doing you idiot? You are giving the FBI an insight into what the Benefactor has paid dearly to keep quiet. I need to give him a stern warning.*

"Warren, Bob seemed very interested in learning about Tom Rowe."

"Yes, I wonder why."

"How much did you tell Tom about the chillers?"

"Actually, I told him just about everything I know about them, both the old ones and the new. We talked a lot about the sensors on the chillers. How they worked, what they were measuring, what would happen if the sensors gave the wrong information."

"This is sounding very suspicious, Warren."

"Reuben, did you talk much with Tom Rowe?"

"At first, I didn't think so, but now I am wondering if I told him a lot more about the chillers than I thought I had."

A serious look was on doc mike's face as he addressed the Cigar Team. "Guys, it was shortly after we had taken Tom and Damian into Manhattan with us that the chiller sabotages started."

That's right doc, did we show him how to sabotage the old chillers?" asked a worried-looking Warren.

"That's a distinct possibility. Warren. We need to mind our Ps and Qs from now on."

"I agree with you, doc."

"Roy, do you know more about Tom Rowe?"

"Well, you know, he said his father was Egyptian. However, he never really talked about his father, or say why his mother and he left Egypt."

"I would hate to believe that Tom Rowe was a terrorist."

"Me too, doc. He seemed like a true down-to-earth person. I asked him to help me find Damian a girlfriend. He helped Damian and Shelly meet."

"Yes, I agree, that doesn't sound like a terrorist unless he was trying to fit in with the Cigar Team because he wanted to learn as much as he could about shutting down computer centers in Manhattan."

"Do you really believe that, doc?"

"It's hard to believe he joined the Cigar Team because he knew he could learn enough to shut down computer centers. If that wasn't his original motive, what was it? Could it have something to do with ActSof?"

"Doc, you are well beyond me."

"Same here," replied Warren.

"Okay guys, we are at a wedding, not reading a mystery novel. Let's just have some fun."

"You're right, doc, I need another beer."

"I'll join you, Warren."

Kachen finally found Pat and pulled him aside. "Don't you realize that Bob Hollis is the FBI and you are blabbing your mouth off about things you should not be saying to people. You could ruin everything."

"Yes sir, I didn't mean to ramble so much. It just came spilling out."

"You go spill more out of your mouth and I will shut it for good. Do you understand?"

"Yes sir."

Let's get back and enjoy the festivities."

"Absolutely!"

A shaken Pat Sherman tried to re-enter the festive evening, but his pale face and slow stiff walk made him look like a sore thumb.

"Pat, are you all right?"

"Yes Damian, I think I just drank the wine too fast."

"Well, pull it together, we are going to step outside for the fireworks and cigars. Personally, I am going to have some brandy."

"In that case, I'll have some pasta to settle my stomach and join you later."

Across the way, Louane brought Bob to her mother and father. "Well I see you two have been having a nice quite time by yourselves."

"Yes, we have, daughter. I see you have finally gotten Bob away from the cigar smoking clan."

"Actually, VJ it was enjoyable and quite enlightening. How are your businesses doing?"

"The businesses are doing very well. I wish my country was doing half as good."

"Yes, we notice the unrest, especially in Cairo, itself. I recall some months back that three officials were assassinated."

"That is very true. However, they were corrupt and part of the cause for all the turmoil."

"Really, do they know who planted the bombs?"

"The police know that it was the work of the rebels. It has caused a big stir within the government because the corrupt faction believes that any one of them can be a target and that nobody can protect them all the time."

"Has all of that helped to curtail the corruption?"

"It has suppressed some of the more overt activity, but it will start up again." VJ wasn't usually this talkative about his affairs, he was a tough businessman who walked a gray line between legal and illegal.

"What about the positions of the officials? Have they been replaced?"

"Only on a temporarily basis. The leading official was an elected position. His replacement will have to be elected before this year is out."

"Do you see any true candidate on the horizon?"

"I have a favored candidate and I have been working with many of my business associates to support his campaign."

"I hope you are successful."

"We have better than a 50/50 chance—but enough of this, I am so happy to see Shelly has found an outstanding young man to marry. I have had some brief conversations with his parents. They seem to be well rounded people with strong moral standards. I expect Shelly and Damian will have a fruitful life ahead of them. They are both very sharp minded and seem to be well established in this high technical computer world."

"Yes, it almost seems to come to them naturally."

"I would say the same. It is almost as if they are always on the same page all the time. They know what each other is thinking. It appears that they have already formed a union between themselves."

"That is a great way of stating their relationship. They both seem to be on a fast track to success in their chosen field."

"That is for sure. I have briefly talked to Damian about his company's software accounting products. I intend to follow through with Damian and set up my businesses with their accounting products."

"That's outstanding, I can see it now, when Damian and Shelly go to Cairo to install their software accounting products, Louane will be right there alongside of them."

"That's a definite possibility."

"Bob, they are getting ready for the fireworks. We need to get everybody outside," Louane interrupted.

"Okay, Louane." Hollis walked through the crowd and announced that a surprise was planned on the patio. The crowd gathered, chattering excitedly. Across the wide expanse lawn fireworks started. All eyes turned to watch. Damian, Pat and the Cigar Team lit their cigars and sipped their brandy as they watched the fireworks.

'This is a great touch, Damian."

"Yes it is. Warren, it is VJ's idea."

"I haven't had a chance to meet him."

"That can be arranged. He's coming over to have a cigar and meet the team."

"Wow, we are becoming popular."

At that moment, VJ arrived and Damian handed him a cigar. "Please Damian, introduce me to your friends."

The team made the rounds of introductions again.

"Who is this young fellow over here standing next to Roy?" VJ asked doc mike.

"I'm Pat Sherman," he said, overhearing the questions. I work with Damian at ActSof."

"You are the one working on networks or something like that."

"Yes, that is me, sir."

"Please, call me VJ."

"Yes, sir."

"Now I can use a little brandy. I hope you all have enjoyed the fireworks."

"Nothing like smoking a cigar, sipping some brandy while watching fireworks."

"I'll drink to that, doc."

At that moment, Hollis joined them. "Well VJ, I see you have met the Cigar Team."

"Yes, and they can help me save some money on my utility bills at all my stores."

"Have a cigar, Bob."

"Thanks, Damian. Do you have a light? Thank you."

"You need to sip some brandy while your smoking a fine cigar Bob."

"Thank you, Warren. I hope all of you are enjoying the fireworks. VJ insisted that we had to have fireworks. Great move VJ."

"It appears that the rest of the crowd are also enjoying the fireworks."

"Yes, it seems so. It has become a part of our American culture."

"That is why I wanted them Bob. It's a lot better than gun fire."

"I wish these were the only kind of explosions that we would have."

Bill Tilghman, the president of ActSof, joined the group. "I have been waiting for this the whole night."

"Have a cigar, Bill."

"Thank you, Damian. Do I finally get to meet your cigar smoking friends?"

"Yes sir, this tall fellow is Warren Baron, he is the foremen for the energy conversion crews. Be careful, he might shake your hand off. This is John Lipton, he is an energy manager of a holding company that own a string of hotels. This fellow standing next to my dad is Cosmo Iacanari, the football player I have told you about. He is boss of the energy company where I worked. This is Reuben Steiner and doc mike. They along with my dad do the engineering work for the energy company."

"Gentleman, I toast you all with this fine brandy and great smoking cigar."

"Here come my girls," VJ said as Louane and Shelly whisked VJ away.

"Dad, we see that you have been mixing with the Cigar Team and Mr. Tilghman," Shelly said to him.

"Yes, I have been enjoying myself with their company. I haven't had time to talk with your Mr. Tilghman. I would like to talk with him more."

"In a little while, now Mom wants to have another picture of the four of us together. She has cornered the photographer and is waiting for us."

"Another picture. Soon I will go blind from all those flashes of light."

"Now Dad, we know you do not like to have your picture taken, but as you have said, this is a very special occasion, and these pictures are just for us to see."

"I have spoiled you two girls terribly. Let's go find your mother and the captured photographer."

Bob continued his conversation with the Cigar Team. "Bill, I have been talking to your new employee, Pat Sherman. He is taking over for a Mr. Tom Rowe?"

"Yes, we lost Tom. We believe that he must have been in the Towers when the planes hit. We haven't heard from him and have no one we can contact to find out if they know anything. Tom was very good at this near real time networking technology. That is one of the key pieces that we needed for a next generation product line. We have already started to roll out that entire product line due in a great part to Damian and Shelly."

"Somewhere I heard that Tom was from an Ivy League University."

"Yes, in fact, that is how we found Tom. Our research people were tracking several different technologies and came across two of Tom's papers. They were just what we were looking to find, so we quickly made contact with him."

"Seems like providence was shining on you."

"Actually Bob, that is a very good point. Not only were we so fortunate with Tom, but we also found Shelly through Tom."

"Really, how did that happen?"

"I'm surprised that Damian or Shelly didn't tell you. Tom, who was born in Egypt, wanted to pick up some literature on the country. He found a bookstore in Brooklyn that had the book that he wanted, and he and Damian went there on a lunch break. At the store, the book was set aside in the backroom. When Damian and Tom followed the clerk into the backroom, Shelly was at the computer and her radio was playing one of Damian's favorite songs. Damian struck up a conversation with her about artificial intelligence. This is one of the key technologies we need. Damian invited Shelly to talk with some of our research people. That was all they needed. Shelly and my people immediately started to bond in their tech world. As far as we at ActSof were concerned, we found a gem in the rough. So, yes, providence has shone down on us."

"That is quite a story Bill." *In fact, it is very interesting. This is too big of a coincidence. I need to check into this more. Is it possible that somehow this could be part of the financial terrorist act that the CIA has been talking about?*

"It is much more than just a story to ActSof. It has propelled us into the forefront of near real time network accounting."

"So, finding Tom and Shelly has made a significant difference in your company's ability to produce the capabilities that you had been working for your next generation of products."

"You hit the nail on the head, Bob."

"Even so, having the products is one thing, but getting companies to buy them seems to me to also be a very big task."

"Once again, providence has shone upon us. Even though we only have a small marketing group, we must have been at the right places at the right time with what these companies needed and wanted."

This is way too big a set of coincidences and dumb luck. Something else is happening. I really need to find out what that something is. "Bill, maybe you just have the Midas touch."

"I believe I just have good people who really enjoy their work."

"Oh, speaking of enjoying, the time has come for Damian to whisk his bride away."

"You're right Bob, there they go."

Chapter 2

"Bob, I've got to tell you that wedding reception was the best I've ever attended," Cory said enthusiastically.

"I'm glad to hear that, Cory. Not only was it a great party, I'm almost dumbfounded about the information I gained that night. I sure didn't plan it that way, but it must have been the first time that we had so many people of interest in one place at the same time."

"I agree with both of you. These were some very interesting people with interesting backgrounds there," put in John.

"Like what, John?"

John straightened in his chair. "First of all, this heavyset guy Kachen Mihad. He kept moving around from table to table listening in on conversations. I saw him get with Pat Sherman after you talked with Sherman. It looked like he was lecturing Sherman. After Kachen was done, Sherman turned pale."

"Do you have any idea of what they were talking about?"

"I didn't hear anything, but my guess it had something to do with what Sherman told you."

Hollis paused and rubbed his forehead, as if he could massage the memory out of his brain. "As I can remember, Sherman told me about his job at ActSof. I asked him if someone could upset a company's finances. His answer was a big time yes."

"Somehow Kachen and Sherman have a connection, Bob."

"Right, John. I wonder if it has anything to do with this financial coup that seems to continue to elude us."

Cory jumped up. "Wow, that's impressive and a little scary, Bob."

"Right, Cory, if there is really something here, it has been right under our noses all the time."

John wasn't as excited as Cory about the information. "So, where do we go from here, Bob?" he asked quietly.

"First, let's discuss more of the items we came across at the reception. When I was talking with the Cigar Team, they mentioned Tom Rowe. He worked with Damian and Shelly at ActSof and apparently died when the Towers were bombed. He's the person Pat Sherman is replacing.

"The first thing the Cigar Team said was how impressed they had been with Rowe. He was very intelligent, well educated, and always looking for something new."

"I'm with you on that, Bob. They were very impressed with Rowe, and since Damian brought him to the Cigar Team, they assumed that he was a special person," added John.

"Yes, and I heard similar things," put in Cory.

Hollis sat back in his chair. "All of this makes me more and more suspicious of Rowe. According to the Cigar Team, he showed a great interest in the air conditioning systems that cool computer and data centers."

"Listening to Reuben and Warren, it sounds as if Rowe kept trying to understand the key components of the cooling systems."

"That's right, John. Rowe wanted to learn about the high-risk points of the cooling system and then focused on the chillers."

"Yes, and shortly after that, a series of chiller failures caused many computer centers in buildings that housed financial firms to shut down."

"Exactly, Cory. Then just as suddenly the failures began, they stopped."

"Yes, almost as if somebody ordered them to stop."

"I think you're right, John."

"Bob, we need to uncover as much information as we can about Tom Rowe."

"I agree, John. That's your assignment, but before you get into that, we need to meet with Horton and his software people. They should be in the conference room by now."

A short time later they entered the conference room and greeted Fred Newman, the head of Jeff Horton's software group.

"Hi, Bob. Jeff says you have a new direction you want investigated."

"I certainly do, Fred. You know Cory and John."

"Oh, we've met many times. Usually they talk with Charles Koury and Dennis Smith, here, my main analysts," Fred said, pointing to the two men who sat at the conference table with him.

Hollis shook hands with the two men. "Glad to see both; where is Jeff?" he added just as Horton entered the conference room.

"Well, I see we are all here. Bob, let's hear about this new direction of yours."

"We're ready. John, please begin."

John moved to the front of the conference room and rubbed his hands together. "The CIA has been telling us of a major financial coup that will happen in Manhattan. Now we think we've been looking for over a year in the wrong place to find the group behind this coup.

"We asked ourselves, why choose New York? Why not some other major city in the world? Because whoever is behind this coup has a mole in the FBI here in New York, and possibly has people strategically placed in several companies through which they could control financial transactions."

"Holy mackerel, now that is a major supposition!" said Fred, surprised. However, if it is true, it is one heck of an operation."

"Fred, the more we look over our information, the more it seems likely," put in Bob.

"You truly seem convinced of this, Bob." Fred, looking across the table at Bob, saw just how serious he was.

"Yes, we think a secret organization somewhere within the New York area is manipulating things to organize and execute a major financial attack centered in Manhattan."

"Wow, this is amazing!" said Newman excitedly. I've never thought about it being a Power Group that was working on this coup. We've concentrated on individual hackers. You're talking about something more organized and complex than we've ever considered."

He settled in his chair and put his elbows on the conference table as he contemplated the possibilities this new theory brought up. "Something like that would take a great many resources."

"That's what we have concluded, Fred—and I like your term 'Power Group.' It really fits. This is not somebody's garage operation. It's big, with many people and many moving parts. It would take a lot of people with special talents—and that means there has to be traces of them somewhere."

Newman, always restless, sat back in his chair again, scratching his eyebrow. "Ah, so you believe there must be patterns somewhere."

A smile grew on Bob's face. "You've said it, Fred!"

Once again, Newman leaned forward. "Patterns are found in data. Do you have any idea where to look for this data?"

John stepped into the conversation. "We have some thoughts, Fred."

"Okay, John, where do we look?"

"Where to look is something we wish we could tell you. What we have is a lot of disjointed pieces. There is no clear picture. But, while we may not have a picture, we do have information on those disjointed pieces."

Newman again scratched his right eyebrow. "Okay, I get the sense that over a long period of time your team has gathered a lot of information. I doubt that you can show it to us now. So, what do you have in mind?"

"Fred, we are figuring this out as we go along," said Bob. "The first thing we wanted to do is to tell you we believe there is a new direction to pursue. Our next step is to have Cory work with Charles and Dennis. We'll also contact our CIA partners. Remember that Sauly Omara was our link to the CIA, especially some of its data bases."

Newman relaxed and sat back in his chair. "Now we're talking, Bob. Charles and Dennis worked with Sauly on several searches."

"Exactly. We want to reestablish that connection. We have a new person replacing Sauly. Her name is Janet Orr. She has no experience in what we have just been talking about. Cory has the experience, and Janet has the technical capability, so they'll work together with Charles and Dennis."

"Sounds like a plan, Bob."

"Glad to hear you say that, Fred. Cory, please take Charles and Dennis to meet Janet."

Horton, who had been patiently listening, stood up. "Gentlemen, this goes to the top of your work queue. Is that clear?"

"Yes sir, Jeff," Newman said. Bob and Fred stayed to talk with Horton as the others filed out.

"Bob, Fred, I am very interested in this new idea. My gut tells me this is the way to proceed. Before, I felt we were always a step behind; I believe this is why. We need to get with NYPD and see if they have any leads on a possible local group with a lot of resources who could set up such an operation."

"Good idea Jeff, I'll get with my NYPD contact and see if we can uncover something," said Bob.

"Stick with this, Bob, I doubt you will see much of anything at first, but somewhere, you'll find the NYPD has something that can help us. Also, get back with Fred Hendricks in D.C. and see if he has anything on organized crime related to what we've discussed."

"Absolutely, Jeff."

Horton turned to Newman. "Fred, I know you have informal connections to other agencies."

"I'm with you Jeff, I've been thinking about that as we sit here."

"Gentlemen let's make this happen!!!

A short time later Bob was making phone calls to start the ball rolling. His first call was to Fred Hendrick, Head of the Law Against Organized Crime Division for the FBI, stationed in Washington, DC.

"Hello Bob, how are you and your people doing?"

"A little shaken, but we believe we are on a new path. We believe that a powerful group with a great number of assets is somewhere in the New York area, and that they have been manipulating a complex operation that will allow them to attack the financial center inside of Manhattan."

"Do you see them as terrorists?"

"Not in the normal sense that we usually think of a terrorist. We believe they are after the money."

"That's interesting, Bob. I assume you have some clues that brought you to this jump in thinking."

"As you are aware, we had a mole within my department. We have other information that people with specialized skills, particularly in computers and networking, have been planted in strategic places."

"That's intriguing, Bob."

"We also believe this Power Group, as we are calling it, has funded some of the terrorists both in the States and in the Mideast."

"That's a lot of believing. However, it could be possible if someone had the assets."

"That's why I have given you a call."

"Let me think. You want to know who could have such vast resources within organized crime?"

"I knew it wouldn't take you long to figure it out."

Hendrick pulled up a file on his computer. "You called me awhile back to see if organized crime had any connections to terrorists. At that time we had nothing. All we saw were some isolated local instances. That got me thinking, so we started looking for things that could connect terrorists with organized crime."

"Did you find anything?" Bob asked quickly.

"After many months of frustration, no. Then we started to think a little differently. What if organized crime were funding some terrorists? We asked ourselves why would organized crime want to support terrorists, unless they got something in return? We concluded that the terrorists could provide diversions by requiring the authorities to use their resources to go after them instead of going after organized crime."

"Fred, that has also been in the back of our minds. Did you find anything?"

"We haven't found a true smoking gun. What we have found is that the terrorists have been using the resources of organized crime to obtain more sophisticated weapons, as well as using some of organized crime's infrastructure. This has been invaluable to the terrorists. We have been working with the Anti-Terrorist Group here in D.C., and with your boss's people.

"We believed there was no major connection between organized crime in the States and the terrorists, but there could be some connection in the Mideast. Our best guess is an organized crime group that has global participation. We are ready to hand this over to your boss, believing this group would most likely be centered in one of a handful of coastal metropolitan cities—New York is high on that list."

Hollis was scribbling notes on a paper pad as fast as he could. "Fred, this supports our new thinking and gives us a motive. Thanks, I'll alert Jeff."

"Good luck, Bob, I believe you are on the right track."

Hollis immediately called Horton. "Jeff, I just had an amazing conversation with Fred Hendrick. They have been doing some research to see if organized crime had any major connection to the terrorists. They think there's a good possibility that an organized crime group headquartered in the New York area could have been funding the terrorists in the Mideast. They wanted us to be chasing the terrorists, rather than concentrating on this organized crime group."

Horton pushed the budget report he had been working on to the side of his desk. "That supports your new direction. Did Hendrick have any suggestions on who this group might be?"

Hollis heard the excitement in Horton's voice, but knew he had to be a little cautious. "His people have just started to focus on finding out who this group is. They're looking at large metropolitan cities on both coasts. I doubt they've narrowed their search down to any one group in particular. They plan to hand this over to us and our Anti-Terrorist Group in DC."

"That makes sense, Bob, especially since we are the first ones in the FBI to make significant ties to the CIA. Keep me informed even if you just hit some dead ends."

"Will do, Jeff." Bob said, and immediately called his contact at NYPD, Captain Walter Johnson.

"Hello Walter, it's Bob Hollis. Yes, things have gotten interesting. We have a strong belief that a powerful crime group in the New York area has been working with the terrorists—and is the group planning a major financial attack in Manhattan."

"Really Bob. That's almost as big a story as the last one you told me," Walter said skeptically.

"Walter, I just finished talking with Fred Hendrick, the head of the Law Against Organized Crime Division for the FBI. His people are investigating the possibility that organized crime in the States has been funding Mideast terrorists. New York is high on their list."

"Ah, so you are giving me a call to see if we have any good candidates who could be carrying out such a threat."

"You've got it. Hendrick's people believe that the group has global enterprises and is funding terrorists to divert law enforcement from their own activities."

"As wild as that sounds, it makes a lot of sense. Let me do some probing around here and then get back to you."

"Appreciate it, Walter."

While Bob was contacting his resources, Fred Newman was also talking with contacts outside of the FBI. First on the list was an old school friend who now worked at NASA.

"Hello Fred. Are you calling about our next conference?"

"No, Bill. I'm working on some new pattern work. It has to do with organized crime. We are trying to see if some Mideast terrorists have any connection to organized crime in the States."

"That's an interesting twist. Here at NASA, we haven't followed organized crime for over a decade," Bill said sarcastically.

"Okay, smart guy. I know you're designing new software to look for hidden signatures inside of other objects."

"We've had some success when we can use a known signature. The sharper the signature we can define, the better the results. I assume you want to look through something like financial data or personnel movement data?"

"You've got that right."

"The closest thing we have to that is looking for black holes inside a Nebula cloud. We track star orbits then work backward to find the focal point."

"That is interesting. If we can find a focal point, that would be fantastic. Is this software available?"

"No problem, I can send you the code along with some user notes and signatures."

"Outstanding, Bill. I really appreciate this."

"Good luck, buddy. Let me know how well it works. Who knows, maybe NASA will start tracking organized crime."

"Sure thing, Bill."

The new theory had set off a flurry of activity throughout the FBI. In another part of the building, Janet Orr was being introduced to Charles Koury and Dennis Smith.

"This is the first Dennis and I have heard about this new approach. Have you been able to get started?" Charles asked Janet.

"Yes, I've started to look into Sauly Omara's connection with the CIA. I've searched some of Omara's files and gone over some of the work that he had carried out with the two of you."

"When we worked with Omara, he always sent us the data from the CIA. We never had direct access. Dennis received more data than I did."

"Right, both Charles and I put all that data on a stand-alone computer system so nobody on the outside can get to it," added Dennis.

"That makes sense. It's why I couldn't find any large databases."

"Yes, it was a prerequisite of the CIA."

"And they still want us to keep it that way. It took a lot of doing to have them clear me to have access to their database."

"Cory has an outline that we can use to get started."

In another part of New York, the activity was also causing concern as Kachen Mihad placed a call to Max.

"I need to see you."

"I will get back to you in ten minutes."

The phone rang in exactly ten minutes and Kachen heard a voice: "Go to the fourth meeting place at 6:30; ask for Phillip Morris."

6:30 pm
Somewhere in Brooklyn

As Kachen entered the room, he saw Max sitting behind a desk; two seats were placed in front of it. He sat down uneasily, moving around in the chair as if to find a more comfortable position.

"Thank you for meeting with me," he said, and got straight to business. "I attended the wedding reception of Shelly Nasser. I was introduced to her brother-in-law, Bob Hollis, an FBI agent. I overheard a conversation with Hollis and some people called the Cigar Team. They were talking about Tom Rowe and his sudden disappearance. I could see the expression on Hollis' face as everybody talked about Tom Rowe. I believe he will start an investigation into Rowe, as well as to start to keep a close eye on ActSof.

"Also, your new man, Pat Sherman talked too much," Kachen continued. The disapproving tone of his voice telling Max just what Kachen thought of Sherman. "He gave Hollis too much information. I took Sherman off to the side and set him straight. However, I believe Hollis has learned too much and will now put all of us under the FBI microscope."

Max absorbed the information, stroking his hair as he tried to maintain his composure. "You were right to call this emergency meeting. The Benefactor will be very grateful."

Relief showing on his face, Kachen added, "There is something else. When I realized Shelly Nasser's brother-in-law is an FBI agent, I suspected that Shelly might have been a mole at my brother's bookstore, so I gave her some false information about Tom Rowe. If she is a mole, I expect somebody to show up at the house Rowe used. I placed some of my men there to see if anyone shows. So far, though, no one has come by the house."

"Interesting. I know that you and Anu used Shelly to distract Damian Naparti so Anu could do his software implant. Now it seems we may have accidentally open too many doors for the FBI."

Once again Kachen shifted uneasily in his chair. "That is my concern. It gets even worse. We did not realize until the wedding that Shelly's father is VJ Nasser, a powerful man in the Mideast. He has many friends and many assets. He is not someone to cross."

This news shook Max; he stood up and paced the room. "We did not know that Shelly Nasser was the daughter of VJ Nasser. This is another twist that we had not counted on. We need to increase our information gathering. This meeting has been very informative. You need to keep your vigilance and as of now, do not make any movements involving Hollis or the FBI. I need to take care of some items and I'll be back in touch with you in the next two weeks."

As Kachen left, Max picked up the phone. "We need an emergency meeting. Tomorrow is good."

September 25, 2001
Franklin Lakes

As Johnson met Max at the front door and escorted him into the library where Cap's son, Cisco, was waiting, Madame was hidden in the shadows of the stairs. She quickly headed to her control room to observe the meeting.

"What I just heard is scary, and we may need to get in touch with John Harrison," Max told Cisco.

"I just have received a message from him. The New York FBI has established a special working relationship with the CIA. It's been upgraded with more resources to search for organized crime connections to Mideast terrorists."

"It's more serious than I thought," said Max, just as the others arrived.

"Gentlemen, our man tells me that the New York FBI has started an investigation to connect organized crime with global enterprises that are supporting Mideast terrorists." Cisco calmly stepped back from the conference table after he spoke and waited for responses.

"This is what I have been afraid of hearing! I knew they would get around to it sooner or later," Cyn said emphatically. "However, why just the New York division, why not the whole of the FBI?"

"We don't know, Cyn. We need to discover why—that's your task."

"Absolutely." Cyn moved over to the wet bar and poured himself a stiff drink of Scotch.

"Meanwhile, we need to hear from Max, who called for this emergency meeting."

Max moved to the head of the conference table while running his hand through his hair. "I've just talked with Kachen Mihad. He attended a wedding reception for Shelly Nasser, and learned Shelly's brother-in-law is Bob Hollis, the former boss of Abu Ladin when Ladin was masquerading as Sauly Omara."

"Why didn't we know this before?" asked Cyn.

Once again, the calm cool Cisco spoke. "Cyn, we had no reason to believe so."

"Believe so, really! This is just another example of underestimating."

"You're absolutely right, Cyn. However, we know it now and we need to go forward from here."

"So, where do we go?"

"Cyn, I have much more to discuss from my talk with Kachen," put in Max.

"Sorry, please tell us."

"Thank you. Kachen also overheard other conversations. There was a lot of talk about Tom Rowe, who as you know, was really Anu Ladin. Something in all the talk aroused Hollis' suspicions, and he pursued information on Rowe with some of the other ActSof people who were at the wedding. What he learned apparently caused Hollis to ask even more questions, included talking with our new man, Pat Sherman. Sherman talked too much, according to Kachen. Hollis actually asked Sherman if someone inside ActSof could have implanted something in the software to cause a financial crisis."

Numbers, usually much calmer than the excitable Cyn, was visibly shaken by this information.

"How could things have gotten so bad so fast," he injected. "We might as well have given him a roadmap of what we've been working on for the last four years."

"Okay gentlemen, we need to calm down and do some real planning about our next steps," said Cisco.

"I agree with you, Cisco. I have been listening to all of this new news," said Red, attempting to add some calm to the panic that was steadily rising in the room. "First of all, it sounds like the key individual is Bob Hollis. This also tells me that is why Harrison said the New York FBI had the lead in this new investigation. We've always known that eventually the FBI and or the CIA would turn their eye to organized crime's connection to Mideast terrorists. So, we do not need to panic."

"I agree with Red. Although isn't it quite a coincidence that Shelly, Hollis, Damian, and both the Ladins were so closely tied to each other. Is there anymore, Max?"

"Yes Cisco; there's one more coincidence. Shelly Nasser's father is none other than VJ Nasser."

Cyn jumps up out of his seat. "Wait a minute, *the* VJ Nasser?"

"That's right, Cyn."

"How did we not know this?" Cyn said accusingly.

"Nasser is a common name. And VJ has always been very private. There was no reason to make the connection," Max said defensively.

"Do you think that VJ has been aware of all of this from day one, maneuvering on the sideline and just waiting to make his move and take over the Big Kill?" Cyn asked.

"That is the million-dollar question—or in our case the trillion-dollar question, Cyn."

Cisco interrupted before the accusation became too heated. "Okay, we can sit here all day and speculate until we are blue in the face, but first, let's concentrate on the FBI and CIA.

"I am with you on that, Cisco, but what do we do about Bob Hollis?" said Numbers.

"We can't just eliminate Hollis. The investigation is much broader than just one person. He may be the impetus, but he is surely not alone," said Red.

"I agree with you, Red. Since things are already in motion, we can't just stop it. Therefore, we need to slow it down on the one hand and on the other hand continue to stay under their radar."

"We have been staying under their radar by being ingenious about our money movement. We need to develop even better ways to do the same thing," Numbers said as he took off his spectacles and slowly wiped them with his handkerchief.

"It sounds like you and Red have just defined your primary task."

"I agree with that, Cisco. I also think that Cyn and I need to do a similar thing with our people movement."

"Well, Max, you just got you and me a new job," said Cyn.

"For now, let's just concentrate on these two things. When we get a better understanding of where we are, we'll have a clearer idea of what to do next. We'll keep a regular meeting schedule of every two weeks," Cisco said, dismissing them.

After everyone left, Madame joined her son in the Library. "That was quite a bombshell we heard from Max. I can understand the FBI and CIA getting better at looking for us but to find that Shelly Nasser is the daughter of VJ Nasser and that her brother-in-law is in the FBI is hard to cope with."

"It is a big surprise and a scary one at that."

"Even so, I was very happy to hear Red speak about remaining calm. I am also proud of you controlling the meeting and not letting Cyn get too far out of hand. We need to do some serious thinking about how to proceed with this new information."

September 26, 2001
Versailles, France

That chalet of Margo Nasser's outside of Paris turned out to be much more than just a chalet. It was a luxury estate in Versailles. As Damian and Shelly arrived, Damian couldn't believe his eyes. The so-called chalet was massive. It had a large indoor swimming pool with a ten-foot diving board. The opening foyer was floored with inlaid Italian tile and boasted a crystal chandelier. The foyer opened up to a dining area with a table that could seat twelve; an even more impressive crystal chandelier hung over it. Off to the side of the dining area were a semicircle of a sofa and plush set of comfortable chairs with a sparkling mahogany circular table. The view to an outside hanging garden was provided by a series of Arcadia doors that led to the patio in front of the hanging garden.

"Hello Shelly and Damian. My name is Clorese," said a tiny, middle-aged woman with blue eyes and light brown hair. "Miss Margo told me to expect you. I hope the car set up at the airport was satisfactory."

"It is more than adequate," said Shelly, smiling.

"I am Miss Margo's housekeeper," she explained to Damian. "I have been with her for over twelve years. I have prepared some refreshments. Would you prefer to have them here or in the kitchen nook?"

"The nook sounds good," Shelly answered, as a stunned Damian followed silently into the kitchen, where a huge island was the center of the room. A row of refrigerators and freezers on the opposite wall then wrapped around to a sink. Next to the sink was a large cabinet followed by a set of Arcadia doors that opened up to another patio. Going further into the room there was a nook area with a table that fit six people.

"Please make yourselves comfortable. I will get the refreshments."

"This is a large kitchen," a wide-eyed Damian remarked.

"Yes, Miss Margo does a lot of entertaining."

"Without wanting to pry. Who does she entertain?"

"Mostly businesspeople. I don't know who they are but many of them have been here for many years."

"So this is why this 'chalet' outside of Paris is actually a luxury mansion?"

"I really don't know. I stay out of Miss Margo's business. All I know is that you and Shelly have the run of the house and that I am to let you know of the many things of interest here in Versailles. We can talk about that later. For now, please enjoy your refreshments and settle in."

NYC FBI Headquarters

"John, have you found something about Tom Rowe?"

"Maybe," replies a nervous John Thompson.

"Maybe?"

"Yes, maybe. The address he gave for his home residence is a phony. According to ActSof, Rowe was staying with his mother. She worked at Dow Jones in Princeton. However, Dow Jones has no information on anyone named Rowe and ActSof suddenly lost all information on him."

"So as of now, we have no information on Rowe. This is a little unusual. Everything else has shown us that if a crime group is behind this operation, they have been very efficient. If they did insert Rowe into ActSof, I would expect it to be clean with impeccable backup material," Bob summed up.

"That is why I said maybe I found something."

"Do you think the information was erased?"

"It's possible. But we know Rowe attended an Ivy League university. I have a search for him now at Princeton."

"When do you expect to get that information?"

"I thought I would have it already, so hopefully any minute."

"Well, if it isn't any minute, I am afraid we'll find nothing--that this Power Group also got that erased, leaving us with nothing."

A moment later Corey strolled into the office, humming. "Why such sour looks?"

"We are coming up with nothing on Tom Rowe."

"That's not good news. I have something to add to that. I just got word that your search of Princeton University has come up empty."

"This tells me that there really is a Power Group behind all of this." Frustrated, Hollis hit his hand on the desk.

"I'm with you on that, Bob but they can erase files but not people's memory. I'll get with ActSof and check with the people who interviewed Rowe and see if I can get some new leads."

"Cory, what have we done so far on searching the CIA database?"

"Two things. Fred Newman has some new pattern searching software from a friend at NASA, and also Janet, Charles, and Dennis have been exchanging ideas on how to proceed. I'm impressed just how well they work together."

"As of now Cory, it's the only thing that we have going for us. John, get the best pictures you can find of Rowe and go visit each and every teacher, possible classmates, and anything else you can think of at Princeton."

"I'm on it, Bob. First, I'm going to talk with Harry Simpson at ActSof. He interviewed Rowe when he first started there."

September 27, 2001
Versailles, France
Damian and Shelly slowly made their way downstairs and into the kitchen about 11:30 a.m.

"Well, good morning. I figured you two would sleep in this morning, so I didn't start cooking until just a few minutes ago."

A half-awake Shelly smiled at Clorese. "It smells delicious, Clorese. Are those my mother's blueberry crepes I smell?"

"Yes, they are, Miss Shelly."

A yawning Damian added, "I'll have some also."

"Later, after the two of you finish eating and get settled, I recommend you visit the Chateau de Versailles.

"Oh Damian, you won't believe this place. I love the Royal Court at the Palace," said Shelly as she started to fully awaken.

"How do you know about the Palace?"

"My mother has taken me there several times."

His eyes now wide open, Damian responded. "Several times! So, you have been in this quaint chalet before."

"Yes of course!"

"You never told me about it."

"I wanted it to be a surprise."

"Oh, it's a surprise all right. What other surprises do you have planned for me?"

"Well, my mother often met with some of her business friends at the palace."

"Really, just what kind of business is your mother in?"

"I think I need to let you two alone," put in Clorese.

"Thank you, Clorese. My wife and I have much to talk about."

"My mother deals in fine art. She has a lot of connections around the world. Many of the things at the palace have features that some of her clients are interested in. So, my mother takes them on a tour, and they talk about the different artwork they would like to have."

As he rubs his forehead, Damian asked. "Then what does your mother do to find these clients what they want?"

"She connects with her contacts and tracks down art objects."

"Would one of these contacts be your father?"

"As a matter of fact, he is one of my mother's best contacts."

"Oh, that's interesting! They are separated and yet they aren't really separated. Does your father also like fine art?"

"Yes, he does. I like fine art also. However, I was never interested in the business."

"Not now, but some day we need to talk more about all of this."

Hoboken, NJ
ActSof

"Harvey, I'm trying to find out more information about Tom Rowe. His sudden disappearance is unsettling to a lot of people," said John Thomson, speaking on the telephone.

"Yes, and I'm one of them. How can I help you?"

"Somehow his files here at ActSof were lost. I was wondering, where did he go to school and what department he was in?"

"He went to Princeton. He was in the computer science department. His advisor was Linden Mercer."

"Do you have his phone number?"

"No, but I have the number for the computer science department."

"That will do. Appreciate your help."

Thompson hung up and called Princeton, where he learned that Mercer had died in a car accident six months previously. He arranged to speak to a few of the man's students the next day.

Versailles, France

Even though it was late September, it was a beautiful sunny day, so Damian and Shelly decided to have a swim in the outdoor pool.

"The heater is working well; the water is very refreshing. Does your mother use this pool often?"

"Yes, so do her business friends. She has some special occasions in which she invites several of her clients to discuss the art she has information about."

"I'm getting the idea that this is your mother's business center."

"That's a good description."

"I have brought you both some snacks and drinks," Clorese interrupted. "I need to meet the truck that is delivering the groceries."

As Shelly got out of the pool to get the snacks, the grocery truck arrived. She could hear Clorese talking to the driver.

"Clorese, who is that young women at the pool?" the driver asked, looking through the kitchen window.

"That is Miss Margo's younger daughter, Shelly."

The driver with a lustful look on his face replied. "She is gorgeous. Is she married?"

"That is her husband in the pool. They just got married last Saturday."

A disappointed looking driver replied. "Too bad. Is her husband French?"

"No, he is an American and they will be living in the United States."

An even sadder look on his face as he said, "Oh, that is too bad, also. What do they do in the States?"

"He is a doctor and so is she."

As his eyes lite up, the driver continued his pursuit. "You know, I have been having some trouble with my back."

"She is not that kind of doctor. She has a PhD in Computer Science."

With a confused look on his face, the driver asked. "What is that?"

"I have no idea. It is what Miss Margo told me."

NYC FBI Headquarters

"Janet, have you gotten access to the CIA data?"

"Yes Cory; Charles and Dennis are setting up a series of databases to accumulate the data. You know that it has to be a stand-alone and connected to nothing on the outside."

"Yes, I remember Sauly saying the same thing."

"Charles is taking the lead on building some early signatures to use for the pattern searches. Meanwhile, Dennis is studying the search engines of the NASA software. It's important to understand how to implement the signatures so the algorithms can utilize them."

"Sounds like Greek to me. Glad you understand all of this," said Cory. He shook his head as if to clear it as he walked away.

In the meantime, John was giving Bob more bad news.

"Bob, I just talked with Harvey Simpson at ActSof and got the name of Tom Rowe's advisor at Princeton."

"Very good."

"Not so much; his advisor Linden Mercer was killed in a car accident about six months ago."

Once again Hollis slapped his hand on the desk. "John, this is smelling more foul all the time."

"Right, but it bothers me that someone would go to the trouble of trying to erase any memory of Rowe at Princeton. There are too many things and people involved to completely erase all knowledge of him there."

"I'm calling Fred," Bob said, as he dialed and asked the software expert to join them.

A few minutes later he and John were bringing Fred up to speed on Tom Rowe.

"Someone has been trying to erase Tom Rowe from Princeton. However, this seems a little foolish because there are people who must have had classes with Rowe, talked with him, while he was there," John concluded. "How can someone believe they can erase all of the information about one person. It is too sloppy, and this Power Group is not sloppy."

"Who did you call first at Princeton?" Fred inquired.

"I called administration."

"It would be very easy to write some code to make any files on Rowe come up empty."

"Really, that is amazing."

Hollis leaned forward in his chair, hands on his desk. "So, what does this buy them?"

"Most likely, time. My guess is that they believe Rowe left some information, most likely on a database at Princeton, that they don't want people to see."

"Now that makes sense, Fred," replied Hollis with a fresher tone. "So how do we go about finding this information?"

"Legally, we need a court order."

"We don't have enough information to get one."

"Then I guess it's old fashioned police work to find some clues and track down where this information may be stored."

"Thanks, Fred. John, I believe you have your work cut out for you."

A rejuvenated John jumped up from his chair. "I'm on it, I have a meeting setup for tomorrow at Princeton."

Franklin Lakes

Max headed for the Library and joined Cisco. "I have been briefing Sherman on everything we know about Tom Rowe. Some of the first files Red got from Princeton are giving Sherman an idea of Rowe's style of coding. It's quite different than what ActSof uses, so it has been helpful."

"So now Sherman needs to search through Rowe's work at Princeton and see what type of password he would use."

"That's it; a slow process. We can't just redo what Rowe did."

"I know," answered Cisco. "According to Red, Rowe set up some traps to keep someone from either undoing what he did or putting in something else. That's why Sherman needs to understand Rowe's techniques so he can get past the first security level set up by Rowe and then get to the key password."

"I really don't understand this stuff."

"Neither do I. It's Red's area of expertise," said Cisco.

A moment later Numbers joined them, followed by Cyn, who almost immediately said, "I hope somebody has some good news. My new plants at the NYPD tell me that there is a massive effort to look for us."

"It's good to see you too Cyn," Numbers said sarcastically. "Red is coaching Pat Sherman to break through Rowe's labyrinth of security to get to our imbedded code."

"I don't understand a thing you just said but you seem to believe it," replied Cyn, shaking his head.

With an unusual smile on his face, Numbers replied, "Hopefully Red can help you understand. For now, we need to get into some other business. Harrison, our security man, tells me the FBI have made some major strides in tracking Rowe. They now understand that Rowe left information at Princeton we don't want anyone to find."

As he stomped around the room, Cyn looked directly at Numbers.

"That is a real problem. By the way, where is Red?"

Still with that unusual smile on his face, Numbers said, "He is going to be a little late."

"Red has been setting up some roadblocks against the FBI at Princeton," Cisco put in. "For now, we need to see what progress Numbers has made."

Numbers slowly wiped his spectacles, then he took his time setting them properly on his face. "First of all, there is no money flowing into the US. Ali Ki's major flow of money is into Southeast Asia, then it goes to Japan. There it is broken up into small pieces. This looks like some long-term planning."

"I see similar movement to Japan with their people," chimed in Cyn.

"I've been routing our money to follow their movement to Southeast Asia, then to Japan, then back to Luxemburg through the companies we set up in Japan last year. By increasing our number of companies there, we have been able to break up the money flow into smaller portions. Meanwhile, I haven't seen any increase in the FBI search of any of the money flows."

Cisco, relieved, said, "Good, it looks like we are way ahead of the FBI on the money movement for now. Even so, the word is that the FBI is starting to search for more patterns, especially on the money flow back to the States. I believe this is our biggest risk for exposure."

"I agree with you, Cisco. I'm wondering about setting up some false money flows," said Numbers.

With a quizzical look, Cisco asked. "How would we do that?"

"There are large money flows from many world operations such as OPEC, the South American Cartels, the aircraft industry, to mention a few. We can route some funds into the same streams to make our money look like it came from some hot activity in the Mideast."

"I see where you are going with this, Numbers," Cyn said excitedly. "Then the FBI will get tangled up following other major money sources, once again tying up their resources."

"That's what I have in mind, Cyn."

At that moment, Johnson opened the door for Red.

"Sorry I'm so late."

"Have you completed your roadblock of Rowe's files?"

"I have selectively hidden all the files that I have not perused as yet. The ones I have searched are scattered in five different places. This will keep the FBI busy for at least a couple of months."

"Red, help me out. What are we looking for in Rowe's Princeton files?" asked Cisco.

Red took a deep breath, knowing he had to avoid computer jargon. "During Anu Ladin—Rowe's—time at Princeton, I worked with him on setting up masking software that identifies a set of particular transactions. Then it delivers those transactions to a focal point server. We take the information from that server, process it, and send it on to its original destination. After the information is processed at the original destination, the return information comes to the focal server, where we can process that return information and send it back to the originator of the transaction."

Shaking his head, Cyn blurted out, "Whoa, is this how we are skimming off the financial transactions?"

"That's right, Cyn. So now I am looking for the files Anu had modified to do just what I described."

"Wow! Now I understand why we are so concerned. Do we know on how many files he did this?"

"The quick answer is no. He may have erased all of those files. However, we cannot take that chance."

"This software stuff is going to give me a heart attack yet," replied Cyn as he wearily sat back in his chair.

"You're not the only one, Cyn! If it wasn't for Red, I believe I would have had a heart attack months ago," said Numbers as he uncomfortably moved around in his chair.

"Max, you've been quite for a while," said Cisco.

"Yes, I remember when we first set up the prince. Cyn kept telling us to be careful."

"What's on your mind, Max?"

"The U.S. is mobilizing. Volunteers are flooding blood banks and military recruiting stations. Millions of dollars are being raised for the families of victims. A new patriotic sentiment is surfacing. People speak of simplifying their lives and spending more time with family and friends. The U.S. government, instead of lashing back immediately, is forming a coalition including countries in NATO. This is a more orderly way than the government has operated in the last decade. We need to be a lot smarter, too."

"Glad to hear you say that, Max. I am with you a hundred percent," said Cyn.

"So, what do you have in mind, Max?"

As he ran his hand through his hair, Max spoke. "I wish I knew. I do believe we need better information than we've had in the past, even though we thought we had great information."

"We have lost our best source in Abu Ladin's Sauly Omara impersonation. It is far too risky to try and put another source inside the FBI. We have also never been able to get anything inside the CIA."

"Why don't we bug ActSof? If Hollis believes ActSof is tightly mixed in with the Big Kill we may be able to get some earlier information by listening in on what is happening there."

"Great idea, Red. I'll get on that immediately."

"By the way, Max. About Rowe's advisor at Princeton, have we closed off all loose ends?"

"I have been wondering about that myself, Cisco. The accident went well. Now I wonder about his computer files."

"That's a good point, Max," said Red. "I haven't checked Mercer's computer files, but I'll start that now."

NYC FBI Headquarters

"Hello Walter. I was just getting ready to call you," Bob said as he answered his phone and hearing the NYPD officer's voice.

"I figured that you were, so I decided to call you instead. We have been looking into your crime connection. Needless to say, there are quite a few in the New York area. However, most of them are local and some are national. The majority of international are with South America and Mexico. There are a few that appear to have connections in Southeast Asia, even fewer in the Orient. What we haven't seen is any of them with connections in the Mideast."

"I was afraid you were going to tell me that. I got the same sense from our people in Washington."

"Bob, if you think about it, other than oil, there really isn't a lot in the Mideast for a States-centered crime organization in terms of direct business. However, what if they were trading something?"

Hollis sat up in his chair. "What do you have in mind, Walter?"

"Let's look at drugs. What if the terrorists in the Mideast are helping to bring drugs from say Southeast Asia or the Orient and then transporting them through the Mideast?"

"Then they bring them into the States."

"That's the thought, Bob. So, we started to look for locals who could be getting their drugs from the Mideast. Unfortunately, we haven't yet identified anybody, but the word on the street is that drugs from Southeast Asia come through the Mideast to New York. Understand, this is not firm. It's more like an undertone."

"That may be just what is happening. The crime group would want to keep that under wraps as long as they could. There could be something here. Do you have any candidates?"

"That's what we're looking into now. Realize we are doing this from the bottom up while you follow the money and terrorist movement."

"That's about right, Walter. We are working with the CIA to track terrorist movement, and to some degree money movement. So far it's heavy on people movement. We're trying to find better ways to track the money."

"I'll send you the list and some details we have uncovered. It may take awhile but in the end the word on the street will tell us a lot more."

"That's what we are counting on, Walter."

September 28, 2001
Princeton University
Computer Science Department's Office

At Princeton, John entered a small conference room and introduced himself to Ron Bates and Jason Miller, two Princeton grad students.

"I am interested in learning more about Tom Rowe. He is a person of interest in an ongoing investigation."

"I knew Tom, we worked in the same lab together," said Jason. "Actually, we really only talked about technical issues. We never really got together socially."

"Same here," added Ron. "He was easy to talk with if the topic was technical, especially the software here at our lab."

"That is interesting; other people have said Rowe was very outgoing and friendly with his co-workers."

"He wasn't unfriendly, he was just focused on his work and classes."

"How well did Rowe and Professor Mercer get along?"

"They worked well together. Actually, I wished I worked as well as Rowe did with Professor Mercer. Rowe just had a way of coming up with some interesting approaches that always impressed him."

"I agree with Jason, in fact Professor Mercer said Rowe sometimes seems to think like a wily veteran, as if he had someone coaching him."

Thompson's antenna went up at this comment. "What did he do with all these impressive approaches?"

"What do you mean?"

"Where or how did he use them, and where did he put the files."

"He used them to accomplish an algorithm to perform something he needed his program to do. Then he would store the information as a file in memory."

"Did everybody use the same memory?"

"Everybody had an account and could store files under it on the university data center. We also have some local databases here in the lab, and then there are some within other databases in the computer science department."

"So, Rowe could have used many different databases?"

"Yes, he also could have put them on a flash drive."

"Are those devices kept here in the lab?"

"They could be anywhere."

"Did Rowe have some type of lockup?"

"Don't really know. We don't have any designated personal lockup."

"Has anybody replaced Professor Mercer?"

"Not really, we've been allowed to work in the lab but there are at least three other professors here, too."

Once again, Thompson could sense that things were eluding him. "Then I believe that my next move is to talk with these other professors. Jason, Ron, thank you for meeting with me. You both have been very helpful."

John returned to the department office and requested a meeting with the professors using the lab. Unfortunately, none were on campus that day. He made a few follow-up appointments and headed back to the office where he reported his findings to Hollis and Fred Newman.

"It sounds like Rowe had somebody coaching him from outside the University about coding," John told them.

"Any idea who it might have been?"

"No, and that is why I needed to talk to you. According to the students, Rowe would come up with some excellent software techniques to solve very difficult problems."

"So, you think that my people could look at some of Rowe's files and study his coding to see if we can identity his coach."

"You hit it on the head, Fred," said John, smiling.

"Bob, you need to get us a warrant so we can access these files."

"But these files are not just in one place, and as we had talked before, we believe that the Power Group has been methodically going through all of Rowe's files."

"So even finding the files is going to be a big effort."

"Right."

"John, this means the warrant is going to need a lot of detail."

"I agree, Fred. I am setting up interviews with three professors who are now using Professor Mercer's computer lab. Next Monday, I'll get started on preparing a warrant. Hopefully I can get more information from the three professors."

"Sounds like a plan."

Chapter 3

October 1, 2001
NYC FBI Headquarters
"Beverly, I need to put together a warrant that will allow me to search through many databases, storage rooms, and any furniture to look for information connected to a Tom Rowe. Rowe is a person of interest in an ongoing investigation that is believed to be a software attack on the financial institutions in Manhattan, NY."

A very busy Beverly responded to John Thompson calmly, "Okay John. Take this and list the items you believe are of interest in your investigation that exist at Princeton University. Next, take this form and establish the overall reason for the larger investigation. Then, use this third form to establish that Tom Rowe is a person of interest.

"The best person to help you is Teresa Simmons. When you get all that together and have your boss sign each form, then we need to get to a judge in Mercer County, the county in which Princeton University is in.

"Oh John, Princeton will resist this, so be ready for a fight."

Franklin Lakes
Cisco rubbed his forehead. "Mom, do you think VJ Nasser knows about the Big Kill?"

A very stoic Madame slowly responded. "I really don't know. However, it sounds a little too convenient to me that his daughter is right in the middle of all of this."

"Yes, but all of our sources tell us that both she and her new husband seem to be oblivious to VJ's operations, yet alone to ours."

"I know, even so, we are dealing with some very intelligent

people. We need to keep our surveillance on Shelly and Damian as a high priority. They may be a distraction."

Cisco got up from his chair to pace. "Really, you think it could go back that far?"

"I wouldn't put anything pass VJ. He has global connections and deals in information. He could have sniffed out what we were planning. His resources are that good."

Cisco looked at his mom whom seemed deep in thought. "What do you have in mind, Mom?"

"I have been going over our next steps. Every time I go through the options, it tells me not to eliminate anybody."

That remark seemed to come from nowhere. "I don't understand, Mom."

"First, we are not going to eliminate any of these people— Shelly, Damian, or Hollis. It would draw too much attention from the authorities, and VJ, too. Even so, I would like to see that pesky cop who uncovered Abu taken out."

"Oh, I see. We take care of the cop. Instead of eliminating the others, we increase our surveillance on them and let them show us what is really happening."

"Exactly! What is our update on Princeton?"

"Red is laying out a false trail that should keep them occupied for weeks. If he finds anything else that Anu left behind, we'll destroy it."

"This could be a bigger risk than we originally thought. This software stuff is getting to be more and more of a pain," she said with disgust.

"That's why we have Red and his people. I have a lot of faith in them. They've always kept us ahead of the authorities. In fact, the next thing we have in mind is to overload Hollis and his people with a lot of false information on Actsof, as well as money trails. Numbers is working on a scheme that will cloud any patterns or signatures the FBI is looking for."

Cairo Egypt
"Abdul, your campaign is going very well. You need to stay away from any talks about the terrorist groups. There is still too much unrest in the communities. Instead, concentrate on the flow of funds. We will have people in the crowd who will ask questions about that." VJ stood in the middle of the room. With the presence of a commander, he ordered **Abdul Moqued, his candidate, to do his**

bidding.

Moqued fidgeted. "I understand sir. Even so, how do I not talk about terrorists if someone asks that question?"

"Our people in the crowd will see that it doesn't happen. Ignore those questions without looking like you are ignoring them."

"I can do that sir," replied Abdul like a son who had just been lectured by his father.

Versailles, France

Damian was bothered that he hadn't known about his mother-in-law's wealth or occupation. "Shelly, how long has your mother been dealing in fine art?"

Unaware of his concern she nonchalantly replied. "Well, not sure, but Mom was working in fine art before she and my father separated. So, it must be a couple of decades."

"How did she get interested in it?"

"As best I can remember, Mom has always been interested in fine art."

"So, she has been interested in fine art for decades and then when she and your dad separated, she started dealing in fine art?"

"That's right. Why are you so interested?"

Damian knew he needed to proceed slowly. "Don't you find it a little suspicious that your parents separate and yet are involved together in a high-priced business."

"This is starting to upset me, Damian!"

"Well, why does your mother work? Your father has more than enough wealth to take care of her."

"Now you're really upsetting me. I'll be in the pool trying to cool off."

Shelly went to the outside pool. Damian right behind her.

"Shelly, please."

"Please what?"

"I am not trying to upset you. However, I am a little concerned."

"About what?"

"I'm having a hard time trying to resolve the fact that your mom is working in a highly speculative arena that is usually done by people who have a large inventory of fine artworks. I don't see that here, and yet she seems to have found a niche in that arena."

Shelly stopped walking, paused, and started to think. "I never really thought about it that way. Mom enjoys being part of the fine arts world. I never considered the business side of what she was doing, let alone what my dad has to do with the business. I am aware that Dad has some contacts that Mom never liked."

Damian moved next to Shelly and put his arms around her. "That is the part that bothers me, Shelly."

"Yes, I see your point. I just never thought about it before."

"I wish I never started this conversation," Damian said. His concerns about his mother-in-law's business were not worth ruining his honeymoon. "Let's make a pact to not discuss this topic again."

"Thank you for that, and now I will race you up to the bedroom."

NYC FBI Headquarters

"Charles, what is the status on the CIA databases?"

"They are all set up and ready to use, Cory. Janet and Dennis are running preliminary tests to exercise the NASA software. Dennis believes they have a good feel for how to set up the signatures."

With a smile on his face, Cory replied. "That sounds great. When will they start using the databases?"

"Most likely tomorrow. Today, they are running some signatures on some of the old data Sauly used."

Anxiously, Cory replied. "We need to find something. Every trail we find seems to dry up, as if somebody has already gotten there ahead of us. I need to talk with Dennis and Janet. See you later Charles."

He immediately phoned Dennis who filled him in on their progress, including drug traffic flow from the Mideast to the East Coast.

October 2, 2001
Franklin Lakes

Red arrived early and walked to the stables where Cisco waited. They mounted up their horses and headed to the waterfall.

"It is good to see the leaves changing color. I always like this time of the year."

"So did your dad. He especially enjoyed the rustic reds."

"Yes, me too. We have always had a great variety of colors. I remember Mom would like to paint some scenes at this time of the year. I never had the talent to paint like Mom."

"The only painting I have ever done is on a computer. Ah, I can hear the waterfall. Now that is a sound I enjoy hearing."

"I believe the horses have the same idea."

When they returned from their ride, Max, Cyn, and Numbers were waiting for them.

"Good to see everybody. Our Mr. Harrison has informed me that the FBI is looking at drug traffic from the Mideast to the East Coast seaports," Cisco said.

Cyn jumped from his chair. "That is not good news, Cisco. My sources at the NYPD have heard the same thing and are on high alert. The NYPD is rousting their snitches to focus on the drug traffic."

"Yes Cyn, I figured that is what would happen. Max, do we have anything to worry about?"

Max tried to remain calm. "Right now, no, but that will give the FBI's pattern search something extra to work with. They will start to find something as time goes on."

That was not what Cisco wanted to hear; even so, he remained calm. "Numbers, is there anything we can do to slow them down?"

Numbers slowly removed his spectacles. "My false patterns of money flow will confuse them. However, we may want to lead them down a winding path that looks promising but takes them away from us. Red, I am going to need your help on this."

"Cyn, what else have your NYPD sources heard?" Cisco continued.,

Cyn still hadn't calmed down. "The NYPD is continuing to look for us. They have strong convictions that we are in an area near Manhattan. They are concentrating their efforts on the typical mafia families in the greater New York area. Even so, they do not believe that any of these families are us. They believe that we are a group who interfaces with one or more of these families."

"That is scary, Cyn that they have gotten this close to figuring out who we are. We know they are sniffing around for drug connections to the Mideast, and now they are looking for the families as the drug outlets. Do they know how close they are to us?"

With an unhappy look on his face, Cyn replied. "No, they are just hoping to find some leads to follow. They have no clue as to how we get the drugs to the different families."

Cisco responded. "Even so, pretty soon they will be knocking at our front door."

"We knew that someday that the NYPD would do this. That's why we have established contacts at the head of the families only, and we never make any exchanges the same way twice. Each head of the family knows that if anyone else within his family knows about us that we will cut off his supply. This threat is our biggest buffer between us and the families."

"Yes, Cyn, I know that. However, as my dad would say, there never is any never. We cannot guarantee that the buffer will always hold."

Numbers decided to speak. "I understand your concern. Once again, I believe we need to drop little hints that the drugs are a foreign cartel who has no residence in the states. We have already set up protocol with the families to contact us through a foreign exchange in the Cayman Islands. They have no idea where we are located."

Excitement flickered across Cisco's face. "You want to drop some innocuous hints that we are not located within the US?"

"That's what I'm saying, Cisco."

Shaking his hands in the air, Cyn bellowed. "Gentlemen, I would be very careful with such a ploy. It could blow up in our face."

"Yes Cyn, we would have to be very careful indeed! My father would have probably said no. For now, we need to put it on the back burner. In the meantime, Numbers, what progress have you made with the false patterns of money and people movement?"

Once again the spectacles come off. "It's been slower than I hoped. I'm looking for candidate paths. I haven't found what I want just yet. My best candidates are large aerospace companies. They are global. Red has set up some simulation routines that I'm using."

With a confused look on his face, Cisco asked, "What are you simulating?"

"I'm picking a company and injecting money and people flow into their typical movements. Then the simulation runs through days and months of activity. As of now, I'm not satisfied with the patterns that the simulations have shown me."

"Oh, I think I see what you mean, Numbers. Do you have any idea when you will find some patterns that you like?"

Red collected himself and cleared his throat. "We have about a dozen simulations running right now. Numbers and I believe that by the end of the week, we will have what we need."

"Good to hear that, Red. Numbers, how are our assets doing in Europe and Southeast Asia?"

"Things are doing very well. Our expansion plan is right on schedule. Our profits are where we want them. The money movement is slowly shifting toward Japan as we planned. The terrorist money has jumped significantly since the plane crashes into the Towers. If they are not careful, they will expose themselves."

"That reminds me, my sources at NYPD have heard that the FBI has turned up the effort to find the terrorists' money. They have already localized some of the big funds in the European banks. Expect to see them converge on particular banks in a few days."

"Have they seen any of our money movement, Cyn?"

"I have not heard any talk about our money movement. Have you heard anything, Numbers?"

"No, as soon as we can get our false patterns up and running, we should be nearly invisible to the FBI."

"Cyn, any word on why the FBI is concentrating on the greater New York area?"

"It all comes back to the fact that the CIA still believes Manhattan is the target for the Big Kill. Since they notified the NYC FBI Headquarters, Hollis has been the focal point and has spearheaded every effort to uncover the Big Kill. Other than that, it doesn't appear that the FBI has uncovered any other reason to focus on the area. In fact, until lately, the FBI didn't have an inkling that we existed, yet alone where we are located."

Cisco rubbed his hands together. "Sounds like they are following their hunches, but to a great degree they are still in the dark."

"Max, is the Ali Ki planning any new targets in the New York area?"

"Since the aircraft strikes, the Ali Ki has gone quiet. Even so, their recruiting seems to have increased because more volunteers are joining."

Cisco's face changed again. "I wonder about the Ali Ki. We knew basically nothing about their aircraft strikes. Hearing nothing now makes me wonder if they have some other major missions in the planning phase. Isn't it odd that our imbedded sources in Iraq have not heard anything?"

"Well Cisco, if you recall, Ali Ki stopped a lot of their communication via phone. It appears that once the prince decides on a target, he chooses a leader, gives him the big picture, and then turns him lose to make it happen. This chosen mission leader works in isolation. As he pulls his team together, they only know their part of the mission. Unless one of the subsets happens to cross our sources, we won't know about it."

"So how do we infiltrate one of the subsets, Max?"

"As of now, I am at a loss."

Cisco got up from his chair. "Those are not the words I want to hear, Max."

"I need to pay a visit to Kachen. He has been one of our best sources."

"I believe you are right Max. I also think a visit to Egypt is in order."

"Consider it done."

Manhattan

Andrew Hollingsworth, a tall, slender Englishman who sported a crew cut, was one of VJ's right hand men. He always affected a tailored suit with a carnation in the lapel and seemed to be looking down his nose at everyone whenever he spoke. "Mr. Nasser, our guests are leaving the airport by copter. They should be here within ten minutes."

"Thank you, Andrew. This is a meeting that I have been anticipating for almost a year. These transactions will increase our assets in Europe by $50 Billion. Your work has been masterful, Andrew. I've told you before, when we are alone, you can call me VJ."

"Yes sir."

"There you go again, Andrew."

"You're right, sir. I have also forgotten to congratulate you on your daughter's wedding."

"Thank you, Andrew. That was indeed a grand time. I am also impressed by my new son-in-law. I have some big plans for him but we'll talk about that another day."

Bronx, NY

"Mommy, daddy is home."

Young Michele ran out to meet her father and jumped into his arms. "Mommy is talking on the phone with Aunt Shelly."

"Well let's go see how Aunt Shelly is doing."

Hollis carried Michele into the house and put her down in the kitchen where Louane had just hung up the phone. "I heard you were talking with Shelly. How's the honeymoon going?"

"Many things to tell you, but let's first have dinner."

After dinner with the children upstairs, Hollis and Louane relaxed with a glass of sherry.

"So, tell me about Shelly and Damian."

"First of all, Damian is in awe of mom's chalet. Shelly said he talked about it for two days. They also have been enjoying Clorese."

Hollis smiled. "I figured all that would happen."

"They are enjoying married life. Shelly took Damian to Versailles. He was surprised by how much Shelly knew about it. He didn't realize how much time we spent in France as children. However, that eventually led to an unexpected conversation between them."

With his crafty look, Bob replied. "Really, now what might that be?"

"You know very well!"

"Yes, I can imagine. I've held truth on our pact not to talk about your mother's business. Why are you bringing it up now?"

"After talking with Shelly, I'm starting to wonder about the business, myself."

"Why is you mother still working?"

"I believe it is for the joy of it. She doesn't need the money. She has always enjoyed fine art. She even thought about running a museum. However, that faded after a while because she enjoys the search and the joy of finding treasures more than just running a museum."

"I can understand that. However, some of that finding can get a little too shady, especially with VJ involved."

"Yes, I know. Even so, I doubt that it will stop anytime soon."

"I agree; but getting back to Shelly and Damian. What's happening between the two of them?"

"Damian is a little shocked by it all. He is also wondering about dad. He is asking himself, *who are these people*? Shelly doesn't know what to do. That is why I have decided to talk to you about this."

"I believe that Damian and Shelly need to do the same thing that we have done. They need to make a pact to not become overly curious about your parents and just let it happen. They need to let your mother do her own thing the way she has for years. I suggest they turn a blind eye to the business and just enjoy the benefits of seeing your mom do the thing that she loves."

"I was hoping you'd see it like that. I do believe it is the best way. It is not like Damian and Shelly will be with my mom all the time. They will most likely rarely see her."

"That's part of my point. Don't make a mountain out of a mole hill. Now, why don't we just go upstairs and enjoy the night."

"Give me ten minutes," Louane said with a knowing smile.

October 3, 2001
Versailles

"Damian, I just had a long talk with my sister. She and Bob talked about my mom and her business. They had the same issues that we are having. So, they decided to make a pact to not discuss mom's business and to go about their lives."

"I am with you on that. I couldn't bear having something like that come between us."

"Neither can I."

"Your mom and dad will be here on Thursday. How do we act?"

"According to Louane, we should ignore mom's business and only follow along if they bring up anything about it."

"Sounds like a plan.

Cairo, Egypt

"Hello, my friend. It is good to see you, Max," said Mohammed Ladin.

Max started slow. "Mohammed, I am so sorry about your son, Abu, and your nephew."

"I have now lost two sons and a nephew," Ladin said sadly.

"Mohammed, how can it be that none of us knew about the prince's attack on the Twin Towers in Manhattan?"

Mohammed snapped back to the leader that he was. "My friend, it has gotten more and more that way. Without your support and contact, we have no idea of what is happening in our Arab world outside of Egypt. We heard nothing of the recruiters who were heavily prevalent here in Cairo."

Max looked confused. "That is unusual. We thought that there would have been heavy recruiting."

"Not so, we believe that there is an influx of people from North America with modern technology talents. The recruiters are busy working with those people."

"Mohammed, do you know of a man named VJ Nasser?"

"Yes, he is very powerful. He is supporting a candidate to replace the corrupt official whom we killed in a car bomb."

"Is VJ involved with the terrorist recruiters?"

Mohammed looked surprised. "No, VJ has nothing to do with the

Ali Ki. In fact, the Ali Ki make sure they do not cross VJ's path."

Max pressed harder. "Are VJ's businesses involved in any illegal works, like drugs?"

Once again, Mohammed was surprised. "No, his business and operations are more subtle than that. VJ deals in very large transactions usually involving land and mineral rights. He has a massive network of people who search for land with high probabilities of mineral wealth that can turn a profit in a short time."

Even so, Max continued to pursue. "What about his stores that he has here in Egypt?"

With a smirk on his face, Mohammed laughingly replied, "The stores are not his primary source of revenue. Originally, he started the different stores here in Cairo because the infidels who owned stores charged too much for their products. VJ set up the same type of stores and undercut them. Since then, he has started stores in other parts of the world. I believe they are fronts that offer VJ and his people the ability to get involved in the local culture. That helps them to do their primary job of looking for minerals."

"Interesting; would you say that VJ is primarily interested in finance?"

"Absolutely, his father was a big financial player."

Max changed direction. "Is VJ a user of modern technology?"

"From what I know about him, he is all about staying on the cutting edge of technology."

Max paused and thought for a few moments before finishing. "This has been very informative, my friend."

"Well then, it is time for some good food and entertainment. The belly dancers are getting ready to start their show."

"So, let us not keep them waiting, Mohammed. It has been too long that I have been away even though I cannot stay long. I have to catch a plane back to the States this evening."

October 4, 2001
Versailles, France
"Well daughter, you are looking especially bright and cheery this morning," VJ, said, giving her a kiss as he and Margo got out of the car at the "chalet."

"I am just so happy to see you and mom."

Margo joined them and teased, "That must be it, what else could it be? Your dad is right. I can't remember when I have seen such a pleased look on your face."

VJ moved toward Damian and shook his hand. "Hello Damian. I hope you have enjoyed your stay here in Versailles."

"How could one not enjoy himself in such a setting? Clorese has already prepared some morning fare to welcome you home."

Shelly and Margo were already deep into conversation as they made their way into the house.

"Hello Madame, I hope your trip was successful."

"Yes Clorese, even so it is a joy to be back home, especially seeing my youngest daughter here."

With a smile on her face, Clorese informed Margo, "I believe she has much to tell you, Madame."

"I certainly hope so."

VJ and Damian had taken the long way around to the back and settled in by the outdoor swimming pool.

"This is a beautiful place, VJ."

"Oh, I am so glad you have decided to call me VJ. Yes, it is a wonderful place for Margo. As you probably have heard, I visit here often. Margo and I stay in close contact. She uses this villa as her headquarters."

With a relieved look on his face, Damian replied. "I am glad to hear someone call this place a villa. I was told it was a 'chalet' outside of Paris."

"Oh, they pulled that one on you," VJ chuckled. "The women seem to enjoy calling it a chalet. I myself have always called it a villa. Clorese and the rest of the crew do a fine job of maintaining its character and usefulness."

"Yes, I agree. Clorese seems to be very comfortable working and living here."

With a serious look, VJ stated. "I insisted on that being the case. I could not have Margo live alone."

"According to Clorese, she is anything but alone here in the villa and in Versailles."

"That is another reason why I like this villa. I hope that you and Shelly will visit it often."

"I would like that very much."

"I was hoping to hear you say that. Even though I call Cairo my home, I am rarely there. My business requires that I travel a great deal. As such, I consider this villa my home away from home. It gives me the feeling of stepping out from the business world and stepping into a quiet place in the country."

Clorese approached VJ and Damian with some breakfast.

"Ah Clorese, thank you. Just in time. I could see that Damian was getting hungry."

Clorese immediately picked up on VJ's humor. "Of course, that is why I brought the food out."

Clorese left the two men and went back into the house.

VJ slowly turned to a more serious note. "I have been very busy with my work lately and I have set up my biggest deal of my career, which I hope will mean I won't have to travel as much as in the past."

"Does that mean you'll be spending more time here?"

"It is a definite possibility. For now, I would just like to enjoy some of Clorese's cooking," VJ said, effectively closing off anymore questions from his new son-in-law.

In the kitchen, however, Margo and Shelly talked non-stop. "You and Dad seem to be very happy together."

"We have been doing a lot of talking. Your father is planning to travel less. In fact, I believe he will be spending more time here."

With a surprised look on her face, Shelly blurted. "Wow, that is a big change. What's brought this on?"

Margo continued her serious tone. "He has been working on a plan for the last couple of years to be able to setup his business so that it almost runs itself."

Wide-eyed, Shelly responded, "That is big. He was always so hands-on with everything in the past. Why the change?"

"He says he needs a change in his life. He says he needs a home."

"I thought that I would never hear that from Dad," Shelly said in awe.

Cautiously, Margo continued, "Well, let's just see how that works out. Enough about me and your dad. How are things with you and Damian?"

With a devilish smile on her face, Shelly replied. "We are enjoying our honeymoon. I just love being with him."

"Obviously, I can tell by the glow in your eyes. Even so, now you are married and things that you never thought about before will start to appear. So, what stumbling blocks have you come across?"

A little shocked by her mother's statement, Shelly looked her mother straight in the eye. "You don't waste much time, do you mom?"

"Shelly, I know life. It has many twists and turns. I can image that Damian was shocked by this house. I also believe that he has to have said something about the arrangement that your father and I have."

"As usual, you are right on target. He didn't realize how wealthy you and dad are."

"I thought that would happen. I assume you've talked with your sister about your concerns."

"Yes, and then Damian and I had a long talk and we agreed to not focus on it and to go about our own life."

Margo smiled. "That really won't be necessary. My business life will be winding down. I have already started that over a year ago. The deeper question is, how uncomfortable is Damian with our wealth?"

Shelly looked at her mother quizzically. "I really don't know. It is a big shock. Damian knew there was some wealth in the family, but not as much as we have."

"It will take some time. As the two of you live your lives, it will fade away as a stumbling block. I just want you to remember that this is the type of stumbling block that ruins marriages. You will need to be patient with Damian and let him work it out in his own way."

October 5, 2001
Brooklyn, NY

A disheartened Kachen welcomed Max. "I have been expecting to see you. Many things have happened, and many things have appeared that have been a big surprise."

"You are right, Kachen. The Benefactor is not very happy. One of the most disturbing things is discovering that Shelly Nasser is the daughter of VJ Nasser."

"That was a big shock to me—I had no idea her father was VJ Nasser. Nasser is a common enough last name; there was no reason to assume the daughter of such a wealthy, well-known man was working part-time in a bookstore."

"So, what do you know about VJ?"

Kachen sat down in his chair. "I know he has a very powerful organization. He is both greatly respected and feared. If he wants someone eliminated, they just disappear. Even the Ali Ki is afraid of him."

"Does VJ have anything to do with the Ali Ki?" Max hoped to confirm what he had learned from Mohammed with Kachen.

"No, VJ has nothing to do with any of the Islam movements,"

Kachen replied quickly.

"Is he against the Islam movements?"

"Not as long as they do not interfere with his business operations."

"How much do you know about his business operations?"

Kachen paused, sat back in his chair. "I know that he has been working on what is rumored to be the biggest operation of his career. It started about four years ago and involves several places throughout Europe and Asia."

An anxious Max asked. "What is it?"

"That is the big mystery. All I know is that it has to do with mergers and some key acquisitions. It is so big that even VJ could not finance it by himself."

That was big news to Max; he continued, "So, he has partners as investors?"

With a smirk Kachen replied. "I would seriously doubt that. VJ doesn't trust partners. He is very much hands-on with his endeavors."

Max was growing even more curious. "It sounds as if VJ is in a tough situation. He needs the finances but won't give up control of his operations."

Kachen continued to smile. "That was the case. However, rumor has it that about a year ago, he came across something that could turn a profit quickly. I have no idea what it is. The rumor is that it could be here in the States."

A worried look came across Max's face. "Where in the States?"

"I have no idea, and I have not heard of any of his finance people having anything to do here in the States."

"Why did you say his finance people?"

"Because they are the ones involved with mergers and acquisitions. They are his most visible people. That is how one knows where VJ is doing his next venture."

Max paused, then spoke openly. "I am getting the sense that maybe this latest quick profit deal is not the same type of business that VJ has done in the past."

"That's very possible. The rumor is that whatever it is just fell into his lap."

Max did not want to hear that comment. "When did that happen?"

"I don't really know. Remember, this is just a rumor."

"By the way, when did his daughter, Shelly, start working for your cousin in the bookstore?"

"That started several years ago. She came to the store looking for a book on Egypt. My cousin was trying to do his own accounting and wasn't doing a very good job. Somehow, he mentioned that to Shelly. She mentioned she could help him. She did such a good job that he hired her permanently."

Max's suspicions increased rapidly. "Really! Did your cousin know her before that time?"

"I don't believe he did."

"Well Kachen, this has been a very interesting discussion. I need to check a few things and get back to you."

October 6, 2001
Franklin Lakes

Max had called for an emergency meeting as soon as he left Kachen. "My news is more disturbing than I thought," he told Cisco as soon as he arrived.

"Let's wait till everybody is here," Cisco replied calmly.

When they were all settled in their favorite chairs with drinks in their hands, Cisco said, "Okay Max, what is the emergency?"

"In talking with Mohammed and Kachen, I have uncovered more information about VJ. Not only is he not involved with the Ali Ki, the Ali Ki is afraid to cross his path. So, we can dismiss him having any involvement with our prince."

Cyn didn't wait for Max to continue. "Well, that's good news."

"That is the only good news, Cyn. According to Kachen, VJ has been working on the biggest project of his career. It started about four years ago. However, it is so big that VJ could not finance it by himself."

Numbers' ears perked up. "That must be one big project; VJ has always financed his own projects. He never has any partners, maybe some small investors but never one large one."

"Your right, Numbers. So VJ had a problem. Then he stumbled across something that could bring him some quick money."

Max barely got the words out when Cyn again blurted, "What gives him the quick money?"

Max was getting a little frustrated with Cyn barging in on the conversation; he took a deep breath. "Kachen doesn't know. According to rumors it just fell into his lap. The bad part is that it is here in the States."

Numbers, always been the calmest of the group, jumped in before Cyn could speak again, showing just how upsetting this information was to the group. "That is really unusual for VJ. He has stayed clear of the States."

"That's right, Numbers. So I asked myself, why now is he interested in the States? I then talked with Kachen about VJ's daughter, Shelly. A couple of years ago she shows up at the bookstore to buy a book on Egypt. Kachen's cousin starts to tell Shelly how frustrated he is with trying to do his own accounting. Shelly volunteers to help him with his books. She does such a good job that he hires her."

There was no holding Cyn back. "That is too much of a coincidence!"

"That is exactly what I thought, Cyn."

"Right; it sounds like VJ sent his daughter to the bookstore to get her on the inside."

"Probably right again, Cyn. Somehow, VJ uncovered our Big Kill and sent Shelly to be a mole. My guess is somehow, VJ noticed Abu's activity and figured out what we were planning."

Cisco had let the conversation unwind but stopped it now. "Okay, this is a little bit of a stretch."

Cyn walked restlessly around the conference table. "We have talked about this before, Cisco."

"Yes, I don't like it, nor do I believe in coincidences, especially where someone as well-known in our world as VJ is concerned. However, I find it difficult to believe that he figured out the Big Kill from some activity of Abu—alias Sauly Omara."

"There is probably more to it, Cisco. We just don't know what those other things are. Even so, it sounds too suspicious to me."

"I'm with you, Cyn," put in Max.

"All right let's assume VJ knows about the Big Kill. So, why did he not do something by now?"

"Well Cisco, I think he is waiting and watching. He has his daughter implanted in ActSof. She probably knows that Anu, as Tom Rowe, inserted something into ActSof's latest product."

"Yes, you could be right, Red. So, what do we need to do from here?"

"We have our man at ActSof. We need to bring him up to speed and have him investigate both Damian and Shelly. The worst thing we can do now is make an overt move that will tip off VJ."

"Good thoughts, Red. You need to get with Pat Sherman, bring him up to speed, and give him some direction on how to investigate Damian and Shelly. Make sure he only investigates and does not take matters into his own hands."

Red, although usually cautious is quick to respond. "I'm with you, Cisco. I'll arrange to meet Sherman tomorrow."

"I'm glad you're ahead of us on this one, Red," Cisco said. "Max, Cyn, we need round the clock surveillance on both Damian and Shelly."

"We already have their phones bugged, including at ActSof and their personal phones."

"Good move, Cyn. Numbers, help Cyn; see if there's been any money flow or major gifts from VJ to his daughter. I am going to touch base with Mr. Harrison. We have a course of action; we'll meet again soon."

After the group had left, Madam joined her son in the library. "Good moves, son," she said in praise. "We don't know for sure that VJ is on to us, but we need to take these actions anyway. Even if VJ is not, we can still learn something that could help us by observing Damian and Shelly."

"Do you think this is enough?" Cisco asked anxiously.

"We may find out soon enough. I am surprised we have not heard more from Cyn's moles at the NYPD. I don't know if this means that nothing much is happening or if we don't have the right people in the right places."

"Cyn seems confident in his people."

"I agree; Cyn has a natural way of reading people. He has always selected people who can penetrate the most difficult circles of interest. Even so, I don't like this. Things usually are not this quiet," muttered a concerned Madame.

As he rubbed his hands together, Cisco stated, "I need to put some pressure on Harrison."

"Yes, that is another source that has been too quiet. It seems everybody is circling their wagons, keeping information only within a select few."

"And that usually means either the operation is small or it will take a long time to unfold. We are very close to making the Big Kill happen."

"You've learned well," praised Madame. "Let's make sure nothing stops us this time!"

Bronx's Zoo

"I want to see the giraffes," Michele shouted excitedly.

"We will see them, but first we'll look at the monkeys. Just stay with your brother and where daddy and I can see the both of you."

"OK, Mommy. Can we feed the monkeys?"

"They don't want us to do that anymore."

"Why not?"

"They are afraid that people might make the monkeys sick."

"I won't do that."

"I know you won't mean to, but they still won't let anybody feed the animals."

The Hollis family did their usual walk through the zoo. As they approached the water show, Bob moved over to a rail bordering the penguins pool. Captain Walter Johnson of the NYPD was already there.

"Your kids seem to be having a good time."

"Yes, they both love the zoo. So, what is happening in the Big Apple?"

Johnson started slow. "We have a lead through one of our informants. We believe drugs have been coming into Manhattan from somewhere in the south. It is always a very big order. It is never done the same way twice, and only with a direct contact with one of the family member's top men."

Hollis's eyes opened wide. "Why are we talking about it here?"

Johnson wasn't happy. "We believe we have some moles in a couple of our precincts, including mine."

Hollis knew the feeling of having a mole. "Is this new information?"

"Less than five people know, including you."

"Is the drug traffic done with only one family?"

"We're not sure; we think it can be with each of the families in all the boroughs."

"Wow, that could be very big! One would think that with that much action and territory that we would have known this a long time ago."

An unhappy Johnson replied, "As I said, we think we have moles and that they have been misdirecting things to keep us from discovering the activity."

Hollis paused. "What is the drug?"

"Heroin."

"So it could be from the Orient."

"That's our guess; it seems to come into different seaports on the East Coast, then is brought up to New York City."

"Could there be a terrorist connection in moving the drugs?"

"As of now, that's our best guess. We believe that the drugs are moved over land through Asia and then down into Africa before coming to the States."

Hollis relaxed. "This is fitting some of our possible scenarios. We need you to select your most trusted people and let us get together to scope out just how we are going to investigate this."

"I'll get to you before next Friday."

"Now, I need to rejoin my family."

Hoboken, NJ

"No matter how great the honeymoon was, it is good to be back home, even if it is a new home."

"It's a nice home, Damian."

"That it is, dear. It will become even nicer as we raise our family here."

"Speaking of family, I need to give my sister a call."

Shelly surprised Louane, not just with her phone call, but with the news that their father was considering semi-retirement and their mother closing her business,and that they would both be spending more time together in Versailles.

"Wow! When did all this happen?" Louane replied.

"Believe it or not, they have been planning it for the last couple of years."

"That's a revelation. I can't wait to tell Bob. We both thought that would never happen. What does Damian think about all of this?"

"Damian says he had a great talk with Dad, and he thinks Dad really means what he is saying—that Dad is tired of always traveling and never really having a place to call home."

"Do you really think that Dad is going to retire or is he going to setup Versailles as his new headquarters?"

"I didn't think about that. However, knowing Dad, I would not put it past him to do just that.

Bronx, New York

Bob was just as astonished when Louane told him the news.

"Even so, I know Dad and I hope he's not using this to setup Versailles as his new headquarters," she added.

"Your dad is very shrewd and cunning. However, he and your mom have been separated for a long time. Maybe, just maybe, the time has come that they have done it long enough."

"I admit, I am a little suspicious. You know that Dad is supporting a political candidate in Cairo. Why would he do that and still be planning on leaving Cairo?"

"When I talked with your dad at the wedding, I didn't get the feeling that he had any motive other than getting rid of some of the political corruption that has been prevalent in Cairo lately."

"Dad can be somewhat underhanded at times."

"Listen, I need to tell you something that I never shared with you. Several years ago, the CIA suspected that your dad was supporting the Ali Ki. There was a very big investigation undertaken by both the CIA and the FBI. We found that your dad was not supporting the Ali Ki but was against what they were doing. So, if your dad could walk away from the Ali Ki, I doubt that he has any underhanded thoughts about Versailles."

"I hope you're right."

October 8, 2001
NYC FBI Headquarters
"John, any progress at Princeton?"

"We have plowed through hundreds of files but have found nothing but Rowe's academic work. We haven't seen anything from an outside source. There is a lot more to go through. Actually, Princeton has been very helpful."

Disappointed, Bob said, "Too bad, I was hoping to find something. Cory, anything on the patterns?"

"The new software Fred Newman got from NASA is finding some anomalous patterns we hadn't seen before in the CIA data."

Hollis lifted his head. "What kind of anomalies?"

"Financial information in central Europe. So far, we have been able to identify about a third of them. Some are well-known and we can eliminate them. You see, you get a bunch of patterns and you have to separate them from each other through an elimination process. It's time consuming."

Hollis' enthusiasm subsided. "What about financial flow from Europe to the East Coast?"

"We haven't gotten that far. First, we have to eliminate what we see in Europe. Then we can start looking at the remaining patterns and see where they go in the States."

Frustrated, Hollis asked, "When do we get to that?"

"May need another week."

"Well, we are making some progress, I guess. Plus, I've got some new information from the NYPD. They have an informant who claims that the drugs are brought into the New York area by establishing direct contact with the lead man of one of the New York family— different families each time. Plus, the deliveries are always done differently, both place and medium. Each delivery is exceptionally large."

"Wow Bob, that is a major change," said Cory

"Yes, it is, Cory. In fact, they think the delivery is just a drop. Nobody is there from the family. Later the family moves the drugs, usually heroin, a piece at a time."

"Do we know who owns these drop offs?" asked John.

"We don't; so far it is never the same place."

"That seems a little risky, Bob. Somebody has to own it just to keep anybody else out of the place."

"That would be my guess. Even so, it is being done. My guess is that the building is owned by the family and there is a regular amount of traffic so even a large heroin load can be easily disguised."

"If I was the family, I would set up a slew of legal businesses with warehouses all over the area. The NYPD can't watch all of them all of the time."

"Makes sense, John."

"The other thing is, you said the contact is directly with the head of the family or his lead man, along with the fact that it is a drop not an exchange. Such a deal has to take a lot of trust and cooperation. Such trust takes a long time to form."

"I'm with you on that, John. It probably has taken a long time to set up such a deal. So, we are dealing with a powerful group who has a very high degree of trust from the New York families."

Thompson persisted with his questions. "Does the NYPD have any idea who this group could be?"

"They are at somewhat of a loss. They are aware that we believe this Power Group is located somewhere in the area but they don't have enough definite information to point to anyone."

"It seems we are constantly dealing with ghost."

"You can say that again John! In fact, my contact, Johnson, is concerned that this Power Group has some moles in his precinct."

That was shocking news. Thompson leaned forward in his chair. "So, what is Johnson doing about that?"

"Everything we have just talked about is only known by a few people at the NYPD. Johnson is keeping this under wraps, which means he has to move slowly and cautiously."

"That means it will be a long time before we can get anything back from the NYPD," said Cory, discouraged.

"You're right, Cory. This is why we need to get those patterns we have been talking about."

"I wish we could move faster, Bob. It takes time to go through even the refined, processed information. But the NASA software is doing a great job. We'll find us something we can use--eventually."

Hollis sat back in his chair. "I hope you're right, Cory, because most everything else seems to hit a blind alley. Okay guys, let's get back to work."

Hoboken, New Jersey
ActSof

"Welcome back. It's good to see the two of you. How was France?"

"Harvey, it was amazing, and that little chalet outside of Paris is a mansion in Versailles," said Damian.

"Oh Damian, it is not a mansion," put in Shelly.

"It is to me. It has an indoor swimming pool and an outdoor swimming pool. The kitchen is larger than our old, original building."

"Yes Harvey, it does have a large kitchen and some very nice large rooms but it still is not a mansion."

With a smile on his face, Harvey responded. "I'll take your word for it, Shelly. Now, let's start talking business. Tilghman wants us to get into cyber security."

Excited, Damian threw his hands into the air. "Really! He has finally decided to do it."

"That's right, Damian, and he wants you and Shelly to take some courses at Stevens. You get to go back to your old haunts, Shelly."

"Who else will be taking these courses?"

"Pat Sherman will be going with you two."

"When do we start?"

"You need to talk with Pat; he has all the information. I believe the workshops start next week."

Curious, Damian asked. "Isn't this the middle of the semester?"

"Normally, yes. However, Stevens has just put this material together and is doing a series of workshops."

"Well Shelly, let's go find Pat."

Franklin Lakes, New Jersey

Red and Cisco mounted up and headed off into the cool fall weather. The leaves on the trees had already started to change. The ground was getting a little harder and the brisk air was refreshing. The horses seemed to enjoy the brisk air as they made their way through the woods headed for the waterfall. As usual, they rode silently, enjoying the day. It wasn't long before they arrived. Leaves were flowing on top of the water and the sunlight bounced off the water. They dismounted, sat by the waterfall, and let their minds wander awhile. There were no sounds of rushing traffic or people talking in the background, just the quite of the woods and the sound of the waterfall. The horses drank from the stream. The two relaxed men mounted their horses and headed back to the stables.

Numbers arrived just as Red and Cisco returned to the stables. Johnson escorted everyone to the library and offered drinks.

"I want to enjoy this one before Cyn shows ups and starts tearing my plans apart," said Numbers.

With a chuckle in his voice, Cisco replied, "Yes, I know Cyn has been unhappy lately. He worries too much."

Cyn and Max entered the library, Cyn shouting, "Who has good news for me today?"

"Hello, Cyn, good to see you. Have you and Max set up the surveillance on Damian and Shelly?"

"It's in the works. They've returned from Versailles. Sherman has been thoroughly briefed. He tells us that ActSof is sending him, along with Damian and Shelly to Stevens to learn more about cyber security, whatever that is."

"What do you think of that, Red?"

"I like it. This gives Sherman a great opportunity to build the type of working relationship with Damian and Shelly that we need."

"That's our thought too, Red. Sherman has been researching Shelly's earlier work on their intelligent engine software. The workshop will give him a great opportunity to get the firsthand information on how her software algorithms work."

A smile crept across Red's face. "That's good news Max."

"I thought you would like that."

"We're setting up a team to watch Damian and Shelly outside of their time at ActSof or Stevens. It will be in place tomorrow."

"Glad to hear it, Cyn. I have a feeling that Damian and Shelly are going to show us more about Rowe and his work than anybody else."

"That would be a good thing since I still have not found anything that leads me to Rowe's password."

Frustrated, Cisco addressed Red. "I find it hard to believe that you have not been able to uncover that lousy password."

"Believe me, no one is more frustrated than I am. I'm the one who told Anu to choose his password carefully and not tie it to any of his known everyday things," Red said apologetically."

"Well, he seems to have done a great job of that."

"I don't understand this software stuff and I don't trust it," Cyn complained—again.

Cisco interceded. "Most people feel the same, Cyn. However, it is running the world and will for a very long time. We need to work with it."

"I hear you, Cisco, but as good as you say it is, it's also a nightmare."

"To you and me, yes, but to Red it's pure heaven. So Cyn, has VJ given Shelly any money to speak of?"

"VJ gave Damian and Shelly a new house just outside of Hoboken. We're talking at least $200,000. He has also setup certain trusts for future grandchildren. Then he decided they both needed new automobiles. After that, he believed a new house needed new furniture so he outfitted it completely. Since it was still a little on the warm side for September, he had a local nursery sod the lawn, put in bushes, and set up a terrace in the backyard."

"Very good. So VJ has taken a little different turn than he did with his older daughter, Louane. You need to see if VJ has also set up trusts for his two grandchildren by Louane."

"Good point, Cisco. It looks like VJ has stepped out from the shadows, just as you thought. He's also spent more time with his wife in Versailles. So maybe the rumors that we have heard about VJ getting ready to retire have some merit."

"Could be. This could change everything. What bothers me is that maybe VJ has really latched onto our Big Kill and figures to make a killing to finance his latest and largest project. Then he can retire."

"Yeah, I'm, afraid you may be right."

"Even so, I doubt he knows that we know. Numbers, what good news do you have for Cyn?"

"Red put together a program for me. I've set up false money trails. This will keep the government busy for months. Next move is to do something similar with people movement. Red and I are working on that now."

"Well, it's great to get some good news—emphasis on some."

"I thought you would like that, Cyn. I've also gotten some feedback from Harrison. It matches what Max told us about the Ali Ki's recruiting via the internet. These are not just gun carriers but educated people with technical talents—especially in computers. It seems somewhat ironic that the prince is getting this influx of technical talent and he himself is probably hiding somewhere in a cave in Afghanistan."

"What about his lieutenants? Do we know where they are located?" Cyn asked.

"Nothing yet, apparently that information is being kept close to the vest. Let's let it go at that. We have work to do. This meeting is over.

As everyone left, Madam, as usual, joined her son in the library. "Do you think that VJ really knows about are Big Kill?" he asked.

"I don't know, son. However, too many little signs are showing up that I do not like. We need to keep a close eye on VJ—not an easy task. With his entourage and connections, he is very slippery."

"Cyn believes our people should keep track of VJ and his wife."

"Our best bet could be Pat Sherman getting close to Shelly at those cyber security workshops. If she is working for VJ, Pat may be the one able to discover that fact."

"It may be the break that we're looking for. If it is true that Shelly is working for VJ, we can use her."

"Provided VJ doesn't know that we have a second man at ActSof who can get very close to his daughter. For now, let's just go about our business, son."

Chapter 4

October 9, 2001

Hoboken, New Jersey

"Hello Pat. Shelly and I need to get up to speed with this cyber security workshop."

"This is exciting. Tilghman talked to me last week and said he wants to get into cyber security. Our software people have been working on this for at least six months. Tilghman wants us to lead the way in developing the products—but I imagine you know all this."

"Yes, Tilghman briefed Shelly and me about a month ago. We knew he was looking for the right way to get us up to speed and we suggested that you also needed to be in the loop since you're our lead network person. So, do we have some upfront material we can study before we go to the workshop?"

"Yes—both hard copy and softcopy. Both of your computers have all the files. Stevens recommends we look over the intro section to start; it's about fifty pages. I've gone through it twice already, and it's finally start to sink in."

"Well, it sounds like we need to get started. Under what is all this material stored?"

"It's all in a folder labeled 'Stevens Cyber Workshop.'"

"That is simple enough. When is the first meeting?"

"Next Monday; all the directions are in the instructions."

"Pat, don't forget that tonight the Cigar Team is meeting. Shelly and Bob Hollis will be there. We meet in North Jersey at the JR Cigar Store."

"Looking forward to it—I've already got the directions."

Brooklyn, NY

"Kachen, have you been able to obtain any more information on

VJ's big project?" Max asked Kachen during their meeting at the fish market.

"I have no news."

"The Benefactor believes that VJ is planning on retiring soon and that this big project will be his last one."

Kachen looked suspicious. "That would be very big news if it happens. I'm told VJ never talks about what he will be doing in the future. Why do you think he is preparing to retire?"

"He has started to come out of the shadows. He makes a big appearance at Shelly's wedding. He buys them a new house and completely furnishes it. He sets up trust funds for his grandchildren. This last year he has spent more time with his wife in Versailles. We believe that his latest project is his lead-in to retiring."

Kachen leaned back in his chair. "You could be right. I remember that some of my people have commented that VJ has been rarely seen in Cairo over the last year or so."

"Kachen, I need you to alert your friends in Cairo to pay more attention to VJ's people. The Benefactor needs to know as much as we can about VJ and his plans for his near future."

"Consider it done."

"Also, how is your cousin at the bookstore?"

"I really don't know. I have not had much contact with him lately. Why do you ask?"

"We are a little suspicious that VJ's daughter just happens to have been working for your cousin in a bookstore in Brooklyn when she was going to a school in Hoboken, New Jersey."

Kachen paused. "Ah, I see your point. Maybe it is time that I pay my cousin a visit."

"Take care of yourself, Kachen, and let me know if you hear anything of what we have just been discussing."

"Will do my friend."

Northern New Jersey
JR Cigar Store

"I have been looking forward to joining you and the Cigar Team," Bob told his new brother-in-law as the greeted each other that evening at the Cigar Store.

"Everybody else has arrived and are across the street at the barbeque place."

"I thought that you usually had pizza on cigar night."

"Usually yes, but this is an old haunt of Warren's. He's been wanting to get us up here for almost a year now. He grew up in the area and says this little Mom and Pop place has the best spareribs in New Jersey."

"Let's join them."

Across the street, they greeted the team.

"Have you all been in Manhattan lately doing any jobs?" Bob asked.

"We were just discussing one. It's next to that 66-story building that we worked last year. Roy and doc have been setting it up. We will be starting it next week," said Reuben.

"What are you going to be doing, Reuben?"

"Their chillers need to be replaced and their air handling system along with control system need to be updated."

"Is that a big job?"

"It is just as big if not bigger than the one we did next to it. Since we are coming into the colder weather, we can take the chillers one at a time offline and start retrofitting the air handlers. We will build out the new control system in sections as we refit the air handlers."

"That's all Greek to me," Bob smiled. Have you heard of any problems like they had last year with the chillers being sabotage?"

"We haven't heard of anything like that. However, building owners are not taking any chances. More and more of them are upgrading their systems not only for efficiency but also for security."

"That sounds like it could provide you with a good market."

"It has so far, and we believe it will continue for several years. What happened to the Towers on 9/11 has worried many of the building owners. Each of these skyscrapers have many firms with significant computer facilities. When the Towers went down a lot of people lost valuable information."

"Wouldn't they have their data backed up?"

"Most of them do, especially the larger firms. They have backup files for a least a month. However, they do so many operations in one day that actually aren't backed up that they can lose significant data."

"Didn't think about that, Reuben. Damian, does ActSof have backup for your software and its data?"

"It's part of our new product line. The information isn't stored in only one location. This is where the networking comes into play. Pat is our new lead man on networking our new products. He's taken over for Tom."

Hollis' antennae went up. "Oh, so how does that work, Pat?"

"Our products are networked to many locations for a given customer who has multiple locations. Usually, we and the customer set up more than one master location. As transactions occur, duplicating processes run in the background and send the information to the different masters which are located at different geographical locations. So, if something happens in one location, other locations will not have been affected and thus the information is not lost."

Trying to follow as closely as he could, Hollis gathered himself. "Does everybody have this feature?"

"No, but many companies are quickly moving in this direction. What happened to the Towers has just accentuated the importance of having a more secure and flexible information system."

"What part of this networking do you do?"

"I concentrate on one major facet. My job is to ensure that the system can perform the main function it was built to do and be able to carry out the duplicating and transfer of the same information in near real time."

With a confused look on his face, Hollis replied, "It sounds very sophisticated." He hoped he didn't sound too clueless.

"It is, and if not done properly, can cause a great many problems."

Hollis changed direction. "What does Shelly do in all of this?"

"Damian and Shelly can tell you more about what they do than I can."

"Someday I just may ask them about what they do. However, I probably wouldn't understand much. It's very complicated to me. I would think that somebody could throw a monkey wrench into a system like that and cause a lot of problems."

"That's why we have security programmers and why ActSof will be getting into cyber security."

Hollis was surprised at this news.

"Bill Tilghman started the company working on cyber security about six months ago," Pat continued. "Damian, Shelly, and I are going to be taking a course at Stevens on cyber security starting next week. We will help to establish a new product line and merge it with our main product."

Hollis's suspicions were growing. *Was Tilghman involved in the conspiracy, or was he just a pawn?*

October 10, 2001

NYC FBI Headquarters

The next morning, Bob told his team everything he'd learned at the Cigar Team meeting.

"That is interesting news, Bob. My gut tells me we need to find a way to get closer to ActSof," John said. "I've been investigating Pat Sherman. Like Tom Rowe, he's is a computer science major. He grew up in Newark and did his undergraduate work at NJIT. He and Tom attended the same computer conference back in April of 1999."

Hollis moved forward in his chair. "That's interesting, John. Can we tie Sherman and Rowe together any other way?"

"Haven't been able to do that yet. I'm contacting some of the speakers and members of the technical committee. It's a long shot but maybe they can put them together."

"Stay with it, John. There is something about ActSof that puts them right in the middle of this financial problem. I want you to check out who really owns ActSof, where they got their startup money, how they became so successful so quickly, and why so many firms have bought their accounting products."

"I'm with you on that, Bob. So far, everything I've seen about ActSof says they're clean. It may very well be that they have been infiltrated by this Power Group we are chasing."

"That reminds me, Captain Johnson has a short list of the families that the NYPD believe are receiving the drugs from the Middle East. It looks like both the Bonanno and the Gambino families are prime candidates."

"What is the NYPD doing with respect to these families?"

"They are tracking down every piece of property that these families own or frequent."

"Well, that's a start. So, what can we do about these families, Bob?"

"I've already called Fred Hendrick in Washington to get a list of all known assets of both families and send them to the NYPD."

With a smile on his face, Cory spoke. "This is beginning to sound like a real lead, Bob."

"Yes Cory, I believe we are onto something that has alluded us for a long time."

October 12, 2001
Hoboken Police Station
Phil Smith followed about ten feet behind his boss Lt. Chad Puleri,

as they headed to the door of the Hoboken Police Station. As Chad stepped out of the building, a shot wrung out and he collapsed, a bullet in the chest. Phil rushed to the doorway, gun drawn, and crouched, peering out the door to try and locate the shooter. He looked at Chad; he wasn't moving. It was obvious he was already dead.

Two officers had taken cover behind two parked police cars. The first officer, Carl Jennings, yelled "I can't see any shooter. I've scanned all of the buildings across the street. There're no windows open—I doubt it came from inside any of the buildings."

The second officer, Bert Johnson, responded, "I can't see a shooter, either. My guess is the shot came from the top of the building directly across from us."

"The two of you enter the building, I'll cover you," shouted Phil. Without hesitation, the two officers moved swiftly across the street and entered the six-story building.

Other officers were now coming out of the station, taking positions behind the parked cars. "Does anybody see anything?" Phil yelled.

"I don't see anything," responded one officer, and several others chimed in with their own affirmatives.

"It looks like the shooter was here," Officer Jennings shouted down from the top of the building across the street.

"Cordon off the area and get forensics up there," responded Phil as he looked at his partner and mentor lying dead next to him. Tears started to form in his eyes as he bent over Puleri.

A moment later, the medical examiner appeared and checked Puleri for any signs of life. He stood up. "Phil, I'm so sorry."

Phil collected himself. There was nothing more he could do here. Chad would want him to catch whoever had killed him. He dashed across the street, entered the building, and headed for the roof. "Have you found anything?" he asked when he got to the top.

"The shooter stood here, braced his gun on the ledge. You can see the scratch marks left by the stand that he used," replied Jennings.

"He must have been here for some time because the gun stand has been moved around; you can tell by the pattern of the scratch marks," added Johnson.

Forensics arrived at the rooftop. "Find something so I can find the scum who shot Chad," Phil commanded. "Let me know as soon as you do."

Phil left the rooftop and headed back into the police station. Chad had already been moved as Phil headed to Chad's office. The Captain,

Harry Afferio, saw Phil and quickly walked to him. "Phil, anything you need, you've got it. Just find who did this, and don't take any grief or stalling from anybody."

"Thanks Captain," replied a teary-eyed Phil. First thing, is to go over some of Chad's recent cases."

"Good start, Phil. Pete Henderson will be assigned to help you."

October 15, 2001
Hoboken, New Jersey
After the funeral for Puleri, Phil continued reviewing the dead man's cases. Only the death of Sauly Omara's girlfriend stood out.

"The feedback that we got from the FBI indicated that the Omara case," Smith explained to his captain, "was part of a major scam to embezzle money from many of the firms in Manhattan. Omara was put in place by a Power Group with enormous assets. So, when I look at the hit on Puleri, it was a first class, professional hit."

"You think that this Power Group put the hit on Puleri?"

"Yes, and I need to touch base with my FBI contact and bring him up to date."

"Waste no time doing that and see if we can be of any help to the FBI in tracking down this group."

"I'm on it," he said and called his contact at the New York FBI Headquarters.

NYC FBI Headquarters
"The officer who headed up the investigation into the death of Sauly Omara's girlfriend, a Lt. Puleri, was assassinated last Friday in front of Hoboken Police Headquarters," Tom Hanks, head of security for NYC FBI, told Hollis. "His assistant thinks it could be this Power Group you've been trying to find."

Hollis sat back in his chair. "Why does he think so?"

"He's gone through all of Puleri's files, and nothing else stands out. In addition, he says the hit was first class—a professional hit."

Hollis paused. "I see. Cory needs to meet with Smith and see where we can go from here. Thanks Tom, you may have given us another angle to track down this Power Group."

Hollis called Cory and explained his assignment. "Cory, before you go, any progress on our pattern work?"

"Yes, we have some interesting things to talk about. Janet and Dennis should have some information for you in the morning. They have a series of runs in now."

"Good, please get with Lt. Smith as soon as you can."

Stevens Cyber Workshop

"Hello Pat. I see you have some workstations ready for us."

"Yes, I got here early so I could get us some good seats. Seems like I didn't need to do that since they'd already assigned us workstations."

"Oh, you didn't set these up?"

"No Damian, everybody's location was already set when I got here."

"Guys, my school is very organized," Shelly bragged. "Since they have the three of us together, I expect they anticipate we'll be collaborating with each other."

The class learned they would be working on actual accounts of cyber-attacks by hackers both inside and outside of the U.S. "You will see how the hackers have been attacking firewalls, planting sniffers, slowly adding code over a period of time to build ghost applications that track information and then send it to their hacker," the teacher explained.

After class, as the three met at a coffee shop near the University, Damian wasted no time. "I recommend that after each session, we discuss what we all have observed."

"I agree, Damian. When I was going through the course material, I was immediately overloaded," said Pat.

"So was I, Pat, even though while doing my PhD, I had some training in cyber-attacks," said Shelly.

Pat's antennae were up. "You mean in your AI work?"

"Yes, it was part of my course work."

"Did you get into any password work?"

An unsuspecting Shelly continued, "That was a big part of the course—looking at different ways hackers can find your passwords."

"Did you set up any password protection in your AI work?"

"No, but I believe it's something we need to consider at ActSof. What about you, Pat? Have you done that with your network coding?"

"Some, but mostly I utilized known mechanisms. Now, I think those mechanisms will be easily overcome."

"You're right, Pat. Our security people have been saying that for the last six months. That's another reason Tilghman wants us to get some more background in cyber security—so we have a better understanding so we can serve our clients better," said Damian.

"Well Damian, from what I have seen, it may be imperative to have that knowledge."

"I agree and I can see how this workshop will help us work with our clients to protect their accounting systems."

October 16, 2001
NYC FBI Headquarters

"Good morning, Janet. Good morning, Dennis. Jeff will be here shortly. He wants to see what progress we have made," Hollis said.

A nervous Janet responded, "I hope he isn't disappointed. We are really just getting started."

Jeff Horton entered the conference room. "Good morning everyone. Are we ready to start?"

"Cory isn't here; he is tracking down a new development in Hoboken. Janet and Dennis have been exercising the NASA software on the CIA databases," said Hollis.

Janet explained to Hollis and Horton that they had found patterns in Europe, Africa, the Mideast, Southeast Asia and the U.S. "This activity can be seen in the data of two years ago. We reran each of the same scenarios with data that started six months ago. This activity is different than the activity that existed two years ago," she concluded.

Hollis moved forward in his chair. "Different in what way?"

"The movement between large U.S. companies and Europe has increased. At first we thought it might be an increase in trade between the U.S. companies and Europe so we explored that activity but we did not find anything."

Jeff actually raised his hand. "So, what does that mean?"

"We're not sure; it seems as though someone is moving money through these large companies."

With his hand over his eyes, Horton complanied, "I don't understand?"

"Somehow, somebody is purposely routing funds through the same banks that the U.S. companies have been using for the last decade and making the funds look like the U.S. companies are doing the transfers."

Jeff was stunned. "Really! Is there any way to identify who this is?"

"We haven't gotten that far, sir. It will take a lot of digging to unearth whomever it is."

"How recent is this latest money flow?"

"Just in the last couple of weeks. It is almost as if someone knew we were looking for them. If it wasn't for the new NASA software, we would not have seen this anomaly."

"What would you have seen?"

"We would have thought that the U.S. companies were illegally moving funds."

Jeff turned in his seat and looked at Hollis. "This is startling! Either they've chosen a new method to move funds or they wanted us to go on a wild goose chase."

Dennis finally spoke. "It's a definite possibility that someone wanted us to go off in a direction to waste our time and resources."

"So, what do we do now?" Jeff asked.

"We continue to track these anomalies and start to see what patterns emerge. If we are right, we'll be able to uncover the source."

With a broad smile on his face, Jeff once again turned in his seat. "I am beginning to like this pattern stuff. What do you think, Bob?"

"I believe they have found something. This pattern correlation and un-correlation is beyond me, but it may just be what we need to uncover this Power Group."

"I hope you're right, Bob. My gut is telling me that we have, for maybe the first time, gotten ahead of this Power Group. As of now, we share this with nobody. We keep the lid on it. Is that understood by everybody?"

Everybody replied, "Yes sir!"

"Good work people. Carry on."

Hoboken, New Jersey

"Cory, good to see you again," Smith said, walking into the conference room where Cory waited.

"Phil, I wish it was under better circumstances."

"So do I, Cory. Puleri was more than just my boss. I learned so much from him. He was the best mentor I have ever had, and a darn good friend. He paused and took a deep breath. "Since it happened, I have gone through all of Puleri's cases—talked with everybody here who worked with him on his cases. I've had people cross reference names, locations, methods of operation and some other factors. We stacked that information up against the assassination. We found no strong connections except possibly Omara."

"If that is the case, then you and anybody who had any connection to the investigation may also be a threat."

"We thought about that, but any official correspondence between the Hoboken Police Department and your office had only Puleri's name on it. No other name was ever mentioned. The only way my name was known was because I personally contacted my friend who spoke to your Tom Hanks."

"Yes, Tom is the head of security at our NYC Headquarters. Tom contacted my boss and that is how we learned about this."

"There've been no other attempts on any other member of our crew. Of course, we've been on a high alert since the assassination. Even so, nothing indicates that anyone else is being targeted."

"What have you found from the hit itself?"

"At first we thought there was only one person across the street on the roof. Our forensic people were up there within a few minutes."

"What made you think the shooter was waiting there for some period of time?"

"We saw some scratch marks on the ledge. It appeared he moved the gun around a few times. However, later some experts said that a shooter might establish sighting and then pull the gun down knowing just where he wanted to place it when the time arrived. He wouldn't want to risk exposure of the gun or his face for any extended time."

"So, you aren't sure how long he was there?"

"Right."

"What did your forensics find?"

"Almost nothing. No usable fingerprints, no cigarette butts, no shoe marks even though it was a dusty roof. No shells or oil from a gun and no trace of anyone in or around the building who didn't belong there. Whoever it was disappeared like a ghost."

Cory sat back. "I can see why you think it was a professional job."

"It was swept clean. A whole section of the rooftop had been swept clean of all dust. Nobody in the building saw anything or anybody out of the ordinary. It was just another typical day as far as everyone in the building was concerned until the shooting. Even after the shot was fired, nobody saw or heard anything that could be connected to the shooting."

"So, the shot was audible. The shooter didn't use a silencer. That's odd."

"That's what we thought at first. Why go through all the trouble of setting up the site and then not use a silencer? That's when our experts said because the shooter was never on the roof. It was just made to look that way. We now believe the shooter was in the 22-story building behind the six-story building."

Cory sat up in his chair. "Wow, now that is some serious planning."

"Right, and by the time we figured that out and got to the other building, whoever was there was long gone. We concluded there were at least two people. A spotter and a shooter on the 20th floor in an unoccupied room in which, once again, we found nothing to tell us who was there or how long they were there."

Cory paused and said thoughtfully, "Well Phil, I agree with you that this was a top notch, professional hit."

"Right and none of Puleri's other cases showed anywhere near this sophistication. That is why we think it was your Power Group."

"Have you found anything since?"

"A couple things have been bothering us. Why did the shooting take place here at the police station? How did they know about Puleri? Why was Puleri the only target? We think they wanted to send a message. 'Stay out of things you know little about.'"

"Do you think there is some hidden information in what your original investigation had uncovered that didn't mean anything at that time?"

"Actually, yes. We're reviewing the files on the Omara case. The people who staged the crash scene were not the same caliber as the people who did the assassination. The crash was done without any planning; it was a real-time response to a situation that had to be taken care of immediately. The people were probably local. The assassination was well planned by someone higher."

"That's an interesting thought. Do you have anything that says the hit team was not local?"

"First of all, the shot was long—from a few buildings away. That requires an expert marksman. Second, it was done early in the morning and in broad daylight when there was plenty of activity to mask the noise of the gun shot near the 22-story building. The third thing was how did they know it was Puleri they were aiming at? They must have had significant preparation to identify Puleri. It doesn't fit any of the local talent."

"So what's your plan to track them down?"

"That's where we need a little help. We've questioned everyone locally for any unusual visitors they might have seen. They had to case the area and go through some on-site rehearsals—that would take about a week. They were cautious, so we doubt they lodged in the immediate area. We've cast our search from Newark to New Brunswick and from the Hudson River out to Interstate 278. We have a bunch of maybes and could be's so far. What we don't have is any indication of someone with the necessary talent coming into our area."

"Ah, so that's where the FBI comes in. We can do that. I assume you already have a list of people traveling into Newark airport during that period?"

"Yes, and you can have anything else that we have put together."

Stevens Cyber Workshop

"Did you see how easy the hackers broke through the passwords?" Pat asked, as he, Damian, and Shelly waited for their coffee to arrive at the coffee shop after their workshop.

"Yes, I did, and it is a little scary."

"I'm with you on that one, Shelly. I can hear our security people's voices echoing in my head," said Damian.

"It seems just about everything I have done in the past was the wrong way to set up my passwords," added Pat.

"I had the same feeling, Pat. At Stevens, I didn't worry much about my passwords. I've changed my mind," Shelly said.

Sherman started probing. "What about some of the other people at ActSof? Have they ever talked about their passwords?"

"What do you mean Pat?"

"Have any of them talked about how they selected their passwords?"

"I don't ever remember anybody talking about it," said Damian.

"What about you, Shelly? Did anybody at Stevens ever discuss how they selected their passwords?

"No, Pat. However, maybe I should have paid more attention."

"Pat, are you having trouble with your passwords?" asked Damian.

"Actually I am. Tom Rowe had some files I can't get into because they're password protected. I need to know what is in those files."

"I didn't know that about Tom. I don't have any idea what would be in those files. Shelly, do you?"

An innocent Shelly answered, "The only thing I can think of would be the interface to the code I brought from Stevens. Tom was very cautious; he would go over the link points with me many times to make sure he had them right, so maybe he did password protect those files."

Sherman almost wet his lips but stopped himself. This was what he'd been after. "I can see why Tom would want to protect that information because when he would insert it into the overall script it might be hard to find again."

"Ok Pat, we need to get those files to our security people and see if they can open them for you."

"Great idea, Damian."

Franklin Lakes

It was unusual for Cyn to be the first to arrive. Johnson met him at the door and escorted him to the library, then reported to Madam. By the time Cisco came downstairs the rest of the men had also arrived.

"What brings you here early, Cyn," asked Numbers. "And why are you pacing?"

"I'm not happy about our surveillance on VJ. He is not in Cairo; he is not in Versailles, and he is not in the States."

Smiling, Numbers replied, "Okay Cyn, I give up, where is he?"

"This is not funny, Numbers! We don't know where he is!"

"What do we know, Cyn?" asked Cisco.

"He was in Versailles with his wife. Then yesterday he wasn't there. His private plane did not arrive in France; it is still in its hanger in Cairo. His car, and his wife's are still at the villa in Versailles. However, there has been no sign of him since noontime yesterday. In the meantime, several guests have arrived and left. VJ did not leave with any of them. We're tracking each one down as we talk."

"You're right, Cyn, this is a little unusual for VJ."

"That is what's bothering me, Max. VJ just doesn't go with somebody without his people, who by the way are still at his Paris office."

"Is there an outside chance VJ is not feeling well and is just a little bedridden?"

"We thought about that, Max, but we haven't seen anything that would lead us to think that. No, he has left the villa and we don't know where he is."

Numbers once again tried to needle Cyn. "Do you have any other good news?"

"Actually, Numbers, I do have some other news but it isn't good either. Our sources at the NYPD tell me that something is going on behind closed doors there and is being kept very close to the vest. Whatever it is, it has to do with the New York families."

"The New York families! You mean our customers!"

"Yes Max, our New York Family customers."

"Do you have any idea what?"

"Not a clue!"

The big man stood up and went to fetch a drink. "This could be worse news than the missing VJ. I don't like this happening in our backyard. This is too close for comfort."

"Exactly, Max. So, does anybody have any idea why there is a sudden interest in the New York families?"

Everybody was silent. An uncomfortable feeling pervaded the entire room. Finally, until Cisco broke it. "So, people, what do we do about this situation?"

"First thing, Cisco, is not to panic. We need to get more feedback from our sources not only inside the NYPD but also from our snitches in the street," said Max.

"Max, that sounds like both you and Cyn."

"Absolutely, Cisco. Cyn, you and I need to talk to some old friends of mine. We'll get back to you when we know something."

"Before you to leave, Red has set up a mechanism that has allowed me to put up false movements of our people and over two dozen of Ali Ki's people in France, Germany, Iraq, and Yemen. This should cloud the FBI's tracking for a month or more," Cisco added.

"Glad to hear it. I would like to get with you, but Max and I need to find VJ, said Cyn.

"You're right, Cyn, You and Max need to go. Numbers, do you need anything else from Red?"

Yes, Cisco, I've already talked with him."

"Good, we will wait for word from Max and Cyn. Meanwhile I will contact our security friend, Mr. Harrison."

The group disbursed as Madame joined Cisco in the Library.

"Now I am really getting upset. This sudden move by VJ is totally uncharacteristic. Son, we may have underestimated how much VJ knows about our plans," she said.

"Yes Mom, I have the same lousy feeling. So, what do we do?"

"Max and Cyn have never failed us before, and they won't now," said Madam. "With the work that Numbers and Red are doing with the false patterns, the FBI will be walking around blind again.

"This news about the NYPD and the New York Families is a bit of a surprise. Cyn has done a great job over the years of keeping more than an arms-length between us and the Families. However, we may need to change our complete method of operation. Red should set up a wireless link between us and the Families—something very secure. No more people in the middle between us and the Families."

"I'll get Red on it."

October 17, 2001
NYC FBI Headquarters

"Bob, the hit on Puleri was professional," Cory concluded as he discussed everything he had learned from Phil Smith.

"And Hoboken has no idea who did the hit, yet alone who sent them?"

"That's it. We need to help them find the professional hit team. I've talked with our people in Washington. They expect to have some information for us early this afternoon."

Hollis still wasn't overly interested in the hit on Puleri. "Let's hope we can get some leads," he said dismissively. "Meanwhile, Horton really likes the work that Janet and Dennis have done. It's possible someone has attempted to create false money movement trails. Janet and Dennis think they can identify who has done it."

Cory was impressed. "That's one for the good guys, Bob. By the way, have Janet and Dennis found any patterns for the people movement?"

"They haven't really started those patterns yet."

Hoboken, New Jersey
ActSof

Anxiously, Sherman approached Damian. "Have our security people found the password for Tom Rowe's secured files?"

"They haven't found anything yet. They are pretty sure he used one of the passwords that our group gave him."

"That's interesting. I hope they are right. I believe he has some important information in those files."

Damian sensed Sherman's urgency. "Let's give them a call," he said, as he turned to his phone. After a few moments of conversation, he smiled and thanked the person on the other end.

"Did they find it?" Sherman asked anxiously as he hung up.

"Yes, the password is #*2001&%. So, let's go see what Tom had in those files."

Sherman immediately went to his computer, called up Rowe's files, and entered the password.

"Well there they are. I see ten files. Five of them have the word 'network' in the title. Two are from Shelly's work at Stevens—this file is a spreadsheet. It's coming up now. It looks like a schedule and work accomplished. Let's see what is in this PowerPoint file. It's coming up. This is an involved logic tree and a series of graphs. Wow, there must be nearly a hundred pages here."

"What is in the last file, Pat?"

"It looks like a Word file—a write up on Tom's algorithm and the type of coding he was using to build his network engines. It's big. This is what I have been looking forward to finding," he said excitedly. Damian, this is just what I needed. I really appreciate you getting the password."

"Glad to hear that. I hope it helps."

As Damian left, Pat quickly scanned each of the files. He didn't immediately see something that could lead him to the sacred password the Franklin Lakes group was searching for. Even so, he now had access to a host of information Anu had believed he needed to protect. Pat sat back in his chair, took a deep breath, and started the search.

NYC FBI Headquarters

"Wow, can you believe this list? There must be over a hundred suspected hit men on it!" John told Cory as he looked over the information.

"Any of them moving into the New Jersey area?" asked John.

"Nothing directly. Five flew into JFK. One group flew into Philadelphia, another into Avoca. Looks like two into Pittsburgh, one into Cleveland, and one into Cincinnati. There's nothing into Delaware but four have flown into BWI, three more into Dulles and three more into Regan—all of between Sept. 22 to Oct. 15."

"Cory, how high is the probability these people are hit men?"

"About ten percent, John."

"Where are these flights coming from?"

"Most of these are from within CONUS. The flights into Kennedy are from France. One of the flights into BWI is from Egypt, another one is from Sweden. There are some from the airports further south. Two are into Miami from England, one is into Houston from Brazil."

"Okay, send this information to Phil Smith, then talk with Fred Hendrick in Washington and let him know what we've learned about Puleri's assassination."

A short time later a busy Bob Hollis asked John what he had learned about ActSof.

"ActSof was started by Bill Tilghman and his best friend Jacob

Nevins. They are co-owners of ActSof and the Grotto Restaurant. They are friends from childhood. Nevins runs the Grotto and Tilghman runs ActSof. They pulled their money together in the early 90's and started working on some financial accounting software. They first used it for their restaurant. Then they started selling it to other restaurants. The restaurant was handed down through the Nevins family. Tilghman's family had a lot of land. They sold some of it and invested $2 million to expand the restaurant staff and establish ActSof."

"When did that happen?"

"September of 1992—that's when Tilghman left the restaurant and devoted full time to ActSof. Originally, Tilghman did the marketing. ActSof hired Harry Simpson as lead engineer to develop the new software products. Throughout 1993 and 1994, they hired more engineers and support staff while Tilghman found someone to help with the marketing."

"How well did they do?"

"They were struggling along. They were acquiring a few clients but were still living off the original funding."

"So, I guess they had to find some more funding."

"That is the way it was looking until they obtained a big contract."

Hollis' antennae went up. "Who was this big contract with and how did they get it?"

"It was a restaurant chain centered in Newark. Tilghman takes the credit for getting the contract."

"What do you mean takes the credit?"

"Well, there really isn't much I could find as to how they got the contract. It is almost as if a benefactor showed up and got them the contract, but there is no trace of who the benefactor was."

Hollis sat up in his chair. "Hm, sounds a little fishy to me."

"Well, it gets a little fishier. Tilghman hired three more people to do the marketing. It's as if they had the Midas touch. Contracts with other chains continued to flow in. It wasn't all at once, it just flowed in in a timely manner. So, Actsof kept expanding and kept delivering quality products and service. The clients are very happy with ActSof and have become loyal customers."

"Do we have any idea why these clients chose ActSof?" Hollis asked with a suspicious look on his face.

"I've talked to two of their early clients. Nobody knows why they decided to go with ActSof."

"Once again John, it sounds too fishy to me."

"Yes Bob, I agree. I believe there is a secret benefactor who is invisible at this time. I intend to stay with this."

"Do that, John. Anything on the connection between Tom Rowe and Pat Sherman?"

"Still working on that."

Hollis sat back in his chair, as he rolled things over in his mind, he became more and more convinced that the Power Group was the invisible benefactor for ActSof. So was ActSof a member of the Power Group or were they a puppet?"

Hoboken Police Station

"Corey, I got the hit men info you sent me. This is terrific. Now we can pull some pictures and start to show them around that 22-story building. Maybe we can get a hit on the hit men."

Smith hung up his phone and with a large grin on his face started talking to his people.

Franklin Lakes, New Jersey

Red again, headed to the stables as soon as he arrived. This time, however, Cisco wanted to talk business as they rode.

"Sounds like you have been very busy Red."

"Yes, I have, but now I really need to take this ride of ours." Once again it was a crisp October day in Northern New Jersey. The horses were snorting and more than ready to get onto the trails. The turning leaves had begun to fill in the forest and the dirt paths have hardened from the cold nights. As they went further into the woods, the sounds around them changed to the quiet and calm of the backwoods. Red slowly grew easier. There was no hurry here. Time passed as they enjoyed the reds, burnt oranges, and yellows of the leaves.

"My dad always loved this ride, especially the waterfalls. He would take me along and we would just sit and listen to the water careening over the falls and splashing down onto the rocks below. You know he came from Germany and his dad would take him for rides in the Black Forest and teach him about the animals that lived in the forest. Dad would say that sitting by the waterfalls would help him remember back to those times. Ah, I can hear the falls now."

"So can I, Cisco, and I remember the many times that your dad and I would sit by the falls together."

At the house, Numbers and Max arrived and relaxed in the library waiting for Red and Cisco.

"Good to see you, Max, I hope you have some good news," said Numbers.

"There is some good news but also many questions."

"Hello gentlemen, Glad to see you both have made yourself at home. Red and I have much to share. Has anybody heard from Cyn?"

"Yes, I have, he is on his way. He has been checking with some of his street contacts."

"I see the gangs all here."

"Didn't hear you come in, Cyn."

"I saw you and Red walking up from the stables, so I just took my time getting here to the Library."

"I have talked with our security man. The Ali Ki is still celebrating 9/11. They are getting ready for a major recruiting push. In fact, they don't know how they are going to handle the influx."

"I'll believe that. Their funding reserves are the lowest in recent years."

"That makes sense, Numbers. Our security guy says they have stepped up fundraising as well as concentrating on drug traffic. They seem to have no plans for the U.S. in the near future. There is still no new information on where the Prince is other than somewhere in Afghanistan. As before, there is no electronic connection to him."

"Does our security guy have any information on VJ?"

"No, Max, apparently VJ and his people have been very stationary. Have you found VJ?"

"Yes, I have. He is back at the Versailles villa with his wife. His brief excursion was with one of his wife's clients. They were looking at some fine art together at the client's house. VJ stayed the night and returned the following evening."

A surprised Cisco responded. "Really Max, that doesn't sound like the VJ we know."

"Agreed; it is not like VJ to spend much time with his wife's clients. However, this one is a major player in the financial world. You probably know him, Numbers, his name is Francois Dassault."

Numbers snapped his head around. "Very much so. He is a billionaire and a lover of fine art. He is well connected within the financial community of Europe and a believer in technology."

"Sounds like someone VJ would like to be better acquainted with."

"Very much so, Cisco."

"So, gentlemen, what does this mean? We have VJ breaking his normal routine and putting himself in the hands of someone he does not know, but who is a billionaire client of his wife. Numbers, what are your thoughts?"

Numbers slowly removed his spectacles. "Both of these men never do anything without thorough and deliberate long-term planning. I don't see them getting together as a coincidence."

"Very interesting, Numbers. You believe there has been something in the works for a long time?"

"My guess would be at least a couple of years. Maybe even as long as we have been working on the Big Kill."

An unhappy cloud seemed to settle on the room. "What else do you know about Dassault?"

"At least four years ago he invested heavily in software companies. About two years ago he bought a group working on artificial intelligence."

"This gets more intriguing! Putting these things together, what do you think the two of them are planning?"

Cyn left his seat. "I'm wondering if they are planning on doing the same thing that we are with our Big Kill."

"I don't believe that, Cyn. Dassault walks a narrow line between legal and illegal. Even though we have wondered if VJ has been after our Big Kill, I just don't see Dassault doing that."

"So Numbers, you do not believe that VJ and Dassault our planning their own Big Kill?"

"That's right," replied Numbers in a confident tone of voice.

"Even so, you do think they are planning something very big?"

"Yes, I do. Dassault is not going to be bothered by some little transaction."

"So, here we are again, with more questions than answers," injected an agitated Cyn.

"If these two are doing some heavy planning together, if we watch their people and see when both sides get together, we could be able to learn more."

"Good idea, Max."

"I'll take the lead on this, Cisco."

"Maybe we can get more answers instead of more questions."

"Well folks, I have another mystery for you. Someone is trying to track our money transfers, and I have no evidence of who it might be."

"I knew it. It was just a matter of time," Cyn bellowed as he headed for the bar and poured himself a double scotch.

"All right, Cyn. So maybe someone has the capability to track us.

Who could this be?"

"My guess is the FBI.

"Why do you say that, Red?"

"I have heard through the grapevine that the FBI has just gotten some new software search material from NASA, who has built some of the best algorithms for finding patterns within large databases. Their purpose was to find some patterns in the movements within a galaxy. Such a capability could be used to track the type of patterns of money and people."

"Oh wow, now we are really facing some serious adversaries," said Cyn as he put down his drink. "So, what do we do now?"

"We need to change our entire method of operation with respect to our money transfers."

"How do we do that, Numbers?"

The cool minded banker looked up at Cisco. "We need to setup a whole new list of cover companies. We then need to drain the funds from some of our major holding banks and scatter them throughout the new companies. We have to drain most of the funds in person. This will be tricky and will take some time."

"Oh, I knew this computer magic would be our undoing. So now we have to go back to old fashioned methods."

"This time I think you are right, Cyn. I just don't see how we can drain the funding in person without sending flags all over the place."

"The way we do it is to electronically transfer much smaller amounts to many different accounts at different banks. We then drain those accounts in person and shut down the accounts."

"Numbers, we must be talking hundreds of people," stated Cisco.

"I know Cisco, I have established a cadre of people who can make this happen. Red and I have also established a host of companies globally. We started this as a backup in case we needed such an action."

Cisco relaxed. "Excellent move. That is some of the best news that I have heard in a long time. Implement your plan immediately."

"Consider it done."

"Cyn, any news from your sources on the street?"

"I have been working to understand why there has been some hush hush work about the NYC families."

"Have you found anything?"

"The NYPD is establishing surveillance on different warehouses of the families. They are compiling information as to the normal activities and operations at these locations."

Max suddenly moved in his chair. "Are you sure of that, Cyn?"

"Yes, Max, I am. You know that means they suspect that our drug supplies to the families are being done through those warehouses."

"Absolutely, Cyn. You need to rethink your whole delivery system."

"I have already started, Max."

"Well people, it looks like the authorities are sharing information."

"You're right, Cisco. They are closing in from every direction."

"Yes Numbers. Even so, they still don't know who we are. We need to define our actions and execute them cleanly. This is what has gotten us to the level we are at today and will keep us ahead of the authorities."

"Cisco, I hope you are right. I have been warning everybody for years.   The FBI and NYPD are not stupid, and they have access to very good tools."

"I hear you, Cyn. So, let's just go do our jobs."

"Before we go. Puleri has been eliminated."

"Oh, I forgot to congratulate you on that Max."

"We didn't do it. We had everything planned for today. Somebody else got to him before we could."

The room went silent. "This is strange, Max!"

"You're right, Cisco, and we need to find out who it is."

"Another player in the game. This is getting worse instead of better."

"We don't know that, Cyn. Puleri could have crossed someone who has nothing to do with us or our business."

"That is another big maybe."

"Cyn, you are starting to turn red in the face. Please calm down. Regardless of how some things seem, we are still cloaked from the rest of the world; we are still in control of our own destiny."

"I am with you, Cisco."

"So am I."

"We are all with you, Cisco. Even so, you have to admit that a lot of things have been happening that we didn't want to see happen."

"That is true, Red. As much as we plan, we can't control everything. Take for instance, **Osama bin Nedal whom we help setup as the Prince, has taken full control of the Ali Ki. He set up the 911 hit on the Twin Towers and put our Big Kill out of commission, and yet we thought we had everything under control.**

"So you see gentlemen, even our best laid plans and efforts can fail. Let's not get distracted. 'Osama bin Nedal has gone on his way and we need to continue to move in our own direction. We all know what we need to do. One more thing, Cyn, find out why the NYPD is putting so much emphasis on the Families' physical assets."

"I'm on it. Gentlemen, I am tired of the FBI. It's time to be more proactive."

"What do you have in mind, Cyn?"

"Just a few thoughts that I need to work through."

As the group left, Madam as usual joined her son in the library. "You handled that well, son. Cyn can get overexcited at times. Even so, he is right. As Red said, too many things are getting away from us. I don't believe we are losing control. We just need to remember to be patient."

"I agree, Mom. We have been watching Actsof and we don't see any unusual activity. The same can be said for Narparti and his wife, Shelly. I really believe they have no idea of our activity."

"I believe you are right, Son. Even so, I am still concerned about VJ. I want to know what he is planning. I wonder if he has had anything to do with Lt. Puleri's assassination."

"Numbers believes whatever VJ is up to, it has been in the works for several years."

"I agree. That sounds like VJ. He doesn't do anything on the spur of the moment. His disappearance with a prominent financial person in Europe must have been planned. I'm beginning to believe that VJ will be spending much more time in Versailles."

"Yes, Mom. Max says the same. Between Max and Cyn, we will uncover what VJ has planned."

October 18, 2001
Paris, France
Dassault's Office

"Welcome, Mr. Nasser. Mr. Dassault will join us shortly. He is conferring with some of our people in Canada about your discussions with him earlier."

"Yes, Francois and I talked last night on the phone. I would like to introduce you to Andrew Hollingsworth, my chief of investments."

"Pleased to meet you, Mr. Hollingsworth, my name is Pierre Rison. I am Dassault's chief investment officer, and this is **Jean LaFell, our chief strategist**."

VJ also introduced his own chief strategist, Herman Rodenbach, as the door opened and Dassault entered. VJ and Dassault started their people on a discussion of oil reserves in North America, then left to discuss a private project of their own.

NYC FBI Headquarters
Hollis' Office

In New York, the various members of Bob's team assembled to discuss the latest information.

"We hoped to find who has been using this piggy-back money movement. We thought maybe it was two banks in Europe," said Janet. "One in Luxemburg and one in Austria. It looked good until yesterday when everything stopped, as if somebody knew we were tracking them and changed the entire method of moving their money."

At that moment Jeff Horton entered the conference room. "Have I missed anything?"

"We were tracking that piggy bank money movement and we thought we had pinpointed the banks. Then yesterday, it all stopped."

"Why is that a concern, Janet?"

"Well sir, with the amount of money that had been moving, one would not expect to see it suddenly stop. There may be a downturn, but highly unlikely to have a sudden stop."

"So, in your opinion, something made them change the method of moving funds?"

"That is right, sir. We will watch them and see if the movement returns to the piggyback on the large aerospace firms."

"Once again, we think we are getting close and they slip away." Jeff paused, hand on his chin. "Can we see what their new movement is?"

"I doubt it. We don't know who they are. The two banks we thought were involved are very large; many companies run their funding through them. Even so, we plan to set up some computer runs to see if we can identify the companies that suddenly stopped moving funds through those two banks."

"That sounds like something that can pinpoint the companies we are looking to find."

"Hopefully sir, but it will take a lot of computer runs over at least six weeks of data to begin to find some patterns, then we have to eliminate most of those patterns. It just takes time."

"What do you need to reduce the time and effort?"

"Sir, we would need about a dozen experienced people."

Jeff immediately called Fred Newton. "Fred, we need you in Conference room 238 ASAP. Yes, bring him along."

A few minutes later Newman and George Sebastian, a data analyst, arrived to help.

ActSof

"Hello Pat; what have you found in Tom Rowe's files?" asked Damian.

"I almost didn't know where to get started. I just sat back for a while and thought about what I really need to know and came to the conclusion that I needed to figure out what Tom had planned and what he had accomplished. I checked all of his schedules—I'm still going through them. There are almost a hundred pages of schedules and flow charts."

"That's a lot. I hope he had a master schedule."

"Sorry for rambling on, Damian. Yes, it was the first thing I searched. It's extensive." He proceeded to overwhelm Damian with details on his work, in the hopes that Damian would get bored and leave him alone. After a few minutes of talking, he sensed that Damian had bought the whole deal.

"Then Rowe was following through on what was expected of him?" asked Damian.

"It appears so."

"That's good to know. Continue along this line. Tom was very detailed in documenting his work. This will give me some good insight into his thinking and approach."

A short time later, at the Stevens Cyber Workshop, Damian, Shelly, and Pat sat down for their class.

"Sounds like you are making progress, Pat," Shelly said, when Pat also updated her on his work with Rowe's files. "I liked Tom. He was always very thorough. He kept telling me how impressed he was with my work. He always made me feel that I was an important contributor," she said with a smile. "He wanted to know my connection points so he could cleanly interface. He would check my links over and over until he was absolutely sure of the interface."

"Shelly, was Tom absolutely sure that the interface was both functional and safe? I mean safe in that what was crossing the interface was what you believed it to be."

"Yes, he was."

Sherman now had a piece of information that would have taken him days to check by going through Rowe's files.

Chapter 5

October 19, 2001
Franklin Lakes

Cyn scampered from his car to the library, bypassing Johnson, and flung open the door. "VJ and Dassault have gotten together in Dassault's Paris office. Their people met for two hours but VJ and Dassault were not there during the meeting. They were only with them for a few minutes and then they went off by themselves. When VJ's people left, VJ didn't leave for another hour and fifteen minutes."

"Okay Cyn, what does this tell you?" asked Cisco, looking startled.

The only time that VJ is not at the meeting with his people is when he has made up his mind and there are only the minor details to be addressed."

"So, you believe that something is already settled and that VJ and Dassault have something else on the agenda?"

"Yes."

"Let's talk about this with the rest of the group."

At that moment, the library door opened and Red entered. "I have a couple of things I need to talk about."

"Good, why don't you and Cyn grab a drink and let's wait for Max and Numbers."

Cyn and Red poured themselves some sherry, then moved to their usual seats. About ten minutes passed and both Max and Numbers entered.

An impatient Cyn jumped out of his chair. "VJ and Dassault have made an agreement on something. Their people have already worked out the details."

"What is it?"

"I don't know, Numbers!"

"Cyn, slow down. Please go over what you do know without any speculation," put in Cisco.

Cyn consciously took a slow sip of sherry. "Yes, you're right Cisco. What I know is that VJ and Dassault's people met for over two hours at Dassault's Paris office."

"Were VJ and Dassault there?" asked Numbers.

"Yes, both were there for a few minutes at the beginning of the meeting. Then both of them left. Their people worked for over two hours after which, VJ's people left without him. VJ didn't leave for another hour and fifteen minutes."

"Where did VJ go when he left?"

"He went back to Versailles."

"What about VJ's people?"

"Aw, I see your point, Max! VJ's people went back to his Paris office and then to their own homes."

"So, since VJ's people didn't go back to the office to work but took the rest of the day off, you believe that whatever the meeting was about was a final wrap-up of whatever they were working on."

"That's right, Numbers."

Numbers slowly took off his spectacles. "Actually, Cyn, I believe that is good news, not bad news."

"Why do you say that, Numbers?"

"Dassault deals only with the big picture. His people do the rest. VJ on the other hand, stays at a meeting until he is satisfied and only minor things need be resolved."

"Yes, I know that, Numbers." Cyn placed his hands on the back of his chair."

"True, but both VJ and Dassault are long-term planners. Whatever the deal is, there's been a lot of activity prior to this meeting in Paris. I doubt that it has anything to do with our Big Kill."

"I hear you, Numbers," said Cisco. "Cyn, please sit down in your chair before you have a heart attack. So, Numbers, you think that this meeting may have to do with the big deal that VJ has been working on for several years and is the reason he is getting ready to retire?"

"Yes, Cisco."

"That's what bothers me, Numbers. The information we have is that the project was so big VJ couldn't finance it by himself. Now all of a sudden, he has, or believes he will get the money and has given it the go-ahead. Either VJ has brought in Dassault as a partner or he's taken a loan from Dassault which he believes he can pay back because he has some new way of getting some quick money."

"I see where you are going with that. The bad news is that VJ believes he has set up either his own Big Kill or will take over ours.."

Frustrated, Cyn muttered, "Finally, somebody understands!"

"Relax Cyn. It's only a possibility," said Red.

"Why do you say that?"

"If VJ is using our software, I would know because I can monitor when it is operating. I haven't seen any activity."

"Wow, that's a relief, Red!"

Calmer, Cyn returned to his comfortable seat and reached for his sherry. The group followed suit as each one relaxed and a moment of silenced prevailed.

Red broke the moment by bringing up a new topic. "I've been going through Linden Mercer, Anu's Princeton advisor's files. Mercer suggested Anu talk to the Cyber people at Stevens. He'd been working with Herman Steele, the head of the Cyber group at Stevens. The first thing that Mercer told Anu was to never use anything of a personal nature to form his passwords."

"What do you mean by personal nature, Red?" Cyn asked.

"Anything like your name or the name of people you know."

"So is that what we have been using and is that why we have not been able to break Anu's password code?" asked Max.

"Right. Even so, I tried other data such as where he lived, the name of the schools he attended, sports he was involved in, and other things."

"And these approaches did not work?"

"Right again, Numbers."

Cisco decided to get to the point. So, where does this leave us, Red?"

"I have found a way to hack into the Cyber group at Stevens and I believe that they do not know that I have been able to do that."

"Well, that sounds like progress and somewhat impressive."

"Thank you for the compliment, Cisco, but it is only a start and it is the best bet we have. I need to monitor Stevens' cyber activity while continuing to look at the files that they are using."

"I hope this works, Red."

Cyn had heard enough computer talk. "This is all well and good but we still don't know what VJ has planned."

"You're right, Cyn; we need to keep surveillance a top priority."

"We are, Cisco. We have gotten feedback from our man at ActSof. Sherman says he's been getting great cooperation from both Damian Narpati and Shelly in helping him break into the encrypted files that Anu had at ActSof."

Max was surprised to hear about Sherman. "He has been able to understand how Anu coded his work!"

"Right, Max, I can verify that. Sherman has been meeting with me for the last two weeks. He can now start tracking the code insertions that Anu made into the ActSof software."

"If he can do that, then he should be able to modify the next release of the ActSof software so we can do the Big Kill," Cisco remarked, grinning.

"Theoretically your right, Cisco. However, practically speaking, it's much more difficult unless you understand what evasive tricks that Anu used when he added his code originally."

"Every time I hear we are getting closer to re-establishing the Big Kill, another software monster rears its head. At times I wish I never heard the word software," said Cyn.

"I hear you. I get that same feeling also."

"People, believe it or not we are making progress."

"I hope you're right, Red," said a frustrated Cisco.

"Getting back to Damian and Shelly, they are either great actors or they know nothing about what VJ has in mind and have gotten no directions from VJ to spy on anybody," Max said, changing the subject.

"Maybe they are acting when they are at ActSof or when they are with Sherman. What about when they are somewhere else?"

"Cisco, even I have to say that Max is right," Red commented. "We have several people constantly watching Damian and Shelly. Their new house has bugs in every room and around the grounds outside. Their computers and all their phones bugged. With all of this, there is nothing we have found that indicates they are marching to VJ's orders."

"Well Cyn, coming from you, that is a major testament. So, we have found nothing from our surveillance of Damian and Shelly. Have we found what the NYPD is doing with their surveillance on the New York Families?"

"Nothing new. As of now, they're recording activity at eleven sites. We haven't seen them at any others. Either they don't know about those or they haven't gotten to them yet. And none of our moles at NYPD have been able to learn who is really leading this action. This is one of the tightest held secrets I've ever seen at NYPD."

"Do we have any idea why it is being held so secretly?"

"Nothing direct, Cisco. We guess they suspect moles within the NYPD."

That comment was one of the last things that Cisco wanted to hear. "Cyn, that does not give me a good feeling."

"I'm with you, Cisco, but we have to proceed with caution to make sure our moles are not uncovered."

"Cisco, Max and I have already set up new delivery methods of the heroin to the New York Families."

"I knew you would, Cyn. I have total faith in you and Max. By the way, Numbers, how is our effort to make our drug traffic look like it is coming from the drug cartels?"

"We have put in a couple of very subtle clues that the drug traffic is being done by the cartels. This is the reason we have some of the drugs going into Africa instead of directly to the East Coast."

"That's the stuff I like hearing. One more thing, our security man tells me that Osama Nedal is moving back into Iraq. They believe he is getting ready to make a new video. Even so, no one knows where he will be. Our moles in the Iraqi camps have heard nothing about his movement. They keep telling us that very little news is coming from outside of their areas while the people at the camps are busy continuing their work.

"That concludes our business. Remember to keep yourself vigilant."

The group left and Madame joined her son in the Library. "Very good meeting, Son. Some things are starting to go our way again. Even so, not only can we not let up, we need to step up our activity."

"What do you have in mind, Mom?"

"We need to find a way to bug the villa in Versailles. It looks like VJ is planning on spending more time there. We need to get inside VJ's head and understand what he is thinking."

"Excellent idea, Mom. I'll get with Max and get it started."

"No need, I have already sent him a message from you to start it immediately."

"That's my mom."

Hoboken Police Station

"They have identified somebody," the caller told Smith.

The lieutenant new exactly what his man was talking about. "Stay where you are, I'll be there in five minutes or less," he said, jumping up from his desk. The caller, one of his men, had found someone who had identified two of the suspects the FBI had given them from their list of possible hit men who had flown into the area at the time of Puleri's assassination.

As he pulled up in front of the high rise his man flagged him. Smith jumped out of his car. "Where is she?"

"The small conference room off the lobby."

"Show me the way."

His heart was pumping as if he was in a race. He could barely contain himself as he was led into the conference room. "Sir, this is Elizabeth Miller, she is the receptionist here in the lobby."

"Pleased to meet you, Miss Miller. My name is Lt. Phil Smith. Please tell me about these two men that you have recognized."

Elizabeth Miller was an attractive brunette in her early thirties with observant brown eyes. She was attractive and very observant. "I saw both several times. They were always well dressed and very polite—always waited for others to enter the elevators before them."

"When did you first see these men?"

"As best I can remember, the first time was last Thursday, the 11th of October."

"Why did you notice them?"

"They were letting others get in the elevators before them—that's not usual. Most of the time people are in such a rush they don't see other people around them."

"Did you have a good look at both of these men at that time?"

"Not at that time. What also got my attention is they were wearing light colored Fedora hats. They were very popular about ten years ago but I haven't seen one in a few years."

"So, you didn't have a good look at them last Thursday?"

"No, not then."

"What time did you see them that day?

"The first time was about 8:50 in the morning when many of the office workers are rushing to get to their offices."

"You said the first time, so you saw them again last Thursday!"

"Yes, it was about 11 a.m. I noticed their hats and their English Covert overcoats. You don't see many Covert overcoats nowadays. There are a lot of similar ones, but these were the English Coverts."

"Are you a fancier of overcoats?"

"Not really, but there are two men who have offices here and they have worn their English Coverts for several years. I always thought they were attractive and so I asked one of them about his. He told me what they were."

"Ah, I see, and therefore, these two men became noticeable to you."

"Yes, that is right."

"Did you see them again?"

"Yes, I saw them last Friday, on the 12th of October. Actually, this time they came in early."

"About what time was that?"

"It was a few minutes after 7 a.m. I'm on duty from 6 a.m. to 2 p.m."

"Did you see them again?"

"Yes, it was a little after 9 a.m. Both of them were leaving the building."

"When was the next time you saw them?"

"Actually, I haven't seen them since."

"You are sure that you have not seen them again?"

"I am very sure; I have gotten good looks at them both times I saw them leave the building. I could see them clearly as they walked out of the elevators."

"Miss Miller, you have been very helpful. Thank you for your time and patience."

"I am glad to help."

Smith and his men headed back to headquarters where he went straight to his office and called Cory. Both of these men had flown in October 10, from Cairo, Egypt.

"Outstanding," said Cory. And I have some additional information.

"What have you got?" Smith asked impatiently.

"Karl Koch is a German citizen and Tim Periot is a Belgium citizen according to their passports."

"So why would they be coming from Cairo?" asked a bewildered Smith. "Could they have been hired by somebody in Egypt?"

Cory paused and answered. "It's a definite possibility. Phil, I am going to do some investigating and get back to you."

"Can't wait to hear what you have found." Phil looked at his officers. "I get the feeling once again this is something much bigger than we have been thinking. My FBI contact has something in mind. He wants to do some investigating and then get back to me." Phil's men were amazed. It was unusual for the FBI to share information this freely.

NYC FBI Headquarters
"Bob, I just talked with Lt. Smith over at Hoboken PD," said Cory. "They have a witness who identified two men seen in that 22-story building—Karl Koch and Tim Periot."

"The names sound familiar but I can't place them."

John Thompson, who had followed Cory into Hollis' office said, "It was several years ago when I was working the Niece case with Interpol. These two are a pair of hit men who have been working in France and Germany. They are true professionals who are impeccable dressers. They only do jobs in urban areas where they have to mingle with business types. They have been linked to several high-profile hits both in France and Germany."

"This sounds big time and I wonder why!" Hollis sat up straight in his chair. "Why would they be paid to do a hit on a New York City cop?"

"I have the same thought, Bob. uleri had no connections to anybody or anything outside of CONUS. According to John, these two guys are very expensive hit men. Whoever hired them must have a major reason."

"There's more. These guys are often called in to do the job in a short period of time. Somebody else does the setup work and hands the plan to Koch and Periot," interceded John.

"Cory, what was the first and last time the witness saw them?'"

"Yeah, the day before the hit on Puleri was the first time, and the last time on the day Puleri was shot."

Hollis stood up. "That fits, John. Even so, why Puleri? Hollis paced the office. "We never met Puleri. We only met with Smith."

"That's right, Bob. However, the paperwork we had from Hoboken had Puleri's name on it as the officer in charge."

"I remember now. Puleri's name was on our interagency cooperation write-up. Human Resources published that information.

So, someone on the outside could have seen Puleri as tied to us."

"I'm on that one, Bob," stated John, quickly exiting Hollis' office.

"Bob, do you think we have a new player in this financial game?"

"I hope not, Cory. We can't find the original players—if a new player has entered the arena, how can we possibly find him?"

"What does a new player expect to gain by putting a hit on Puleri?"

"Let's stay with that, Cory. Let's say you are the new player. You have some operation going. All of a sudden you discover that one of your rivals has some big plan to attack the financial center right here in Manhattan. What would you do about that?"

"I would throw a monkey wrench into their plans."

"How soon would you do that?"

"I wouldn't waste any time. I would put out a contract to either hit one of the group or to take out something of importance to them."

"It doesn't appear that is what has happened. The hit on Puleri doesn't seem to have taken out one of the members of this rival group nor is Puleri someone of importance to the rival group. Instead, he had caused some of the group's well-planned tactics to be uncovered."

Cory sat back in his chair. "I hear what you're saying, Bob. So maybe, just maybe, I decide to expose the rival group by committing an act and leaving subtle clues that lead back to this rival group.

"One of the things that bothered me was that the receptionist became aware of the two hit men because they acted differently than the typical person who worked in the building and wore overcoats and hats that either were out of date or very rare. If I were a hit man on a mission, I would want to be as unidentified as possible. There is no way that I would want to stand out in a crowd."

Hollis walked back to his chair and sat down. "That's intriguing Cory."

John entered Hollis' office on a run. "According to HR, the publication you were talking about circulated only within the FBI, CIA, and the White House."

"John," Hollis put in, "Cory and I have been doing some thinking about the why a new player might put a hit on Puleri."

"So have I. I find it hard to believe that these two hit men would be picked out of a crowd because they wore distinctive coats. Looking through their other missions, they were inconspicuous. In fact, they were never seen together. So why this time?"

Hollis rubbed his forehead. "You've wrapped it in a neat package, John, that says this is not the typical mode of operation for these two. There must be some reason they acted the way they did."

Smiling, John followed through with his thinking. "I believe their contract was twofold. The first objective was to complete the hit in their usual professional way. The second objective was to leave clues that would lead to somebody the person who let the contract wants exposed."

"I'm with you, John," echoed Cory. "This may be the big break we've been looking for handed to us on a silver platter."

"Okay Cory, calm down. If you are right, John, then the one who let this contract must have a set of clues to follow. So let's find them."

"I'll take the lead on that, Bob."

"Yes John, I believe you should."

"John, I'll get you in touch with Smith. I am certain he's been very busy tracking down other leads on the hit men. I told him I'd get back to him—why don't you visit Phil and his people in Hoboken?"

October 22, 2001
Versailles, France

"Andrew, are you happy with your negotiations with Dassault's people?" VJ asked his assistant.

"I am very happy," replied Andrew Hollingsworth. "They have done a very exact investigation into all of the legal strings attached to the plot of land that holds the oil field."

"I'm also satisfied," replied VJ as he relaxed back into his chair. "I'm grateful to Michele for her work in securing the funding we needed."

"I know that you haven't shared with me the details of the work with her but I'm very much aware of your appreciation and faith in her efforts."

"Are our people prepared to meet with the Canadian Government this week to finalize our contract?"

"We are ahead of schedule. The Canadian Government representatives are a little behind. That is why we are not meeting with them this week. I believe there will not be any more delays."

"That is good news, Andrew."

Cairo, Egypt

In the back room of a restaurant on the outskirts of Cairo sat Kachen and several of his Egypt contacts. "I am very interested in what you all have observed of VJ's people."

Leonard Attman, a short man with a white mustache and an English accent who had friends in VJ's Cairo office, replied, "My friends at VJ's office tell me his legal people are working with Dassault's legal people in France—and they are working with the Canadian Government. It's about some land in western Canada. They don't know exactly where or why."

"Leonard, how long have they been working with Dassaults' legal people and the Canadians?" Kachen moved forward in his seat. This was the first time he had heard of VJ's interest in Canada.

"That's a little bit of a mystery. Most of the activity has been in the last four years. However, my friends seem to think it may have started more than a decade ago."

"What do you mean by a mystery?" Kachen questioned..

Attman paused. "From what I understand, VJ's people have been looking at different parts of North America for more than a decade."

"Ah, so the early searches were looking for opportunities in several different places in North America, and this is now a specific location. But it is the first time that I have heard that VJ had been looking at anything in North America." Kachen's tone was reproving. Why had his people not mentioned this before?

"This is why it is so strange to me. None of my friends had ever talked about VJ doing anything in the western continents." Attman tried to defend himself.

"Then this has been a closely guarded secret, is that what you are telling me?" The Benefactor will be most alarmed to discover that VJ has had his eye on North America for so long. Have you heard of any of this Abdalia?"

Abdalia Banefre was a government official in Cairo. "I did not know that VJ's people were interested in North America over a decade ago. However, I do know that his legal people are working with the French Government and with Dassault's people for at least two years."

Kachen had known Abdalia for over two decades. He was observant. "How long have Dassault and his people been doing business in the Americas?"

"At least a dozen years, mostly in South America."

"What you have shared, Abdalia, is also very surprising. I have never known VJ to work with a partner, yet alone someone who has the influence of Francois Dassault. This makes me very suspicious." Kachen got out of his chair and walked over to a counter to pour himself a drink.

Abdalia followed him. "I am sorry if I have offended you my friend."

"You have not offended me, my good friend. I just am disappointed in myself for not having seen this activity of VJ's before."

A relieved Abdalia placed his hand on Kachen's shoulder. "It is my fault that I have not warned you much earlier."

"No, my friend, it is not your fault, but now I would like you to find more details of this activity between Dassault and VJ."

"Consider it done, my friend."

Hassan Ibi, a banking investor at the bank that VJ uses for his business activities, spoke up. "I can say with certainty that there has been no money transfer between Dassault and VJ."

"You can say that, Hassan, with all certainty?"

"Absolutely my friend. As you are aware, VJ's legal and financial people use my bank when they contract outside of Cairo. There have been many transactions within the last year but none with Dassault or any of his companies."

"How can you be so sure, Hassan?"

"I have a very close working relationship with Andrew Hollinsworth, VJ's right hand man. Any type of financial activity between VJ and Dassault would have been executed by Hollingsworth and me through my bank," Hassan said confidently.

"This is very important information, Hassan. Even so, it is a little confusing. VJ has never taken a partner in the past, yet he seems to have been working with Dassault for at least a few years. This in itself is unusual and yet, there seems to have been no exchange of funds between them. If VJ has not gone to Dassault for funding, then why is he working with him?"

"I wish I could clarify that, Kachen, but I have not heard anything that connects VJ to Dassault," Hassan replied, scratching his head as if to search through his mind to find some possible clue.

"I hear you, Hassan. Even so, my nose tells me there is something very big that has drawn these two together in what appears to be very secret negotiations." Kachen sat down in his chair and took a deep swig of his drink.

The group went silent for a few minutes. Cha Hepzefa spoke. "As you know Kachen, I am now the head supervisor over all of VJ's warehouses. I have not seen VJ for many months at a time. this year. Previously, he would unexpectedly appear at one of his warehouses."

"Cha, what are stored at VJ's warehouses?"

"Most of the items are there for a short time because they are for his many stores mostly here in Cairo. However, there are other items that appear suddenly and stay at the warehouse for almost a year. They vary in size from that of a loaf of bread to the size of a large car. These items only arrive with a courier. Most of the time these items are very heavy—even the small ones."

Kachen stroked his beard. Cha was a big man, athletically built and in prime shape. If he said the items were heavy, they must be. "Cha, can you remember where these items came from and where they were sent?"

"I can't remember just now but I can check. The best I can remember that the very large items came from Southeast Asia and China. I'll check to see from where in those areas. The small packages came from many different places. I don't remember where any of these items were sent."

As he continued to stroke his beard, Kachen replied, "Understanding from where these items came and to where they were sent could be valuable information, Cha. Please let me know what you can find."

"It may take time but I will get you that information, Kachen."

Gamil Irsu, the foremen of VJ's security crew had been calmly listening. "Many times, couriers bring items to VJ's warehouses. We are always informed when one will arrive. Most of the time the items are about the size of a grown man. Each package is carefully wrapped to keep it from breaking."

After a thoughtful pause Kachen asked, "Gamil, were these items always delivered by the same courier?"

"As I think about that, there were different companies that delivered the items. I would need to check my files to know the different company couriers."

"Were you also notified when one of the items was shipped from the warehouse?"

"Yes, Kachen. Every time I would say."

"My friends, all of this is very interesting. It appears that VJ has a sideline activity."

There was a knock on the door and Cha moved to open it. Mohamed Ladin appeared. "My friends, it is time to eat and relax. Please join me in the garden."

It didn't take much coaxing; as the group filed out and into the garden, Kachen took the hand of Mohamed. "My good friend, I have been remiss in not telling you of the sorrow you must have endured for the loss of your second son. Please accept my apology for delivering it so late."

"There is no need to apologize, my friend."

"I had become very fond of Anu. He bravely endured many days of training and physical alteration to penetrate the FBI. His work was worth immeasurable help to the Benefactor. Unfortunately, our brothers had plans that caused our many efforts to be silenced."

"It is good to hear you say that about my son. It is also very hurtful that our brothers seem to have left us all in the dark."

"Have you had any contact with them of late, Mohamed?"

"I and many of our followers have heard nothing for months from them. However, enough of this talk, it is time to set things aside and take in the gifts of Allah."

Kachen followed Mohamed, but then moved to a corner to place a call to Max. "My friend, I have learned a great deal. I need to meet with you this Wednesday at our usual place, say at noon time. I will see you then."

Hoboken Police Station
8:45 am EST

"The two men your eyewitness saw are notorious," John told Phil and the technology expert for the Hoboken Police, Fred Haas. "Several years back, I worked on a case that involved them. They are consummate professionals. They are never the people who case an operation. That is always done by someone else and takes several days to complete. Then Koch and Periot arrive, perform the hit, and disappear. They have never been seen together. In fact, any detection of them has required a great amount of investigation. We are astonished a local police department was able to find out this much about them."

John realized how condescending this sounded and quickly added. "I don't mean it that way. We're really appreciative. You all have done a great job."

"What you are telling us is quite contrary to what happened here," said Phil.

"Exactly, Phil. It appears they wanted to be seen."

"Why do you believe this case is so different, John?"

"There is a possibility of a rivalry between Power Groups. One group is setting up the other to take the blame for the hit on Puleri. If this is the case, they may have left some small clues to be found."

"That's a new one on me," put in Fred. "That may be why we have found some other interesting things."

"Such as?"

"We've been tracking any occupants of the room in the building where the shots were fired. The previous occupants were there for six days. They used an account of a company in London. That led to another company in France, and finally to a small company in Northern New Jersey."

"A small company in Northern New Jersey? Really!"

"Yeah, it seems a little too easy. Even so, we have tried to contact the company but have not gotten any response."

"I doubt you will get any. Most likely it was a paper company that has ceased to exist."

"I agree, John. Needless to say, we will turn all that information over to you. We don't know much about the two people who occupied the room. It is vague and I believe it is not going to be very reliable."

"I have tallied those scraps of information. We can view them on this large screen."

"Okay Fred, let's get on with it."

"First of all, this is the main room of the suite," said Fred, turning to the computer. "The large window faces the six-story building across from our building. This is the telescopic shot that we took from the main room to the front door of our headquarter building."

"An unobstructed shot."

"Exactly, John."

"The setup people did their job. We have an enhanced image of the telescopic view. I'll bring it up. You can see a very faint discoloring in the stone on the right side of the doorway. Someone knew Puleri would be walking in front of that stone because his parking spot is in that direction."

"So, they knew he would pass that spot and timed their shot to strike him in the chest. They probably knew his exact height and orientation as he passed by the stone. If it was me, I would have a pedestal set up to hold the gun and a sensor pickup so when he passed a certain point the gun would fire."

"That is exactly what we wanted to show you. This is a picture of the pedestal. We found it in the closet of the adjoining room. There is a suite with two other rooms that join the main room."

"Pedestals have been found at the other suspected hits. It is part of their method of operation. That's why I was able to tell you about their setup. This just adds to the fact that Koch and Periot are most likely the actual hit men." John took a moment and rubbed his brow. "On the day of the hit, were the same three rooms rented?"

"The suite was rented until two days after the hit."

"So, the plan was for Koch and Periot to make the shot, then leave without taking anything with them. The setup crew then tore everything down, taking everything except the pedestal."

"That is what we believe has happened, John."

"The rooms are carpeted. They could have laid down some type of floor covering, removed the window blinds from the main room and placed them in one of the other rooms and had the doors to the other rooms covered with something so there'd be no gunpowder residue. Most likely Koch and Periot put their outer garments in the other rooms and wore coveralls. The net result is you found no gunshot residue anywhere in the main room."

"That's right. We did find some depressions in the carpet in the main room that were left by the pedestal. We also found other depressions surrounding it. We believe they set up a tent around the gun to stop the gunpowder from falling on any part of the room."

"Yes Phil, that makes sense."

"That we were hoping you could tell us, John."

John sat back in his chair. "This suite was a business office not a lodging suite. Why was there no office furniture in the rooms?"

Fred spoke quickly. "We asked the building manager the same question. There are a group of small suites like this one with no furnishings other than window blinds, phone, and computer hookup outlets."

John stood up. "I am totally convinced that the job was done by Koch and Periot and that somebody is trying to get us to believe that it is the Power Group who paid to have it done. So far, we have Koch and Periot flying in from Egypt. Both of them overtly show themselves at the

22-story building. A fabricated paper trail leads to Northern New Jersey. We know the Power Group is close to Manhattan. However, we did not know that it was located in Northern New Jersey. Since you sent the information to Cory, he can get some idea about the fake company."

"So John, you think the telltale clue they left is the fake company in Northern New Jersey?"

"Yes, I do. As I said, we didn't know where geographically where the Power Group was located. If we are right about what this hit group is telling us, we now have a smaller geographical area to focus on. It is still large, but much smaller than we had. However, this raises another question: Who is this other group?"

"It still doesn't tell us who put the hit on a good friend and a great mentor," said Phil.

"I hear you, Phil, but we are on their trail, now."

"I hope so John, we will do everything we can to help you do that."

October 23, 2001
NYC FBI Headquarters

"Cory, can you and John join me in my office?" asked Bob. "I want us to go over all we know about the hit on Lt. Puleri."

"This whole setup showed the true professionalism of the hit," John told him. "Performing it at police headquarters sends a message: 'We can get to you or anybody when we want.' Setting up in the farther building lowered their risk of being seen."

"You're convinced this was a professional hit by a top-level team?"

"Absolutely."

"I agree with, John," put in Cory.

"Actually, so do I," said Bob. "My next question is how much faith do you have in the Hoboken Police and their investigation?"

"They've done a good job so far," said John. I go all the way back to when Smith came to us with the information that showed that Sally Omara was not who he said he was but was really Abu Ladin, a spy we later found was put into our group through the efforts of this unknown Power Group. That was some outstanding detective work."

"Yes, Cory and with egg all over our faces, we were able to climb out of the dark and set ourselves on the right track. I agree with your assessment of Smith and Puleri."

"The work they did to identify the second building, find an eyewitness, and do some quick tracking to trace the money path to a small company in northern New Jersey in a short period of time is really first class. I have a lot of confidence in the people associated with Lt Phil Smith."

"That's what I wanted to hear you say, John. Because if we believe that this was done to deliberately expose themselves, they must have an ulterior motive. We have speculated that another Power Group paid for the hit on Puleri and is leaving us clues to the group we have been chasing."

"So, if we believe this northern New Jersey company points to the elusive Power Group, we are taking a great leap of faith."

Bob sat back in his chair. "I couldn't have put it any clearer than that. But if we are wrong, we will all be walking around with a big black eye."

"Speaking of this New Jersey company, we've found traces of it in seven different counties there."

"Even so, this narrows down the geographic area that we need to concentrate on. I want a full search in the area; I don't want the Power Group to know that we have narrowed our search."

"What do you have in mind, Bob?"

"Well John, I want to go back to the pattern work. Janet, Dennis, and Charles are doing a great job on these pattern recognitions. I want them to take a shot at narrowing down the field without tipping our hand to the Power Group."

"What kind of data do they need?"

"We need to get with Fred Newman and his people to answer that question."

Somewhere in Brooklyn, NY

Kachen parked and slowly walked into the restaurant where he was to meet Max. "Hello, my name is K, I have a meeting with Robert Morris."

"Yes, he is waiting to see you." Please follow me. The young lady led Kachen down a long hallway and opened the third door on the left. She then walked through a conference room and opened the far door and told Kachen to go down the hallway to the third door and knock three times.

Kachen followed her directions and as the door opened, he saw a plush-looking room with luxuriously thick carpeting and an oval mahogany conference table positioned in the middle of the room. Six cushioned chairs were placed around it.

"Please have a seat, my friend. and enjoy some stuffed grapevine leaves."

"Thank you, my friend, I see you are enjoying some of your fine Upstate New York wine," Kachen answered, taking a seat at the table. "I have much to tell. VJ has been very active."

"I am anxious to hear, my friend."

"First of all, VJ is after some land in western Canada. He has been working with Dassault's people for nearly four years and has been pursuing the land for more than a decade."

"That is very interesting. We thought that VJ only recently began working with Dassault."

"In those four years no money or contracts have flowed in either direction."

"That is big news. We know that both VJ and Dassault only deal in long term projects. We believe this project of VJ's is so large that he could not afford to finance the whole project. Then suddenly, he moves ahead. So, where did he get the necessary funds? Dassault?"

"That is what I am telling you, my friend. It also appears that VJ has some other sideline business."

"What kind of sideline?"

"Many objects that have come from China and Southeast Asia. These objects are very heavy and usually about the size of a man. They are carefully packaged so as to prevent any damage. Each time these packages arrive or leave, VJ's security people are involved."

"That is very interesting! Do we know where these packages come from and to where they are sent?"

"Not now, but it is in the works to find that information."

"The benefactor will be very excited."

NYC FBI Headquarters

"Bob, Janet and Charles are setting up in the conference room now and will be ready to start their briefing in a few minutes."

"Very good. Jeff wants to hear the latest update also. I'll let him know we are ready."

Janet was shaken when she got the message to brief the bosses.

"There is no need to be concerned, Janet," Cory told her. Jeff is very interested in the work that you all are doing. This is new stuff for Jeff, and he's amazed at what you all have been able to uncover."

"I'm glad to hear that, Cory. Charles has been able to adjust the signatures with the help of Allan Tubbs and Duncan Witherspoon, the two experts with Sebastian's new post processor."

"We are fortunate that Allan and Duncan have been able to help."
"Allan and Duncan will be here for the briefing."

"They are also pleased—and excited—with the progress the three of you have made."

"I'm concerned you're expecting to get an absolute identification of who has been doing the piggyback money movement," Janet told the group once they had all assembled in the conference room. "Although we can find patterns, they are not always that clear and precise. In fact, most of the time the results are not very precise at all." Janet clenched her left hand as she went through her view graphs.

"Believe me Janet, I know how you feel. I've been in your shoes. Bob and Jeff have too. They may seem to be very confident about things but they know how the real world works and they will be happy to see that the three of you have been able to whittle down the possible world to a small number of candidates."

Before Janet could answer, Fred Newman, George Sebastian, Allan Tubbs and Duncan Witherspoon walked into the conference room. "I see you are ready to give your presentation, Janet."

"I have a presentation, George. But I don't know if I am ready. Regardless of how many times I go over this material, I am never truly sure if we have found something or if we forced it to appear."

"You are not alone, Janet. Duncan and I have the same thoughts whenever we work on some new material."

"I can second that, Allan."

"I see that the crew is here."

"Hello Bob. Is Jeff going to make the meeting?"

"He is a few steps behind me."

"I hope that I have not held up the meeting," Jeff said, entering.

"No sir, we were just about ready to start. We're exercising several runs focusing on the two banks in Europe and then following with the Sebastian post processor. Allan and Duncan have helped Charles adjust the signatures in the NASA software. We have found eight different companies that could be the Power Group."

"What have you found that shows these are true candidates?"

"Well sir, they all have shown a sudden stoppage of activity through the two banks. In fact, all eight have been using both banks."

"That does seem a little coincidental. I would think that other companies would have only stopped using one or the other of the two banks."

"Absolutely, sir. Duncan has come up with a theory that these eight companies are fronts and that in reality the eight, or a large number of them are really run by one entity."

"Wow, now that is a new twist to the thinking."

"Yes sir. First, we did some preliminary investigation of each of the eight companies. Each one is owned by another company. The more we searched the more companies popped up. Of course, they all eventually led to a country where we could not uncover who they really are. They could be owned by still other companies."

"Jeff, I believe it is time to turn this over to Fred Hendrick in DC."

"Absolutely, Bob. This is just the solid type of data that Hendrick's people can use to track these companies. You people have done a great job. We can put this aside for now. Janet, you need to take the lead as our connection to Hendrick's people."

"Yes sir. We also have some information on people movement. We have had some discussions with our CIA contacts. The terrorist groups have had almost no movement over the last three weeks. Instead of moving across large areas, there seem to be more people moving from new places within the circles of interest. According to the CIA, it is a result of the increase in recruiting by Ali Ki. In addition, the movement to Southeast Asia shows that they need to restore their depleted funding."

"The last time we talked you were looking at old data to adjust your software. Since then, have you been running the latest data?"

"Yes sir, we have runs that used data from last June all the way up to October 18, 2001." Janet paused, took a deep breath. "We just received the last three weeks of data on the 19th. We had completed our signature adjustments just in time to run the new data. We then started to look for patterns of drug movement. So far the results are very scattered. We have informed our CIA contacts and they are looking for some new data, also. At this time, we are going through our various signatures and discussing them with the CIA. It will be a few days before we can adjust our signatures and get that new data."

"Excellent work, people. I feel like we are getting close enough to reach out and touch this Power Group," said Bob. "Now, we've got something new. We believe that the Power Group is located somewhere in Northern New Jersey. We have no idea what these people look like nor how many there are, and no help in the area to do any surveillance."

"You can stop right there, Bob. You want to track them using some type of signature to uncover patterns that will lead us to the Power

Group, right?" asked Fred. "That's going to take some thinking." Fred paused for a moment, rubbed his chin, then spoke. "First, we need to have a brain storming session. We need a spectrum of people and some local experts on Northern New Jersey."

"Other than the people already working on this case, the NYPD can help with their crime family background," replied Bob. "We are sure that the Power Group is dealing in the drug supply arena with the NYC families. One big thing we don't have is someone familiar with North Jersey. The closet is Lt. Phil Smith in the Hoboken Police department. He knows the lower portion of North Jersey."

"That's good from a police perspective. You may want to have someone check out the real estate side. I live in the Rutherford area, so I have a feel for the communities up there but even though you have reduced the location to North Jersey, that's a lot of territory to cover. You can count me and Sebastian on your brain storming team."

"I was hoping to hear you say that, Fred. I am meeting with Captain Johnson tomorrow on the same subject. I want to schedule the session for Thursday. I've already booked the large conference room. We do have a trump card. Fred Hendrick has one of his profilers studying this case."

"Sounds like we have a plan. People, great work. We are working on several fronts and we need to keep up the pressure. This Power Group has been eluding us for a long time but we're closing the net on them. We just need to tighten it. I look forward to hearing what the brain storming session will come up with."

Northern New Jersey
JR Cigar Store
"Hello, Roy. Good to see you. Are Damian and Shelly here?"

"Not yet, I expect them any minute. Warren and doc mike are in there waiting for you, Bob."

"Sounds good. I'll see you inside." As Bob conversed with the cigar team members, he learned that Warren had grown up in North Jersey. "How long have you and your family been lived in North Jersey?" he asked Warren, as they sat down to dinner.

"All my life and so has my wife. My family have been in the area for over a hundred years. Originally, they were farmers. We even had some dairy farmers along the way but mostly vegetable farming."

"So, you know the area quite well.

"Yes, you can say that."

"Are there many estates in the area?"

"Many isn't the word. They are everywhere. Quite a few are horse farms. There are some rich people in North Jersey. I think half of the New York Giants football team live there; in fact, some of them also have horse farms."

"Is there a lot of industry in the area?"

"Oh yes. As I said, agriculture is big, textiles are, too. And the medical industry, with a lot of research houses and automated factories. AT&T has always been very big in the area, also."

"That's impressive. If this was once mostly farmland, I image that some families inherited large plots of land. There could be old money in the area."

"There is, no could be about it. That is how many of them became rich—selling off portions of their land. North Jersey is a fairly dense area, so you can just imagine the price of the land."

"When they sold their land off, what did they do?"

"Some left and moved to other parts of the country. Others stayed and invested in different enterprises."

"Before talking to you I always thought of North Jersey as the bedroom community for workers in Manhattan."

"Yeah, they do make up a big part of the population. Some of the towns are overcrowded and have deteriorated over time. A lot of our business has been to upgrade the schools and businesses in the area."

"Who does your marketing?"

"We're part of another company who does the marketing and carries the contract with the client. We concentrate mostly on the engineering and execution. This was the way we operated before doc mike, Roy, and John Lipton started bringing in some of the big jobs in Manhattan."

"So the company that you are with really started in North Jersey." Hollis's excitement level rose as he enjoyed his chili, wings, and beer. "Is that the prime area for your energy work?"

"Absolutely. Mostly just the northeast portion. Think about it. If you head Northwest, you are into the mountains. Very little industry and low-density population. South Jersey is also low-density. That leaves Central Jersey, which is somewhat of a gradual transition from the densely populated Northeast to the lightly populated South."

"Yes, that makes sense, Warren. By the way, these wings are terrific."

Chapter 6

October 24, 2001
Franklin Lakes, New Jersey

Red and Cisco let their horses take them through the woods at an easy pace. At 7 a.m. the dew still lingered on the leaves and sparkled in the sunshine. Both men let their minds wander.

As Max and Numbers arrived, they saw Red and Cisco leave the stables.

"Cyn just got back from Versailles," Max mentioned as they headed into the library. "He'll give us an update on VJ's estate."

"I can imagine it's difficult to put surveillance inside VJ's estate in Versailles."

"Cyn and I did some real deep thinking on who we want to do the job. We'll also freshen up the existing equipment and sensor system we have in place."

"I just saw Cyn pull up into the driveway. We can get started as soon as he arrives and gets his drink. Max has some interesting news, too," said Cisco as Cyn entered the library and went straight to the bar without saying anything. "What's bothering you, Cyn?"

"VJ's estate has more alarms than we thought. The best thing was having our top electronics guys there. The bad news is that it is going to take at least two weeks to do the entire job."

"I suspected as much. I even wondered if we could do any surveillance inside the house."

"Don't worry, Cisco, we will do this job without anybody knowing that we have done it."

"I believe you, Cyn. Take a load off your feet and sit down. Max has some news about VJ."

"VJ has been looking for land in Western Canada for at least four years. We just don't know exactly where or why," explained Max.

"We don't know what they are searching for?"

"No; we have no intelligence on what they've been doing. We do know they are working with Dassault's people—they're the ones interfacing with the Canadians."

"This is sounding like VJ's final coup."

"I believe you are right, Cisco. We thought VJ had never gone into North America, so we never looked for anything there."

"He must have had some very strong motive. What would give him such an incentive?"

"That's a good question, Numbers, but as of now, we have no idea."

"Once again, we find some new information and instead of a conclusion, we get even more questions," said Cyn.

"Cyn, please sit down. Your face is as red as a fire engine. Sometimes the big advantage is finding some information that our enemy doesn't know that we have."

"Good point, Cisco. I have gotten the same sense. Kachen was also surprised to learn what VJ has been doing. We have new information that VJ has kept secret for at least four years. That gives us an edge in my opinion," said Max.

"What kind of edge is that?" Cyn almost spilled his drink.

"How good is this information, Max?" put in Numbers.

"Kachen has always been reliable. He has gotten this information from people who work with VJ's people, often daily. So my answer is this information is real and accurate. And there is more. Even though VJ and Dassault have been working together for about four years, there has been no exchange of funds between them."

"None at all," said Numbers, puzzled.

"Not even a penny. So how can you work with someone like Dassault for four years and not have any money transfer unless you already have an agreement up front?"

"I knew something was fishy between them," said Cyn. "Maybe Canada is just the beginning of VJ's entry into North America."

"On what do you base that, Cyn?" asked Cisco.

"I never trusted the fact that VJ was not doing anything in the Western Hemisphere. My gut has always told me that he was covertly up to something, especially here in the states but made it look like he wasn't even looking at the Western Hemisphere."

"What do you think about that, Numbers?"

"I agree that VJ is very stealthy about his business objectives. I always thought he stayed away from the Americas because he had enough connections in Europe and Asia. It could be possible that he's been secretly working here. He concentrates his resources so as not to spread them too thin. I think that someone—probably Dassault—has given him a tip on something that could be very, very big.

"I've started to look at the assets of each. Dassault is all about finance. He is also been keen on staying pace with technology—to get better tools to evaluate projects and help him to decide where to invest. VJ on the other hand uses technology to better perform the projects in which he has invested.

"I can see Dassault finding something and deciding to do the project himself instead of only investing. So, maybe Dassault contacted with VJ. VJ's people would know how to organize and run a massive mining project."

"Maye we've been on the wrong track. I'm inferring from your thoughts that the project in Canada could be a massive mining or drilling program that would require an exceptional amount of upfront capital—too much for VJ alone, but not for Dassault, who would only invest if he thought the project would pay off in very big gains."

"That about sums it up, Cisco. In fact, this opportunity may have been known for a long time but those who knew about couldn't get, or didn't have, the assets and resources to make it profitable. Then along comes Dassault who devises a plan to make it happen by establishing an arrangement with VJ."

"This makes a lot of sense and explains why VJ has taken on a partner. Very good, Numbers."

"Thank you, Max. We can also thank Kachen for uncovering the Western Canada connection."

Red, who had been quietly listening to the conversation asked a question. "I agree this is an enlightening theory. Even so, where does this leave us with VJ? Is he still a threat to us?"

Red's question seemed to reverberate across the room. There was an unusual silence. Even Cyn was quiet, which in itself was somewhat of a revelation. "Any thoughts?" Red asked after a moment.

"That's a really good question, Red. To be very truthful, I really don't know," said Cyn.

"I can say the same thing, Max," replied Numbers as he lay back in his chair and stared up at the ceiling.

"I really wish that I could have a better answer than yours, Numbers," muttered by Cisco.

"Well I don't believe it. I just do not trust VJ. Even if this Canada thing is for real and Dassault is supplying all the funding, I wouldn't count VJ out of our list of people to be concerned about," said Cyn.

"So, Cyn, you believe we need to push forward with our original strategy to uncover what VJ is doing and is he after our Big Kill?"

"Absolutely, Red!"

"I need to get a refill on my drink and then I need to finish with another piece of news about VJ."

"Oh boy, we still have more mystery to hear about!" Cyn blurted it out and moved to the bar. "I need a refill too, Max." Max nodded to Cyn and then moved back to the conference table. He placed his drink on the table and instead of sitting down in his chair, moved behind it, placing his large hands on top of the chair, leaned over slightly, and began to talk.

"VJ has been dealing heavily in art. Mostly from China and Southeast Asia. The items range from the size of a loaf of bread to the size of a compact car. They don't stay long in his warehouses in Egypt, because they are shipped around the world. These objects are heavy, even the small ones. Each is carefully wrapped. Each is delivered and sent by professional couriers. When a package arrives or is sent via the warehouses, VJ's security people are there."

"This is all new," put in Cyn. We know that his wife has been involved in rare antiques and that VJ has been known to help her but this sounds like we are talking about many art objects."

"That's right. The latest update that I've gotten is somewhere near a hundred objects over the past three years."

"Wow, Max. That is a large number. Perhaps they are not all rare art or antiques. Maybe only a few are rare art."

"Numbers, you know VJ. How often does he have his security people on station at his warehouses?"

"Not often. VJ's warehouses in Egypt are for his commercial stores. Or so we thought. Once again, VJ may have pulled the wool over our eyes."

"What does this mean to us?" posed Red.

"When Kachen's people first talked about it, it didn't seem to mean much other than a stream of revenue for VJ. The more I thought about it the more I thought of VJ's wife. She deals in rare art. This could just be VJ helping his wife with her business."

"I believe it is more than that, Max. I think it is the introduction of VJ to Dassault, who is a major art collector. VJ was helping his wife who then opened the door for VJ to meet Dassault on VJ's terms."

"Now, that makes real sense, Numbers."

"Of course, it does." Cyn sounded more confident than he had all day. "VJ always finds a way to get the advantage. It is his trademark. This shows who is the lead in the Dassault/VJ team. It wasn't Dassault who got the tip about Western Canada. It was VJ. He did his research and uncovered a few candidates. Then he sat down and decided who was the best. Michele had already done business with Dassault. VJ then had his new resource man."

"That makes sense, Cyn; VJ is quite the salesman. It could very well be that VJ has sold the deal to Dassault and that it is Dassault who is putting up the funding while VJ is in control."

"It makes even more sense when one understands that Dassault has had a presence in the Western Hemisphere for a couple of decades."

"Exactly!" Cyn was almost dancing around the room. "Dassault always first establishes a strong political connection when dealing with a project in an area. Yes, VJ has the lead."

"I believe you are right, Cyn. This new information may also have resolved one of our main fears."

"What is that, Numbers?"

"It tells us that VJ isn't looking for a new money stream because he has it. Our fears that VJ knows about our Big Kill and is planning on taking it away from us just isn't happening."

They all sat back in their chairs and let that message sink in.

"This is almost too good to be true," said Cisco.

"Even though it is good news we still need to keep surveillance on VJ."

"I agree with you, Cyn. We should have no let-up in our earlier plans, including surveillance on Narparti and Shelly," added Max.

"Right, gentlemen. We stay with our plans. Numbers, how well are your diversions working?"

"Thought you would never ask, Cisco. Red has put several false trails together. They are so good that even I am having a hard time following our drug movement. Meanwhile, our money movement has been completely changed. We've moved away from large banks. We are in five different groupings of smaller banks in Europe, Southeast

Asia, and Japan. We have not touched anything here in the States."

"Why not?"

"They have never been exposed and the links from the Camens and Nassau are the only offshore links to them. We didn't adjust any of that, so the FBI has no tracking of that money movement."

"Isn't that odd that the FBI hasn't tracked our money movement here in the States?"

"Oh, I believe they have, Cisco, however we don't have much in the states. Most is offshore, with the bulk of it in Europe."

"Well, all of that is good news. This has been a good day. Once again things seem to be going our way. Red, anything from Stevens?"

"I have searched their files and found a few places that referenced Tom Rowe and ActSof. Each time they were referring to a new technique for hacking into a secure network."

"What does that mean, Red?"

"It means that Rowe was aware of some new techniques that could be used to break into the software he used for the Big Kill."

"Okay, but where does that leave us?"

"I am trying several schemes I think Anu could have used to keep someone from breaking into his code. I've discussed this with Pat Sherman. He is aware of certain types of coding that can give him a better understanding of traps that Anu setup when he was at ActSof."

"I think that is good news Red, but it is still Greek to me. What I would like to know is when will we be able to exercise the Big Kill." Cisco wiped his forehead, got up from his chair and headed to the bar to pour another drink.

"I wish I could give you a date for that to happen. As of now, it could take weeks, or it could happen tomorrow."

"How did we get ourselves into such a situation?"

"Like you said before, Cisco. Things happen that we can't control. Ali Ki's targeting of the Towers could not have been foreseen."

"I hear you, Red, but what bothers me is our reliance on software. I know the whole world is going in that direction. Even so, it is very frustrating and just eats at me.

"Max, do we have any update on who is behind the Puleri kill?"

"It was two professionals who often work together. They met in Cairo and flew into Baltimore, then proceeded to Hoboken. There was an earlier setup team that made all the arrangements. They hit Puleri as he was walking out of the building. I'm getting some more information on the two hit men. Early information says these are exceptional, with several known kills. This had to be an expensive kill. Somebody really had a very big reason to put the hit on Puleri with this type of talent level."

"This is not good news, Max. We just uncovered information that VJ may not be a threat, and now it appears that someone else has intervened. The question is why?"

"I may know the answer in a few days, Cisco."

"Well gentlemen, we have covered a great deal today. Max, this latest news on Puleri is a top priority."

"I'll work with you on this one, Max," said Cyn.

The group finished their drinks and left as Madame joined her son in the library. "Well, that was quite a meeting. Very interesting discussion about VJ. It sounds like the most plausible situation. Even so, I am with Cyn on this one. We proceed as planned and increase the surveillance on Versailles."

"I believe it would be foolish not to proceed as planned. I thought that we might not be able to bug VJ's manor in Versailles."

"I have great faith in Max and Cyn. I have seen them do many things that seemed impossible." She pondered for a moment. "This new player may be our biggest problem. How can a small town police officer warrant a professional hit? I just can't fathom anybody we know who would need to place such a hit on Puleri," said Cisco.

"I'm very concerned about this new player. He's appeared out of nowhere. We should have seen something before."

Cisco's mobile rang, cutting of Madame.

"That is not good news, Max," he said and hung up his phone. "Max just got an update on the Puleri hit. There was a witness who noticed the two hit men because they stood out in the crowd."

"That makes no sense unless they wanted to be noticed." She paused, seeming shaken. "That means they left clues to point at somebody. The hit on Puleri will bring in the FBI. Someone is sending a message to the FBI. This is very unnerving. I sense they are pointing to us."

"Max needs to find what the clue is that was left behind. The FBI could be following up on it right now. I need to call Cyn and see if his implants can find that clue."

Somewhere in Manhattan
Conference room in a large hotel

"Glad to see everybody is here," said Bob. "We have a core of FBI people who have been working this case for a long time and others some of you have not met."

He introduced Captain Walter Johnson and Lt. Gino Bonomo and Phil Smith of the NYPD, Fred Newman and George Sebastian of the FBI's data analysis department, Janet, Charles, and Dennis, along with profiler Wendell Gardner, a profiler, as well as Cory, John, and finally Jeff Horton, who stood up to explain the purpose of the meeting.

"We believe we have been handed a clue that the Power Group that has eluded us for years, maybe located in North Jersey. This brain storming session is designed to give us what we need to track and locate that Power Group. We need to find them before they know we are closing in on them," Jeff explained.

"There are numerous large estates through the area. We think a primary base for the Power Group could be such an estate, providing privacy and easy access to the City. If it is an estate, how do we find it?"

"We could start checking the real estate market," suggested Cory.

"That would be good if the group recently purchased the estate. Maybe it would be good to understand the makeup of this group. It may tell us who heads the group and maybe owns the estate," said John.

"Good thought, John. As you have noticed, I have assigned three teams that include a cross section of talents in each group. Let's take that question of John's and meet with our team members to discuss the makeup of the Power Group then report back in 30 minutes."

When the time had elapsed, Captain Johnson gave the first report, explaining the theories he, Cory and Janet had developed.

"This Power Group could not have been formed recently, so if they meet at an estate, it will be a well-known one, even if recently purchased by someone in the group. The head of the group is very likely a businessman, maybe old money. Someone who can mingle with the upper class in North Jersey and Manhattan. He may be well known in that social set—a benefactor who supports causes and charities."

"We agree with your description," put in John, speaking for his group which had consisted of himself, Gino and Dennis. "and we concentrated on the make-up of the rest of the group.

"We believe it will have five or six members, each with a different expertise. Each member will also have many contacts he or she can count on. We believe the types of expertise needed are financial—someone with international connections and experience. Next, a very experienced and creative technical person with an outstanding command of computers and software. A third member needs to have criminal connections to the crime families in Manhattan. The fourth person needs to have connections in Europe, and the fifth person needs to have connections in Asia and the Mideast. And finally, they need someone with connections with the terrorists."

"That is an impressive array of talent and power, John, and it provides a host of patterns to track," said Hollis. "George, your group focused on operations. Tell us what you found."

George, who had brainstormed with Charles and Phil, said, "This Power Group operates worldwide—and that means it's first enterprise is drugs. If they're working in Asia, then the drug is heroin. If they're based in Jersey, the target market is Manhattan. If you're dealing in drugs you've got to launder the money. This means connections to other Power Groups with the same need. The third item is weapons. Their customers are terrorist and rebels. We believe the financial attack is a recent innovation and one they won't give up on. They will try to reestablish that capability as soon as possible."

"This is really great work from all of you," said Hollis. "I think we've got a good picture now. We are looking for a group of five or six people with deep roots in Europe and Asia including connections to terrorists—maybe even Ali Ki," Hollis summed up. "They also may have crime connections worldwide including a massive money laundering operation. Fred, George, is that enough to get started on your patterns and tracking?"

"Actually, Bob it is more than I thought we would get," said Fred. "How good are these profiles we've created, though? If they aren't good, we may go off on a wild goose chase."

"Absolutely, so let us play devil's advocate."

"I see one problem, Bob," said Phil. "We've assumed members of the Power Group all live in North Jersey or close by. If this is such a sophisticated group, they may use telecommunications and be scattered worldwide."

"You're right Phil. It would be the easiest wrong step to take. Let's say that is true. What difference would it make in the patterns?"

"Transportation for one," said George.

"So, we would lose some tracking ability?"

"Very much so, Bob!"

"Is there anyway of tracking these telecommunications?"

"Off hand, I don't know. I would need to get with our networking people. We have been doing a lot of monitoring on the networks, including video. That would leave some very telltale signs and may even be better than tracking ground transportation."

"That's right, George," said Newman. "There are only a handful of companies in the States that own the fiber optics to carry the video for telecommunications. They can be scanned quickly."

"Any other thoughts?" put in Bob. "Yes, Cory?"

"What if the head guy isn't at an estate? Maybe an office building? If these people are so sophisticated, they may have anticipated being tracked and set up in a place that would be considered unlikely."

"Well, let's discuss whether that would be the case or not. Any thoughts? Phil, I see you are thinking of something."

"If I was the head of such a group," said Phil slowly, "I'd have a real business that I would also run so I could have this group of people come and go without drawing any special attention."

"That makes sense. Where would you set up such an operation, and what kind would it be?"

"There are a lot of businesses I could use as a front."

"Maybe not. If these people are as powerful as we believe, their business must be in line with that status," said John.

"So white collar—and most likely in a high-rise building," agreed Phil.

"Then why a high rise in North Jersey when Manhattan is right next door?" asked Fred.

"That's true, Fred. And that brings us back to an estate as the most likely place," said Bob. "This has been a very successful collaboration. I want to thank you all for your help."

As Bob led the group out of the conference room, Captain Johnson stopped him. "I need to talk to you about a new development. We think a big shipment of heroin is coming into Manhattan soon."

"How soon?"

"Within the month."

"Can you trust the source?"

"Actually, it is a series of rumors coming from three different places. The sources have been very true in the past."

"Do you have any details?"

"Nothing yet, just something big. We don't know how, when, or where. Right now, we're keeping everything under wraps and just listening. When we get some updates, you'll hear from us."

"Good, let us know if we can be any help."

"Actually, your tracking capabilities just might come in useful. Nothing yet, but it's another thing to consider. Talk to you soon."

Franklin Lakes, New Jersey

"Hello, Cyn." A restless Cisco anxiously grabbed the phone as soon as it rang. "The clue is a location in Northern New Jersey. What kind of a location?"

"It looks like a dead end is all that we know. I'll keep checking."

Cisco hung up his phone and turned to his mother. "You heard?"

"Yes, somebody is setting us up. They are pointing the FBI in our direction. We need to stop all gatherings here at the estate. We will setup in Manhattan with Numbers." Madame's cell phone rang.

"This is Carl Rutherford. Remember that drink that I owed you? I am in Manhattan tonight. I thought you could join me."

"Yes Carl, my son and I were just getting ready to drive into Manhattan. We'll see you about 7:30 at our old place." Madame hung up her phone. "Something big is happening. Rutherford gave me the hot button signal. We need to get into Manhattan and meet him at our drop point for drinks."

A Restaurant
Manhattan, NY

"Hello Carl, it's so good to see you. It has been too long," said Madame as she gave him a hug and then sat at the small table in the back along with her son.

"I'm glad the two of you could make it into Manhattan tonight. The weather has been very cooperative today. Somewhat a surprise one could say." Carl once again used the agreed upon coded language.

"When the weather is good, surprise or not, I just enjoy it," agreed Madame, ready to relax and enjoy the evening.

"I agree with you on that. I talked to the chef earlier. The new deliveries of lobster are some of the best that he has seen."

"That is really good to hear." The three of them ordered and enjoyed their evening together. About an hour later, Carl excused himself and went through a doorway marked private at the back of the room.

A few minutes later he rejoined Madame and Cisco. "One of the things I enjoy about being here is that when I walk out, the first thing on my left is a great view," he said, pointing Cisco to the doorway.

Curiously, Cisco did as he was told. He didn't understand what was happening, but he knew enough about his mother's contacts to know something important was about to take place. He closed the door quietly, then stopped and stared.

"Dad! Is it really you?" Sitting in a comfortable chair was Cap. Cisco ran to his father, nearly picking him up from the chair in a big bear hug.

"Easy son, easy. I will explain, but first, I need you to return to the table and send your mother in to see me. Tell her to just walk in and close the door behind her." Cisco returned to the table, sat down and said to Madame, trying to hide his excitement, "Go ahead. Just walk in."

Madame, too, went to the door and opened it.

"Oh my God! How can this be?" The couple embraced as Madame, usually so stoic, cried. After a moment, Cap sat her down beside him.

"I have much to tell you. It started with a call from Carl when I was in the Tower, telling me it was of the utmost importance to meet him. I walked down two levels, and everything just exploded. I was thrown into the wall and knocked unconscious. Carl and his people carried me down the stairway and brought me to his estate in Connecticut. I've been recovering ever since. What Carl needed to tell me is that a Colombian mob wants to cut in on our drug market, starting in Manhattan. Somehow, they discovered who I am but are not aware of the group, let alone you and our son. We have been doing some investigating. The Colombians put the hit on Puleri and pointed the FBI in the direction of North Jersey, even though they don't yet know exactly where the estate is. By now the FBI has most likely started to search for us."

"This is almost too much to take in. We had already come to the conclusion that someone has marked us but we did not know who or why. We've moved our meetings to Numbers' office in Manhattan. We're cutting back on telecommunications—none of it from the estate. Our area surveillance tells us that the traffic from our meetings has not given away any telltale signs. The FBI can do all the tracking it wants, and they won't find the estate."

"That's good. You and our kids are safe. Even so, we must remain diligent. These are ruthless people we are dealing with. Setting up Numbers' office is a good back-up but Carl's estate will be even better. We've worked with him in the past, so there are no issues there. I image Cyn and Max are doing their jobs, too?"

"They've done even more. We have learned that VJ and Dassault are working together on what appears to be the biggest undertaking in VJ's entire career. For a while we thought VJ was targeting our Big Kill but now we really doubt that."

"What has happened with the Big Kill?"

"The plane went directly through the Tower office. Everyone there was killed instantly including, Tom Rowe and our Sauly Omara."

"What about Red?"

"He wasn't there when the plane hit."

"Have we recovered the Big Kill?"

"Not yet. Tom Rowe secured the system and we need a password to get into it. But we can talk about all of this later. How are you?"

"I had a concussion. A bunch of bruises, some cracked ribs and a twisted ankle. Carl decided not to try and contact you until we learned how much the Colombians knew about you and the estate. For now, we'll gather everyone tomorrow at Carl's estate. You need to contact everybody. Do not divulge my status. You need to get back to the table. Carl's people will be here soon to take me back to Connecticut." The pair kissed and Madame returned to the table. There she hugged Carl goodbye, whispering her thanks.

October 25, 2001
NYC FBI Headquarters
Jeff Horton's Office

"It is good to see you, Wendell. Your boss has been very helpful in our pursuit of this Power Group. Bob and I are glad you were able to monitor our brainstorming session yesterday. We're interested in your opinion."

"I'm happy to help. You've got a tough nut to crack. Whoever this group is, they didn't just recently get together. They're deeply entrenched and have evolved over a long period of time. That's my take from the information we've received. Your brain storming session theorized that the Group's mainstream of revenue is drugs—and because of the Asian connection that it is heroin. A heroin connection back to the Asian source means old school and old money."

"Wow, that was never mentioned at the session. However, I can see it clearly now. It also tells me that the location in North Jersey is an old estate, not recently purchased but inherited."

"Very good, Bob. I believe you are correct."

"I need to tell our trackers this immediately," Bob said as he moved to phone Fred Newman.

As he hung up, Wendell continued. "I believe our brain stormers got it right on the makeup of the Power Group. But the players can shift from time to time depending on the priorities of the Power Group. There could be more than the small core group. Remember I said they are old school. While they may use technology, they also believe in secrecy. They'll meet *sub rosa in* plain sight. There will be telecommunications or a high-profile location. In fact, I doubt that they ever use their real names in the company of each other."

"You mean that they could all live within a short distance of each other and meet somewhere clearly visible that draws no attention?"

"Very high probability, Bob. Your tracking may show no real results or misleading results."

"That's unsettling, Wendell! I thought we had a very good chance of locating this group, but now I'm hearing you say we may be wasting our time and resources."

"I am not trying to be negative. I want you to use caution when interpreting the results and I think your people doing the tracking need more information to discern the validity of the results."

"Ah, thank you for clarifying that, Wendell. This is why your boss has sent you here to guide us."

"My boss also sent me here to learn. You and your people are engaged in some new territory. We are seeing a small group of individuals who have bonded together for a common purpose and have gathered enormous power and capabilities to control what could be considered world forces. We all have a lot to learn."

"Once again your boss is way ahead of us. He probably realized this long before we even had an inkling of what we are involved in." "Bob, my boss is so excited about what you and your people have uncovered. The material that you're sending us has been given top priority because Fred Hendrick believes you've uncovered a whole new realm of organized crime."

"Fred's been good to us and good for us. Bob has a great working relationship with him and he's responded quickly and with great talent and results. Hopefully together, we can uncover this new threat and fight it without one hand tied behind our backs. Which brings me to ask, what else do you recommend?"

"That is what Fred likes about you, Jeff. You get right to the point. I think you need to take what we have collectively learned and put it to use in your ongoing tracking of money, people, and drug flow. Fred wants me to stay up here for a few days with your tracking people. First, I need to be briefed by Cory and John, though."

"Absolutely, Wendell. Also, Janet was working on some piggyback money accounting. She has been talking with your boss."

"Yes, according to the boss, They are combing through bundles of data to unravel the different companies entangled in this piggybacking issue. It may be awhile before we can have some real results."

As Wendell left to meet Cory and John, Jeff and Bob got back to their meeting.

"Anything new on the Puleri hit?" asked Jeff.

"Our NYPD contacts believe that the Colombians hired them to put pressure on the Power Group that we are after."

"What a small world. You were right, Bob. There was a broader connection and it had to do with Manhattan—I am assuming it's the Colombian drug people who want more activity in Manhattan."

"That's what Captain Johnson thinks. He's positive that is the situation. His sources have come up with the same story."

"In some respects, that's good news. Next time I hope not to have such a negative attached to it."

"Captain Johnson believes there is going to be a big drug drop by the Power Group."

"Do we know when and where?"

"It will be within a month and in Manhattan itself. That is all we know as of now."

"Well, these next couple of weeks will not be boring. Good meeting Bob."

Actsof

"Damian, I just got a call from my father. He wants us to come to Cairo and install Actsof's latest accounting system in his stores."

"I've been waiting to hear that," Damian said enthusiastically.

"He wants us to contact Andrew Hollingsworth, his assistant. Dad already talked with Tilghman, and he's agreed that you, Pat, and I go ASAP."

"Well, that sounds like your dad. He doesn't beat around the bush. In fact, I'll bet that your mom and sister already know about it. We are the last to be informed. It's a command performance," Damian chuckled.

Tilghman entered the room, smiling broadly. "Have you heard from your father?"

"Yes, we have. As usual, he's in a hurry. He wants us there immediately."

"Actually, I'm the one who recommended the rush."

"Really, why?"

"This as a fantastic opportunity to install our new system in a well-established business with multiple sites over a large geographical area." Tilghman was almost dancing around the room. "Damian, this is a great chance to see our system work on foreign soil!"

"Just what have you agreed to do? We don't know what accounting system they use or if they have network connections to their multiple sites."

"Your father-in-law is very tech-minded. He's already sent us all the information on their accounting systems, all their LANs and WANs. He wants a complete workup to include upgrading all the accounting systems and incorporating our near real-time system. His tech folks are already talking with Harvey and our research people. I've told VJ we will need two days here, then all three of you will fly to Cairo on day three."

"Sounds like Shelly and I need to talk to Harvey."

Connecticut
Rutherford's Estate

Madame and Cisco arrived hours early before the meeting to spend time with Cap. "I could hardly wait to see you again," Madame said, kissing him.

"It is so good to see both of you safe and I do know that our daughter is doing well at school."

"Yes, she loves Princeton."

"How are you, Dad?"

"I'm recovering well. I have very little pain left and my mobility has just about all come back."

"Hello Madame and good to see you, young man."

"Carl, I don't know how to thank you."

"There is no need to thank me. For all that you two have done for me over the years, I can never repay you. Even so, the three of you have much to discuss. Your group will be arriving in about three hours. Please enjoy your time as a family." Carl retreated from the library.

"Much has happened. Your son has been running the group and doing an excellent job." The three of them sat down at a large mahogany table that easily would seat ten people. The chairs were comfortable, high-backed captain chairs. "Our business is doing very well. Operations in Southeast Asia have grown more than double our early projections. The heroin trade into the states is also running well beyond expectations. The money laundering in Europe and South America is expanding as we speak."

"I'm glad to hear all that. What I want to know is how you two are."

"I can't tell you how relieved I am that you are alive and well. The shock of those Tower's collapsing gave me a chill that hasn't left me yet," his wife said again, reaching over to touch him again.

"I wanted so much to reach out to you but I knew it was too dangerous. Carl and I had only sketchy information on the Colombians. We were afraid of leading them to you and the family. It was only two days ago that we knew enough to realize that the Colombians did not know of the family or the estate. They only know it is somewhere in North Jersey."

"Do you believe you are safe now?"

"Carl believes the Colombians think I'm dead. Their plan was to eliminate me, intimidate the group, and negotiate a new drug deal for Manhattan."

"A top down thrust," put in Cisco.

"Exactly; now they are rethinking their overall strategy."

"Why are they concentrating on Manhattan?"

"They want to expand their business throughout the Northeast. They figured if they could get a substantial foothold in Manhattan, they could use that as a stepping off place to expand throughout the entire area. They needed to eliminate me before they could make a move on the group. Carl has made sure the Colombians don't know exactly who we are. They know very little about us—even me."

"So now, they have to start all over with their plans."

"Yes, especially since they have learned that the FBI is on their trail. That was something they did not expect to happen."

"Do you have any idea of their new plans?"

"Carl's sources believe they will pull back and regroup. They already have enough attention from the FBI because of their drug trafficking, but this opens them up to the terrorists countermeasure portion of the FBI. Carl thinks they'll close ranks to ensure their existing business doesn't shrink and wait for things to cool down before implementing a new strategy."

"So, what do we do in the meantime? Do we conduct business as usual or do we need to change parts of our operations?" asked Cisco.

"Well son, that is part of what I want us to discuss. For now, we need to not have any group gatherings at our estate. We can base those here. In addition, it would be wise to bring Carl into the group, at least on a temporary basis. You may not remember but about ten years ago, Carl helped us set up laundering operations in Manhattan and Boston. There was no need for Carl to be a part of the group long term. He could build up his own house and we would have several cooperative efforts. In addition, Max and Cyn would have another party to use as enforcers. This was all before Red joined the group."

"Yes, I see where this is going, Dad! This is the right time to bring Carl back."

"Have you talked this over with Carl?" Madame asked.

"Yes, my dear. Carl is ready to join us to establish a protective barrier against anyone else who may want to encroach on our U.S. holdings."

"You have been busy, my dear husband. I have noticed that Maria's car was parked in the garage. How much has she been briefed?"

"Carl and Maria are as close as you and I. They share everything. In fact, Maria is anxious to see you. They have a setup similar to ours for this library. You will both be able to follow the group activity while discussing each of your interpretations of what is unfolding."

"Ah, Maria has come a long way. I can envision the two of us watching and listening. This can be very dynamic. That brings me to a point that needs to be addressed right now. How are you and your son going to run the group? Your son is known to the group as Cisco, by the way"

"Cisco, the name of your horse!" Cap laughed.

"Yes, Red recommended I use the name."

"So, let it be done. To get into the pragmatics, we need Cisco to make my presence known to the group. As for now, I am still in recovery and Cisco will take the lead. Carl will speak for me. I will occasionally struggle to speak. This should maintain the continuity that you two have established with the group."

"Very good, my dear. I will leave you two and join Maria."

"Well Dad, what do I call you in front of the group."

"You call me Cap. We will keep the same anonymity rule that we have always employed. Carl will be called Brady."

"Where did that name come from?"

"Carl is a big football fan. He loves the New England Patriots."

"So, everybody else knows Carl as Brady except For Red."

"That's right. I will stay with Brady while you meet the group here in the library. First you discuss the FBI search for our estate; you have confirmation for that from Brady. We now know that it was the Colombians who put the hit on Puleri and pointed the FBI at us. You then bring in Brady and let him tell his story which will include my injuries. However, we will not tell them that I have recovered but in fact am quite immobile and can barely talk. Remember that they will need to talk and have questions answered. Be patient and go with the flow, but slowly direct it to Brady."

"Understood, Dad. Even so, I know they will be happy to hear you are still alive and will want to see you soon."

"Yes, you just need to be patient and not rush into anything. This is a time for regrouping. We all need to focus on our objectives, keep an eye on our adversaries, establish our priorities, and then execute our plans. We are back in control. I need to leave you now and join Carl. I'm proud of you, son."

Cisco took a deep breath and went to the computer. He pulled up a Microsoft Word file and began recording his thoughts.

A short time later, all of the Power Group had arrived. After explaining why they were meeting in Connecticut, and the implications of the Colombian mafia problem, Cisco brought up the real reason for the meeting.

"So now we know who the new adversary is, but there is a lot more to the story," he told them. "The Colombians want to increase their drug traffic in the whole Northeast, and they see Manhattan as the place to start. They are aware of our connection to the New York Families, so they devised a plan to take control with a top down maneuver by removing Cap, then putting pressure on all of us to control the distribution of drugs into Manhattan."

"Do they have any idea who they are dealing with?"

"Actually Cyn, they have been given bogus information by Brady and his people. Part of that information is that Cap could be alive."

"Whoa! That is a big smoke screen. What is going to happen when they find out that Cap was killed in the Tower?"

"Numbers, you of all people should know that it's difficult to take down an organization if you are not sure who is in charge."

"Yes, you're right, Cisco. So, that means that the Colombians have to rethink their entire strategy and gather far better intelligence."

"Right, Cyn. Brady's people have been tracking them and they know that the Colombians have chosen to step back to protect their assets. They did not anticipate that the FBI would be on their trail."

Cyn clapped and whooped with laughter. "They've shot themselves in the foot."

"This can give us even more room to operate than we have had in the past," a smiling Numbers said, sipping his brandy.

"What do you mean by that?"

"We have always been concerned that a slip up would expose us in Manhattan. Now we have a group running interference for us and they don't even know it."

"Good point, but there's more to this story. Dad—Cap—is alive."

"What!"

"You're joking!"

"What kind of nonsense is this?"

"Back on Sept. 11, when Dad—Cap—was at the Towers, Brady called him to tell him about the Colombians. Cap was walking two floors down to meet with Brady when the plane hit. Brady's men rescued him. They carried him down the stairways to the ground level and brought him here. Cap is alive, but in very bad shape. He is still in recovery."

"I want to see him!" said Cyn, getting up from his seat.

"In good time, Cyn."

"This is astounding! This takes a terrible situation and turns it into a merciful time. I feel better than I have in weeks," put in Numbers.

"I'm with you, Numbers. The Phoenix has risen from the ashes.

Cisco, you have done an outstanding job, but to know that Cap is alive is a real boost. I haven't seen Cyn this excited in years! I want to see Cap but I know it will be worth the wait," said Max.

"Thank you, Max. Believe me, I feel the same," Cisco said as there was a knock on the door and Brady wheeled in Cap in a wheelchair.

"Hello, Gentlemen. It is good to see all of you together. I would like to reintroduce you to Cap. It is difficult for him to talk. He is well aware of his surroundings and his hearing is excellent. Please be aware that he is still in pain."

"It's good to see you, sir. I poured your favorite brandy."

"Thanks, Cyn," was a craggy-voiced reply by Cap as the group began to voice their happiness at seeing Cap alive.

"Dad, it's not only good to see you alive, it's reenergized the whole group. We all needed a boost. We have been doing much and there is much we need to do and do it soon. Right now, we need to hear from Brady."

"Two days before the planes crashed into the Towers, we came across a Colombian Cartel plan to expand their drug business throughout the Northeast with Manhattan as their base of operations. What was blocking them was the stronghold that the New York Families had on the drug traffic in Manhattan. They were able to determine that the families were being supplied by a Power Group located in North Jersey. Their information was sketchy, but they had learned that Cap was the head of the group supplying the heroin."

"But they don't know who makes up the group?" asked Numbers.

"That is correct. We have fed them false information on all of you."

"Why didn't you let us know that Cap was alive?" asked Max.

"We didn't know for sure how much the Colombians knew about Cap and his family, so we decided to stay low, get medical help for Cap, and keep steering the Colombians in the wrong direction."

"Something is just not fitting into place. How did they know the Power Group's connection to Puleri?"

"Yes Max, that puzzled us also. We didn't know the hit on Puleri was part of the Colombian strategy until a couple of days ago. We believe the Colombians have a mole in the FBI."

"Damn, I knew we should have handled taking out the real Omara ourselves instead of letting Katchen and his people do it. It let Puleri into the mix and gummed up our whole operation."

"Cyn, that is history. We need to focus on the now," said Cisco. "Cap believes we need to bring Brady back into the group. We need a combined strategy to keep the Colombians at bay, while we proceed with our operations and new ventures."

"Excellent idea," said Numbers.

"Max and I need to get Numbers and Brady together to build a strategy for our new laundry rollout both in the States and Europe," said Red. "This is going to need a lot of planning and understanding of the special connections we need to have for the laundry flow."

"We cannot underestimate the FBI especially with the new tools they are using. We need to be proactive instead of only laying low," added Cyn.

"What do you have in mind?"

"Can we give them some false leads?"

"I hope you have some, Cyn."

"Right now, I don't."

"Anybody else have any ideas?"

"Actually, I'm not sure if we should go proactive unless we have something really good to distract the FBI that won't put any of us on their radar," said Max.

"I see your point," said Cisco.

"Instead, I think we need to work with Brady on our strategy to deal with the Colombians. They are not just going to give up on Manhattan," said Cyn. "If they had some influence over us, they could have us move their cocaine over our conduits to the NYC families."

"If that is their thinking, they have seriously underestimated who we are or at least who they think we are. But I do think you are on the right track, Cyn. They think we are just some local group who has an arrangement with a source supplier to get the heroin into Manhattan. They have no idea of our other distribution, yet alone how much we control."

"I believe you are right, Max. So, what is the best way to show them what we can do without letting them have any idea of who we are?"

"Gentlemen, I would love to come down on them hard. However, we have always remained in the shadows. So why don't we let the FBI do our dirty work for us?" said Numbers.

"What do you have in mind?" asked Cyn.

"What if we leak to the Colombians that there is a large store of heroin in a warehouse waiting to be moved to one of the families. Then we let the FBI know that the Colombians are going to hit it."

"Get it done, Cyn."

"With pleasure."

"With that it is time for a parting drink. Well done people. We are back in control now."

After the group left, Madame and Maria joined the men in the library.

"Absolutely great meeting, son," Madame said.

"I agree, son. You had them all move through the agenda so smoothly that all of them believes they have orchestrated the meeting and they are energized," added Cap. They believe we know what is really happening and that we are the ones in control. Well done! Now we need to keep our intelligence gathering as a high priority."

"Right Dad, which reminds me. We have a covert operator inside the US intelligence world who has been feeding us information on Ali Ki."

"Excellent, how do we contact him?"

"I'm the only one who can contact him—and it is in an indirect manner. He gets back to me almost immediately and contacts me if there is something that he believes we need to know."

"I am a little concerned with him making the decision as to whether we need to know or not."

"He has a long list of things we want to know about. Mom knows it."

"That's my family."

Cairo, Egypt

"Congratulations Abdul. I am very proud of you. This is a great honor for an honest politician to win this political office."

"Thank you, sir. Without your help, this would never have happened. I am so thankful that you have supported me and the people of Cairo who have been oppressed by too many for too long." Abdul Moqued passed the phone to his campaign manager. "Hello sir."

"Cha, you know what to do. Let them celebrate tonight. Get started immediately on rounding up those who were on the payroll."

"Yes sir!"

October 26, 2001
Actsof
Harvey Simpson's Office

Harvey, Damian, Shelly, and Pat went over the entire procedure for installing their software in VJ's systems.

"Shelly has been talking to VJ's chief accountant and he is well aware of the problems," said Damian. "The fact that no one system is compatible with any other in VJ's corporation has been driving him crazy. He has pleaded with VJ to do what we are doing."

"Even so, every layer below is going to rebel. I've seen it often."

"That's why I recommend establishing an entire shadow system including the link through the network," put in Shelly.

"The more we talk about it, the more I believe you, Shelly. My concern is will Tilghman go along with that?"

"When he sees the numbers, he'll agree with us," said Damian.

"Yes, our numbers. I agree with your numbers, but you have to admit that it is not evident when one first looks at this scenario. I was a little surprised at the results."

"We plan to have everybody doing the shadow at the same time. This way we get everybody together for one day and show them the process for imputing the data into the shadow system."

"But that means everybody doing double work," said Harvey.

"First we train experts. Then we spread them among the local sites to work with the people there to bring up the shadow system. It will be a strain on people at first, but each day it will get a little easier."

"That reminds me of something, Damian. No way can we let those people know that what they will be doing for about three weeks is actually not going into the true shadow system but into a dummy system because they need to learn how to input and run the shadow system before we can let them actually use it."

"We agree with you, Harvey. Damian thought I was crazy when I first recommended that approach but after he did his simulations, he became the biggest proponent," said Shelly.

"Okay Shelly. I am becoming more and more of a believer all the time. This is somewhat of a radical departure from the typical way to introduce a new system."

"We've gone over this material for hours and listened to our people build up and tear down every approach. This is the best strategy," put in Pat.

"You seem very positive about this, Pat."

"Every time I think of the other approaches, I see catastrophe. This is the only one that doesn't have a point of no return because we keep all the separate systems in place."

"I like that, Pat. Now we need to sell that to Tilghman."

Once Tilghman arrived, Damian quickly explained their thinking, and the cost and time savings involved in an unconventional approach.

"We had to find a way to establish a coherent system, control cost, overcome several cultures, and still maintain a daily operation," he summed up their shadow system strategy.

"So what are the numbers?" Tilghman asked.

"The price tag is 2.1 times your quick estimate. The upfront investment is nearly three times your initial estimate."

"We don't have that type of money for the initial investment! It's too large and too soon."

"Sir, I believe my father understands that. I also believe he realizes that he'll need to supply the lion's share of the initial investment."

"Well, he's not my father, so I can't make that call. However, he explicitly asked for both you and Damian—sounds like it could be more than just paternalism. He's a very intelligent businessman and understands the cost of infrastructure. Maybe he is expecting this increase in final price and upfront investment cost."

"I believe he is," stated Shelly with a firm note in her voice.

"I would be very happy for that to happen. Right now, I need to introduce all of you to someone who has been listening in on our meeting. Are you there, sir?"

"Yes, I am," said a voice on the intercom. "This phone connection has worked well. I am glad it has been a secure line."

"Dad, is that you?"

"Yes, Shelly; I have to say that I'm impressed with what you and your colleagues have been able to put together in a very short time against a difficult problem that has plagued me for several years."

"We believe it can be done in one fourth the time that roll-outs like this typically need," said Damian.

"Young man, you don't have to keep trying to convince me. I have heard enough to know this is the best solution. Bill, the job is a go. Damian, Shelly and Pat, my people will be awaiting your arrival tomorrow. Have a safe trip."

Cairo, Egypt

"Hello my friends. It is good to see you all again. Since the last time that we have met, I have spoken to the Benefactor. He was shocked by the information that I relayed to him. He is also very upset to hear such vital information so late. I have told him that such information will never again be late," Kachen told his contacts as they sat in a restaurant on the outskirts of Cairo.

"Has the Benefactor made any threats?"

"Abdalia, the Benefactor never makes threats. He tells you how things will be and that is it. He said this will be the last time such information will be late."

"I understand, Kachen. The last time we met you were concerned about VJ's activity in Western Canada and his interactions with Dasualt. Leonard and I have been looking deeper into these items."

"What have you found Abdalia?"

"It would be best to let Leonard tell you."

"About four and a half years ago, VJ uncovered the fact that some of Dasualt's people had come across a significant find of ore deposits," Leonard began. "I do not know what type of ore but whatever it is it is rare and very expensive."

"Where is this ore deposit?"

"Maybe a hundred kilometers north of the U.S. border, in a providence called Edmonton."

"Do we know where in Edmonton?"

"No, that is the best that we know other than the fact that it is not far from some oil drilling. In fact, that was how it was first discovered. Apparently, it is very deep underground."

"When the engineer who discovered it reported to his bosses, they were not impressed because of the large amount of money needed to mine it."

"So how did VJ find out about this ore?"

"VJ has been looking for ore throughout North America. Some of his people were at the same bar as the engineers who investigated the site. After a few drinks, VJ's people got the story. The engineer was upset that his company was not interested in pursuing this ore. He was happy to talk to somebody who was looking for something like it."

"That makes sense," said Kachen. VJ's people are very good at finding mineral deposits worldwide. They know a good thing when they find it. So, what happened when VJ's people told him about this ore?"

"VJ requested proof that the ore was there and worth mining. After he obtained in-depth feedback, he now believes it is one of the largest deposits ever found of this rare ore."

"I need to interrupt," said Cha. Leonard, did you say this ore is in Edmonton, Canada?"

"Yes, why?"

"Remember the times when VJ's security people would come to the warehouse when certain packages arrived, and when these same packages where sent somewhere?"

"Yes, Cha. I remember."

"Many of those packages came from Edmonton, Canada."

"Really! Now that is very interesting."

"Yes, some packages are small but most are about two meter cubes. They are very heavy. In fact, even the small packages cannot be lifted by hand."

"Very heavy, you say," said Kachen. "As if they were full of this ore. So, where were these packages sent?"

"They have gone to five different places in Europe where VJ sends material for analysis."

"This is exceptional information, Cha and Leonard. VJ has uncovered something so big it has taken him four years to mine enough to analyze to determine if it is worth pursuing. When did these different packages from Edmonton arrive?"

"About two years ago the first small package arrived and was sent to an analysis house in Switzerland. The next package, which arrived about 18 months ago, was also small and was also sent to Switzerland. About a year ago, a large package was sent to France. Since then both a small and large package arrived together. That started about nine months ago. The last one was two months ago."

"Where were these packages sent that came in together?"

"Three different pairs were sent to the three other analysis sites in Europe. I have it all written for you on these invoice copies."

"Thank you, Cha."

"This seems to be very important to you, Kachen."

"I don't even know how important, but I do know that the Benefactor believes it is important."

"The security people were there for about 15 packages. I have them all written down," Cha said, handing a booklet to Kachen.

"I see they have come from many places in Africa, the Mideast, China and Southeast Asia. Several have gone to Paris. I'll need to check these destinations."

As the group dispersed, Kachen made a call to Max.

NYC FBI Headquarters
Bob Hollis' Office

"Bob, any news on the North Jersey search?"

"No, Cory, in fact I just heard from Fred about a half hour ago. They have put together some signatures that they will be running to see if they get meaningful results."

The ringing phone interrupted Bob's meeting with Cory and John.

After a short conversation with Walter, Bob hung up. "It sounds as if the Colombians are going to make a move on one of the warehouses the Power Group is using to temporarily store their heroin."

"The flame's been turned up! Where and when is this supposed to happen?" asked John.

"In the Northern part of Manhattan—it is scheduled for tonight. Captain Johnson is already mobilizing squads. Since we don't know the particular warehouse, Johnson is placing squads at strategic locations throughout the warehouse district. We need to do the same. Our contact is Lt. Bonomo. Set up four four-man teams. Connect with Bonomo and place a team with each of the NYPD squads. I'll stand by here."

"Do we have any idea what the Colombians have planned?"

"Nothing yet, John. Captain Johnson has a big push on to get more information on the Colombians' plan and its execution."

"We're on our way, boss." He and John left just as Captain Johnson phoned in to confirm the plans.

"Things are set for 8 p.m. tonight," Johnson told him. "They want to take the place hostage to get the Power Group's attention."

"What are your plans? Do you let the Colombians acquire a hostage situation and wait to see how the Power Group responds or do you foil the Colombians from taking control of the warehouse?" asked Bob.

"We'll let them start their attack and then shut it down immediately. We can't afford a wild shoot-out."

Newark Airport

"I believe that we have everything, Harvey."

"Yes, I agree, Damian. Your flight leaves in an hour. All the hardware you and Pat requested is scheduled to go on a transport flight tonight and will be picked up by VJ's men at the Cairo Airport storage facility. Then the equipment will be taken to VJ's operation center, which houses all of the accounting activity for VJ's Headquarters. They already have a room to setup the equipment and link you into their Cairo network."

"Hopefully there will be no hiccups and we will be able to start running some of the test pieces that you have planned."

"This is our biggest operation. I know we are ready for it. Good luck and stay in touch."

Somewhere in Northwest Manhattan

"You know Bob," John told his boss as they spoke on the phone, "once we identify this group as Colombians, this becomes a counterterrorist activity and no longer an NYPD operation."

"I am well aware, John. Remember, we have a very nice cooperative arrangement with NYPD. I don't want a turf war causing any rumbles. My question to you is, do you believe that what Bonomo has set up will result in a successful operation or not?"

"He's been very cooperative."

"That's what I was hoping to hear. Are the squads in the original four strategic locations?"

"Actually, we are all in one location. Bonomo got an update on the actual warehouse. We believe that the Colombians have a staged plan starting around 7 p.m."

"What are your contingencies?"

"We have sharp shooters placed in all the surrounding buildings. There's a very light crew and no external dock area. The only way to drive into the warehouse is from the front."

"I find that a little odd. It doesn't sound like much of a warehouse. Then again, that might be the perfect place to store the heroin. What about electronic security?"

"Once again, there's very little that we can identify. We have been doing various scans with IR and with typical security frequencies and there is hardly any in place except for a few in the back and two of them in the front."

"Have we been able to determine who owns the building?"

"According to NYPD, it is owned by a local grocery store. They use it for shipments that come from out of state."

"Ordinarily that would sound very suspicious. However, this Power Group is not ordinary; it just maybe a perfect setup for them."

"Bob, there's some activity. It's a small van from the grocery store. The warehouse doors are opening, and the van has gone inside."

15 minutes later

"Hello Bob. The van just left the warehouse. Bonomo has someone following them."

"Anything else going on?"

"It looks like the warehouse is closing down for the night. We've done some IR scans. There are no guards in place."

"This does not sound like a storage place for heroin," said Bob. "It sounds more and more like nothing of high importance is in the building. However, the Power Group may have gone a long way to make it look like that."

John met a few minutes later with Bonomo and Cory.

"I suspect that the Colombians know the warehouse is closed. That is why they can hit it at 8 p.m. There's no real traffic here—it's quiet and relatively dark. Maybe, the Colombians believe they don't require a large attack force."

"We can expect a slow influx of Colombians on both sides of the building and around the back," put in Cory. The third wave will be quick turning on the inside lights then a large van will pull into the warehouse."

"Let's let it happen and secure the assets on the outside as quietly as possible, then send our squad in."

7:10 PM

A group of four men walked down the sidewalk and headed to the back of the warehouse. About 20 minutes later another group of four came from the other direction. John, Cory, and the NYPD waited patiently until a truck pulled up in front of the warehouse. Two men got out, opened the warehouse doors, and drove the truck inside, then closed the doors behind them.

"How long do we wait?" John asked Bonomo.

"Give them at least ten minutes to secure the inside of the

warehouse. We'll then move on the outside groups and secure them before we move in from the front."

Ten minutes passed and the squads descended on the Colombians with a suddenness that startled them into a quick and quiet surrender. Lt. Bonomo gave the go-ahead and two of his men determined that the warehouse doors were not locked.

"Go!" The doors opened and the armored vehicle rushed into the warehouse with 20 heavily armed commandos pouring in behind it. The four Colombians inside surrendered immediately.

A short time later, at the Manhattan NYPD Police Station interrogations were underway.

"So far all that we have heard is some prearranged story that they were to guard one of their warehouses from some local teen gangs," one of Bonomo's detectives told him, as well as Cory and John. They've all made their one call, so I suspect there will be a deluge of lawyers to descend on us tonight. A drug interdiction squad has been looking for the heroin at the warehouse. They have not found any trace of heroin or any type of drugs."

"This is going to be a long night. As of now, I suggest that we go home, get some sleep and meet back here by 8 a.m," said John.

"I'm with you, John. See you all in the morning."

Cairo Airport
Departure area

"Wow, the airport has changed a great deal since the last time I was here. I believe this is an entire new wing," Shelly said as Andrew Hollinsworth met them and introduced himself and Rene Francois, a networking expert.

"I need your help immediately," Francois told Pat. "Can you come with me to our central location where we are establishing our entire network? We will get your baggage and get you to your lodgings later."

As Pat was whisked away, Hollinsworth helped Shelly and Damian with the bags and took them to a waiting car and on to their hotel, so new that Shelly, again, did not remember it, although she recognized the name as one her father owned.

Their suite, of course, was grander than anything Damian was used to, although Shelly took it in stride.

"Your father has more than just his business accounting upgrade planned for us," Damian said a little cynically.

"I think it is sweet."

"I bet you that your mom is here also. By the way, if your dad's house here is called an estate and that estate in France is called a chalet, I can't wait to see this place." An hour later Hollinsworth returned and drove them to VJ's estate where lunch was being prepared.

"Is anybody else at the estate?" Damian asked.

"I don't know, sir."

"Will you be dining with us at the estate tonight, Andrew?"

"Not tonight, sir."

The gates of the estate were at least ten feet tall and connected to high walls, electronically wired with optical, infrared, seismic, magnetic and acoustic sensors.

As the limo approached the gates they opened and drove past lush shrubbery lining a wide driveway that meandered toward a large complex of buildings.

"I can see the attendants are waiting to escort you to the dining room," said Hollinsworth

"What is that large building behind this main building?" asked Damian.

"Those are the stables, and behind them is an arena for jumping.

"Of course. If you have a large stable, one should also have a large jumping course," Damian said.

"Damian!" Shelly chided him.

"Okay, I'll behave myself."

"Oh, it is good to see the old house again," Shelly said, leading the way into the opening vestibule with a large chandelier hovering over the tiled floor and illuminating the walls. Murals on each of the walls depicted scenes of ancient Egypt. The vestibule opened up to an atrium that rose to the large skylight in the roof. To the right, a curved staircase led to the second level, indoor veranda. To the left, another staircase led to a large sitting room. Ahead, a hallway lined with pictures and paintings showed Shelly and Louane at different ages.

"Oh, I haven't thought about these portraits in a long time. It is so good to see them again," exclaimed Shelly.

"I see someone mounted on a jumping horse. Is that you, Shelly?"

"No, that is Louane. She loved competing in the jumping contests."

"It looks like these are all pictures and portraits of just you and your sister. There are no pictures of your mom or dad."

"Dad's portraits, along with his uncles, aunts and parents are in the blue sitting room. Mom's portraits with her uncles, aunts, and parents are in the rose-colored sitting room."

"Oh yes, that would make sense," Damian's sarcasm got the better of him again

"Damian!"

"Sorry."

At the end of the hallway another atrium with a set of stairways rose to another indoor veranda. "Oh, wow. That is impressive and actually very functional."

"I am glad you appreciate that, Damian."

"Where do these double doors lead?" Shelly opened the doors, Damian walked into the dining room.

"Good to see you both have arrived," VJ said, coming to hug his daughter and shake hands with Damian. "Please sit down," he said, indicating the 20-foot long table with high backed chairs that had the softest cushions that Damian had ever sat in.

"It is good to see you, Damian, and how are you, daughter."

"I am doing very well, Daddy. It is good to see you and the house again. Damian was admiring the portraits in the main hallway."

"I am glad to hear that. Ah, here is your mother," VJ said as Margo entered the dining room.

"Mom, it is so good to see you. I didn't know you were going to be here. Are you staying long?" asked Shelly, giving her mom a big hug.

"At least a couple of weeks."

"Wonderful. I hope we can spend some time together."

"So do I. How are you Damian?"

"I am doing very well, and I am enjoying this beautiful house."

"This house and estate have been in VJ's family for three generations."

"Something else that is impressive."

"How are you finding the climate here Damian?"

"So far it is on the dry side for me. Is this typical?"

"Yes, it is. If you go west from here, you will find the desert, so you need to know where the watering holes are located to cross it."

"From what I can remember from my history lessons about Egypt is that the population is basically centered along the Nile."

"Absolutely, Damian. It has been like that for thousands of years and most likely for a long time to come. You will also find the population density is high along the Nile. Everywhere else it is a very low density. All of our enterprise is located along the Nile."

"Ah, so the networking is also along the Nile. Hopefully whatever fiber that has been layed is also along the Nile."

"That is right, Damian," answered VJ.

"I hope you two are done talking business at the dining table."

"Yes, dear."

"After dinner, maybe we can go to the stables."

"I would love that. In fact, I would like to saddle up and go for a ride in the back forty," exclaimed Shelly.

"What is the back forty?"

"It is what Louane and I called the land across the creek that runs through the estate. There are many trails for horseback riding."

"Sounds good to me."

"I was hoping you would say that, Damian," said Margo. "I know Shelly would love to go riding but I didn't know if you would. So, let us enjoy our meal."

Manhattan NYPD Police Station

"The two outside groups have been holding to their original story of being sent to protect the building from some local teen gangs," Bonono told Cory and John at the briefing the next day. "The four from the inside have not said a word. Their lawyers are talking with the people both from the outside and the four men who were inside the warehouse. Everyone has been fingerprinted. Not a single one of them has ever been in Manhattan before."

"Really, not even one? So how did they get to the warehouse in the first place?"

"Somebody had to drive them there and drop them off so they could walk to the warehouse. The truck probably followed the van and waited while the two outside groups got into place."

At that moment, Bob phoned in. "Hello guys, this is Bob. What have the drug teams found inside the warehouse."

"To make a long boring story short, they found no drugs of any kind. In fact, not even minute traces of any type of drug. This warehouse has never been used for drug traffic."

"Gentlemen, I believe that we have all been used to put a finger on the Colombians—the Power Group has set this up to show the

Colombians who they are dealing with."

"I agree, Bob," put in Captain Johnson. I've gone over our initial leads. Each report indicates that the information we received was vague and passed through many people before it got to our snitches."

"I don't like being used but in this case it has opened up some positive outcomes."

"Right Bob, first of all, we do have a dozen drug pushers off the street. We also have the Colombians committing a terrorist act that puts them under Federal jurisdiction. That helps us with our case loading at the NYPD. Then the Colombians have been sent a message without a shot being fired."

"Well," said Walt. "I believe we have applied enough manpower to this situation. Job well done. John, Cory, see you on Monday. Walt and Gino, thank you for taking the lead on this."

Connecticut estate

"Well done, Max. Tell Cyn the same. This should keep the Colombians off our backs for awhile."

Cisco hung up his cell phone. "The operation came off just as we had planned it to happen. It won't be long before the FBI realize that it has been us who staged this situation."

"Your right, son. Even so, we stay out of New Jersey for now."

Chapter 7

"Please have a seat my friend and enjoy some grape vine stuffed leaves," Max told Kachen.

"Thank you, my friend, it is my pleasure to join you. I have much to tell you. VJ has been even more active than we thought."

"In what way?"

"The relationship between VJ and Dassault is more involved than we imagined. About four years ago an engineer at an oil rig in Edmonton, Canada was investigating an old rigging outside of the then current drilling sites when he discovered a rare type of ore."

"What type?"

"We don't know because at best we have secondhand information. In any case, this engineer went back to the main rigging area and told his bosses what he had found. They then sent a crew to explore the area and report back to the bosses. The engineers were employees of Dassault. After investigating, they told their bosses their findings and to obtain better proof, they needed a large amount of money. The bosses decided that it was too risky so they dropped any further action on the site."

"Were all these people you are talking about employed by Dassault?"

"I believe only the engineer who originally found the evidence was."

"So if this group did not pursue the ore find any further, how did VJ enter into this situation?"

"VJ had a group of his people looking for this ore in North

America. One day his people were at a bar with the engineer who first discovered the location. After a few drinks, VJ's people got the full story. Here, the information gets sketchy but apparently this ore is very rare and very expensive. So VJ ordered his people to get some real proof."

"Do we know how much he has invested?"

"Over the last four years he has received samples from Edmonton that were then shipped to several analysis houses. I have it all written down for you. The size, the destination, even the weight of the crates. You will recognize the locations to where VJ shipped these crates."

"Yes, Kachen, I can see that these are very reputable material analysis houses that VJ has used for years."

"My sources say that VJ believes the site has the largest deposit of this ore ever found. He knew it was too expensive to finance by himself so he was patient and for two and half years slowly mining his way closer to the main deposit. This way he could afford to get better samples with which he could show proof to a major financier."

"And that financier is Dassault?"

"Yes, my friend. Remember the last time we talked, I told you about the many art objects that were arriving and being sent from VJ's main warehouse? Here is another list of those art objects and where they have been sent. Notice the weight, although somewhat heavy is still much lighter than the Edmonton crates."

"Yes indeed, Kachen! They also have been sent to locations owned by Dassault. This information is substantial, Kachen. The Benefactor will be very happy to see what you have uncovered. I need to leave you now. A young lady will join you. Please enjoy your day my friend."

Manhattan FBI Office

"As you know, we have concluded that the Colombians paid for the hit on Puleri for the sole purpose of sending a message to the Power Group and pointing us in the direction of North Jersey," Bob told Jeff, Cory, and John. "Nothing leads us to believe otherwise since the Colombians must have paid a king's ransom for the hit on Puleri."

"Do we have any feedback from Fred's people on the location of the Power Group?"

"Nothing yet. They are still working up their signatures."

"What else do we know about the Colombians?" Jeff asked.

"We are keying off a lot of what the NYPD has told us. The Colombians have been planning an expansion into the Northeast and want to use Manhattan as a base."

"How long has the NYPD been getting this type of information?"

"According to Captain Johnson, over the last 18 months."

"Eighteen months is a long time for the Colombians."

"According to Johnson, they've stayed away from direct contact with the NYC Families. Now we hear they want a direct link to the Families. That is a big move."

"So this is encroachment on the Power Group—a bold move."

"Right, Jeff. They needed to gather some intelligence before they could make their move. This explains the long involvement time and why they decided to have us track down the Power Group for them."

"Yes, that makes a lot of sense. The Colombians needed somebody with the capability to track someone down so they bought the fact that the Power Group has a base in North Jersey but could not get any closer so they chose to bring us into the game. I have to say a very shrewd move even though it is a big risk."

"One thing bothers me," said John. "I don't think the Colombians know how powerful the Power Group is and how far they can reach. If they knew whom they were dealing with, they would not have chosen this path. The Power Group has just sent a big message to the Colombians. 'We can manipulate things and events to upset your applecart any time we want to do so.'"

Everybody sat back in their chair for a moment. Jeff was the first to speak.

"This sounds exactly like what I would believe the Power Group would do. They send the message using a broad hand but actually using very few resources to set up an adversary without firing a single shot. Yes, that is the way I would do it."

"It is almost eloquent."

"Well put, Bob. So, what does all of this mean to our ongoing investigation?"

"I believe it means that the Colombians and any other third party will think twice before they enter into Manhattan."

"Yes, I am with you on that one, Bob. So, what is our next step other than trying to find the North Jersey location?"

"I believe this actually gives us an advantage. This should stop any future activity by a third party, thus releasing valuable NYPD assets. It allows Johnson and his people to concentrate on some new information that has been circulating lately. The NYPD believe the Power Group is going to unload the largest cache of heroin in the next couple of weeks somewhere here in Manhattan."

Jeff, John and Cory were stunned at Bob's news.

"This is totally contrary to everything we know about the Power Group and how they have been operating with the NYC Families," said Cory.

"That's right. Once again, the Power Group is ahead of us and has changed their method of operation to confuse, or even worse to totally fake us out on what they are doing."

"Guys, this is a shift in strategy. We better be sure of this otherwise we could end up with egg on our faces. Let's go over this latest warehouse thing with the Colombians.

"The NYPD drug group found no traces of any type of drugs in the warehouse—not even a trace that there has *ever* been drugs there. Is this correct?"

"Yes, Jeff. The warehouse is clean. It was cleverly chosen to look like a covert operation with the proper associated links to a local grocery store in a semi-remote location, and yet it was totally clean."

"Well guys, if the Power Group can do that, do you think that maybe, just maybe, they could be setting us up with this radical change in drug delivery strategy?"

"Yes Jeff, it is a definite possibility."

"Then I suggest that we get some other means to corroborate this."

"Any suggestions?"

"You have connections with the CIA, Bob. Use them."

"I'll be on that immediately."

Cairo, Egypt
One of VJ's Restaurants
"This must have been a grueling day for the three of you," VJ said to Damian, Shelly, and Pat as a waiter brought them their drinks.

"Long, but also very revealing."

"What do you mean, Pat?"

"You have an amazing mixture of old and new network technology. Far more capable than I was originally led to believe. There is a lot of work to do but you have the assets in place. We need to provide the algorithms for the servers and the routers along with some significant security upgrades. All of this is quite doable."

"I think you have just told me some good news, Pat," said VJ.

"Yes, I have, sir. Your existing investment in the hardware and fiber cable has been well done. These will easily give you growth over the next five years."

"Good to hear. Andrew has been working with some Americans lately to improve our network system. I know that we haven't made all the connections or contacts—I'm not sure what you call them. We want ActSof to look over everything for us."

"Well Andrew, you have done a great job," said Pat.

Connecticut estate

When Red arrived, he was surprised to find Brady's daughter, Julia, saddling her horse alongside Cisco.

"Yours is waiting for you inside the stables," Cisco told him.

An hour later, Red and Cisco entered the library as Numbers was pouring his drink. Cyn burst into the library at that moment.

"All right, where is he and what is so important that we had to have this meeting?"

"It's also good to see you, Cyn. Cap will be joining us shortly," replied Cisco.

"Do you have any idea what this is about?" questioned Numbers.

"No Cyn, we don't," said Cap, entering in his wheelchair. "By the way, great job with the Colombians."

"Thank you, Cap. Max and I enjoyed setting that one up. We are still getting feedback on that maneuver. It seems every NYPD precinct is talking about it."

"What is some of the feedback?"

"First of all, the incident has been listed as a terrorist attack, and that puts the Colombians on the FBI's counterterrorist list. That gives the NYPD a little breathing room because now the FBI can put manpower on the Colombians."

"Well, that's a little bonus for us. With the FBI watching them, the Colombians will need to scale back any movement toward us."

"Absolutely, Cap. That was part of our primary objective and it cost us hardly anything."

At that moment, Max arrived.

"Hello Max. Here, I have poured you a brandy," said Cisco.

"Thank you, Cisco. Have I got a story for you people! I have just met with our good friend Kachen. His people in Cairo have noticed some unusual behavior in VJ's organization."

"You have already told us about that, Max," said Cyn impatiently.

"That was only the beginning, Cyn."

"More on those packages?" Cyn questioned.

"Yes, it starts there."

Max relayed Kachen's new information about the ore discovery in Edmonton.

"What does this have to do with VJ and his rare art objects?" Cyn asked as Max paused in his story.

"Forget the rare art objects. This is totally new. Remember, we concluded that VJ had no dealings in North America? Now we find that he has been there for four years searching for a particular ore."

"Do we know why?" asked Numbers.

"No idea. Whatever he found he started a slow excavating operation. This is where the rare art objects come into place. We thought that the packages for which VJ's security people came to the warehouse were art. It turns out that about 18 months ago, crates the size of a half meter cube started arriving from Edmonton. Then some larger crates, about two meters, started arriving. VJ sends these crates to several material analysis houses in Europe. Kachen's people say VJ thinks this is the largest deposit of this ore in the world."

The room went silent.

"I think VJ took a gamble on the ore field; he opted to keep it under wraps and use a more calculated mining operation to find the mother lode."

"I'm with you," said Brady. I remember VJ from the old days. He has a nose for finding rich mineral deposits. This time it's a big gamble he can't finance on his own, so he's taken an alternate approach."

"I agree, Brady—and he's working to convince Dassault to finance the main operation," said Max. "But Kachen's people have found even more. Those art objects that he's been shipping? Most of them have gone to places owned by Dassault."

As the discussion continued, Cisco received a text from his mother. He glanced at his phone. *Do not let up on VJ.* "This is very good news but gentlemen. We have too much invested in the Big Kill to back off from the surveillance on VJ," he said.

"You're right, Cisco," said Cyn. "I don't want us to think VJ can't also be onto the Big Kill. I don't trust him. He may even have leaked that information to Kachen's people to throw us off his trail."

"We will finish bugging his place in Versailles and find out why he has looked in North America for this rare ore, whatever it is."

"Right, Cyn. This is a major shift on VJ's part. He doesn't do anything without a plan. There has to be something big that sent him into North America. We need to understand what that was."

"Well Max, it sounds like you and Cyn have a lot of work to do. Brady has picked up on your last setup with the fake drug drop for the Colombians."

"We're staying close to the Colombians. They're upset, to say the least. Their entire strategy for the East Coast has been disrupted," said Brady. "The person who proposed this strategy and implemented it is now in disfavor; the Colombians have pulled back on their entire East Coast plan to concentrate on their own delivery systems."

"This is big news," said Cisco.

"That's right, Cisco. We believe they intended to stay below the radar of all local law enforcement and the FBI. This was a major change in philosophy for them. However, when they got caught on the fake warehouse drug deal, they realized they'd stumbled across something and someone with a lot more power and influence than they realized. They're reevaluating their future business and mode of operation here in the States."

"Does that mean they intend to leave us alone?"

"Most likely, but I wouldn't count on it. They're a serious adversary and we shouldn't turn our backs on them."

"I'm with you on that, Brady," said Cyn.

"It still bothers me that the Colombians would even think that we were in New Jersey let alone an estate in North Jersey," added Cisco.

"Yes Cisco, it's bothering us, also. My people still don't know how the Colombians got that much information on us. Someone else knew enough about us to give the Colombians that information—including about Cap."

"That is very disturbing, Brady."

"Yes, I know, Cisco. Cap and I have discussed this for several days and we don't have an answer as to who it might be. Cap is well aware that over the years there have been other family Power Groups operating in many of the places that we've do, but we can't yet point a finger at anyone of them."

"This sounds worse not better. We need to come up with some convincing theories why someone wants to put us out of business."

NYC FBI Headquarters

"Fred, I hear things are going slow with the tracking in North Jersey."

"Yes, they are, Jeff," Fred said. He was meeting with Jeff and Bob. "We are having difficulty getting the signatures we need. In the past we had very large databases to work with. These are much smaller subsets. We're splicing databases together to have a large enough set to even run the applications programs."

"This doesn't sound good at all, Fred. Have we learned anything?" asked Bob.

"Yes. We now know what we can't do. I have some calls into two other agencies, including my friend at NASA. Preliminary feedback says there are too many variables to gain convergence.

"We're working with Cory on searching the various estates in North Jersey. You'd be surprised just how many there are. Some are over a hundred acres while others are just three or four."

"Right, Fred. Cory is actually looking through the genealogy of the estates. Wendell believes the Power Group has existed through many generations."

"So, we can't tighten the loop around the Power Group's location yet. Can we discount anything that we considered before?" asked Jeff.

"A little—not much," said Fred.

"And what about tracking the movement in Europe of money, drugs and people? Any progress there, Fred?"

"I believe we'll get some good information in a week or two. The drug movement is still confusing. We think the Power Group knows we are tracking them and have purposely rerouted everything."

"Does it seem that the Power Group has pulled back from the interaction with the terrorists in the Mideast?"

"There does appear to be less interaction—there's not a great deal of activity right now by known terrorists in the Mideast. Their overall activity has been considerably reduced, and means that the likelihood the terrorists are being influenced by an outside source is very small."

"Have we assumed too much?" asked Jeff. Have we let this group steer us in the wrong direction?"

"I see your point, Jeff." Bob sat back in his chair, put his hand on his forehead and leaned back to clear his mind. "I don't think we've gone astray. I think we've gotten so close to the Power Group that they have gone to a backup mode of operation."

"Bob, are you saying that we are following an old trail that is no longer in use by the Power Group?"

"Not quite that strong, Fred. I think the Power Group has had some pressure put on them both by us and the Colombians. They've had to adjust their local operations, like the drug delivery. Because of the pressure from the Colombians and the NYPD, the Power Group could have decided to change not only their local method of operation but also their links to the heroin coming out of Asia."

"What makes you think that, Bob?"

"A couple of things, Jeff. I am trying to put myself in their shoes. First of all, I would have ways and means of obtaining vital information that can warn me of impending danger and of the lay of the land. So, when the warnings start to pile up rapidly, I would first block or deter any adversary. I would also change some of my routines and pay attention to who may be spying on me. I would think hard about how to fend off an adversary by upsetting his plans."

"Yes, Bob and by planting a false target that was too good for the Colombians to pass up."

"Yes, Jeff; I think the Power Group is feeling very good right now. They've dodged a bullet and taken out an adversary—with our help. So, if they could do that as quickly as they have, they could also change their entire drug operation in a short period of time."

"That's impressive, Bob. So, the work that my people are doing on will only tell us where the Power Group has operated, not necessarily where or how they are operating today," put in Fred.

"A definite possibility. However, we can't just stop and say no more pattern tracking. Even if that is the worst case, it will still give us more information about this group. I would like to know their money flow. Shutting any of that down would hurt them more than anything else."

A noisy restaurant in Manhattan

"Over here, Bob," Captain Johnson called out as Bob entered the restaurant.

"I can barely hear you. The noise level is louder than a jet engine. My ears are still ringing," Bob said, coming over to the table.

"Believe it or not, you will adapt to it. Past a couple of feet and our voices will be swallowed by the background noise of everybody and everything else, so nobody will know what we're saying.

"In the past month my section has handled nothing electronically. Everything has been by a direct encounter," Johnson said, jumping right into the subject of the meeting. "The result is that a lot of people are pestering my folks as to why we have become so closed mouthed. Looking at who is complaining the most has helped us narrow down where our system is leaky."

"Impressive, Walter. This can give you a real leg up on the information you receive from your sources."

"Absolutely. That item I told you about is becoming clearer. The leaky parts are reporting things differently than the non-leaky parts."

"You may have found your own truth identifier. Which of the two seems to be the more realistic?"

"Actually, they seem to be about the same—just in totally different places geographically. We're not jumping to any conclusions at this time but the timetable for each one is essentially the same."

"Is there a need for my people to set something up in any one of these neighborhoods?"

"We don't want to make any moves yet, so that we don't tip our hands."

"Right, Walter. They are cagey. Whatever we do, we need to be ready on a moment's notice—we've set up such an operation already. John is my key man. He's running different exercises with a handpicked squad. It's a costly way of doing business, however Jeff understands the strategy we are using in going after the group."

"I'm fortunate, too. My director has given me a great deal of latitude. The Colombians helped us with that fake drug drop by overplaying their hand. The director was impressed."

"What about the timeframe?"

"It hasn't changed. Something is going to happen within the next two weeks."

"I'll drink to that."

"I'll join you."

Kennedy Airport

"Can I help you with your bags, sir?"

"Yes, I am going to Cairo."

"I see your first name is Kachen. I have an uncle whose name is Kachen. Is this your first trip to Cairo?"

"Oh no, I have relatives there. We see each other several times throughout the year."

"Wow, it must be something special, these reservations were just made earlier today."

"Oh yes, it's somewhat of a blessed event."

"Oh, that's wonderful, enjoy your trip sir."

As Kachen walked off the skyhop made a call on his cell phone.

"He's traveling again. This is the second time in four days."

John Thompson smiled as he turned off his cell phone.

October 30, 2001
Cairo, Egypt
VJ's Headquarters in Cairo

"Dad, Pat needs to talk to you about your wide area networks. He's in your control room."

VJ grabbed the phone, and after a short conversation told his daughter, "Pat believes we have overdone the outside connections," and went to meet Pat.

"The services are five times what we recommended, we don't need all that service," Pat said once VJ arrived.

"I don't understand, Pat. If it is more than what you need, then it should be able to handle what you need."

"Oh, it will do that except that the service will not be available until next week at the earliest. We can have what we need right now if you can call the service provider and tell him to give us the lower capacity service now instead of us waiting for the higher capacity next week."

"Ah, I see." VJ clinched his fists. He immediately called his office, explaining the problem to the purchasing agent, then returned to his daughter to discuss the roll-out.

"We are planning on working with the seven restaurants here in Cairo in the first phase by doing a complete buildup in a shadow mode both at the sites and here in the main computer complex. By the way, the hardware, software, and LAN are top quality. Our people are already installing the hardware at the restaurants as we speak. All the equipment and the software will be operating in two days. Pat is working the operation here at your headquarters and will monitor everything from your control room."

"What is Damian doing?"

"Damian is working with your people who operate all the 36 retail businesses here in Cairo. There are five different accounting systems in these buildings alone. Our people are working on a scheme to establish the shadow system that will allow all five accounting systems to continue to operate while mirroring the updated ActSoft accounting system that will be first exercised with the restaurants."

"If you say so, daughter." VJ had had enough jargon and headed out of the office saying, "Don't forget, we're meeting your mother for lunch."

"Damian and I will be there."

Later at the restaurant, Shelly and Damian joined VJ.

"I thought mom was to be here," Shelly said.

"She is, she is just taking a call from one of her clients in our back office."

"Is everything okay with mom's business?"

"I believe so. She said it was one of her long-time clients. She'll—ah, here she is now," VJ said as Margo appeared.

"Hello Damian," Margo said, giving him a big hug. "Shelly, you look a little tired."

"I am, but I'm all right. Just trying to adjust to the time change."

Just then a call came in for VJ; he took it at the table.

"Yes, yes proceed with all haste. No, advanced notice is not necessary; in fact I prefer not to give any advanced notice. Proceed as planned." VJ hung up the phone and said, "Sorry for the interruption."

The lunch proceeded with small talk about Damian's first impressions of Cairo and the work they were doing.

"We are spending most of our time working on setting up as much as we can and getting very little time for anything else including sleep," Damian joked.

"VJ! Are you responsible for this hectic pace?"

"For once, I can say no. I wanted them to go at a slower pace but they convinced me it would be wiser to proceed quickly in the beginning to allow them to establish—how did you say that Damian?"

"We wanted to carve out a substantial piece of the overall operation that would look like a microcosm of the larger operation. This will tell us a great deal of how to populate the rest of it."

"Thank you for that, Damian. I am not sure of what you have just told me but I see Shelly agrees with you. Seeing the two of you so in sync with each other is truly wonderful."

Margo took a deep breath and looked over at VJ. "When did you decide to do all of this?"

"Actually, my dear, it was at the wedding. I was so impressed by Damian and his colleagues at ActSoft and the cigar team that I decided to go forward first with the accounting upgrade and then with the energy efficiency upgrade. In fact, I have been talking with Cosmo about starting the energy audits."

"Well my dear, you seem to have your plans firmly established. I am just so happy to have our daughter and son-in-law here with us. Damian, when will this fast pace be completed?"

"If all goes well, in three to four weeks."

Another Restaurant
Cairo, Egypt

"Hello my friends. I am becoming a regular customer at this restaurant," Kachen said as he joined his usual group of informants.

"This is too sensitive to be discussed over the open telephone lines."

"Abdalia. yes, I am only jesting with you. I knew you would not call me back unless it was very important and sensitive. I understand that if certain information is leaked, VJ and his people will know from whom and from where it came."

"Yes indeed, Kachen. This is very sensitive information—and I came across it only by accident."

"Indeed, Abdalia."

"Dassault's people have established mineral rights in the abandoned mine outside of Edmonton. Both Dassault and VJ are co-owners of the land and all mineral rights. This is very unusual as you are probably aware, this is not the normal case in Canada for a foreign entity. There has to be extenuating circumstances for such a situation to exist."

"This indeed is very sensitive information, my dear Abdalia. This means that this venture between Dassault and VJ is even larger than we first imagined."

"Kachen, this must be kept very quiet. If any rumor of this even exists, I will be in very serious trouble."

"I can assure you that the Benefactor will not want this information known by many people. Do you know how they are covering their ownership?"

"I only know pieces. The Canadian government is the cover for ownership. I do not know what part of the government is the recorded owner."

"Yes, that sounds like Dassault. Do you know what the spilt is between Dassault and VJ?"

"I am not positive but I believe that it is 50/50."

"Once again, that is significant. Dassault must really need VJ."

"I believe the 50/50 is because VJ did the initial investments and kept everything so quiet that nobody at the nearby oil operations have any idea of what has been happening at the ore site."

"What makes you believe that Haqssan?"

"Since we last talked, I have been doing some thinking about activities at the bank lately. I vaguely remember some activity about four years ago between VJ and a man with what I thought was an English accent, so I went back into the records and discovered that he was Canadian—from Edmonton. I investigated further and found that VJ has had his bank in England transfer money to the firm owned by this man. It is roughly $152 million U.S. dollars."

"I can confirm that, Kachen. Haqssan alerted me and I searched for any traces of this company. They have been well hidden in VJ's personal files. I fabricated a need to have Andrew Hollingsworth verify some large sums of money by going into VJ's personal files."

"Amazing, Leonard. That must be an exceptionally rare event."

"It is. Actually, I have gotten some accolades from Hollingsworth for tracking down the beneficiary of the $152 million money trail."

"How did that come about?"

"Apparently Hollingsworth has known about the ore but not which company VJ was using. According to Hollingsworth, the ore deposit is even richer than VJ first believed."

"My friends, this has been a very enlightening gathering. I suggest we enjoy some fine food and entertainment. I will need to return to the States as soon as I can."

NYC FBI Headquarters
"Come in, Cory. Is John on his way?"

"Yes, he was just finishing a phone call. He should be here any minute."

"Grab a seat, John," Bob said as John walked in. "I've talked with Captain Johnson. He has a feel for who in his district may be our leak. He also thinks the big heroin drop is for real and will happen within the next two weeks."

"Does he know where in Manhattan it will be? Last I heard, his two best candidates were miles apart," said John.

"True, but hopefully we can get some convergence on that soon. Speaking of convergence. Cory any luck with the genealogy and the pattern work?"

"We've run some of the estates. Some have shown the typical passing down the family tree from one generation to the next. Other patterns divide large farmland into subdivisions, still others have divided the large estates so many times that they've become small properties owned by many different families."

"So we haven't found anything that points to our Power Group."

"No; instead we have a list of over 200 estates located all over North Jersey."

"Is this a consequence of not having a large enough database?"

"That's what I keep hearing. They are really frustrated and are trying different techniques to expand the database by combining several together but their efforts have come up short."

"We may just have to let them do their job and hope they have a breakthrough. Most of this stuff amazes me in the first place. So, John, how is our special force?"

"The training is starting to come together. Coordination between the subgroups is very impressive. I've got a great deal of confidence in their ability to recognize the situation and adjust rapidly. We are exercising different scenarios and critique ourselves after each one. Our objective is to cut off any possibility of escape by the targets while keeping any mortal fire to a minimum."

"Glad to hear it, John. Cory, have you been able to participate?"

"I sure have, Bob. John has done a great job of outlining our objectives, our methods of operation, and our coordination within the group. We've had good cooperation with Lt. Bonomo, too."

"Things I like to hear. We need to do this as cleanly as possible. Any bad moves could become disastrous. Keep training, my gut tells me it will be sooner than two weeks. Much sooner.

A restaurant in Manhattan

"Bob, glad to see you have been able to meet with us tonight."

"Hello, Warren. I didn't know the cigar team also met in Manhattan."

"Once in a great while. If some of us are in Manhattan doing a job, we'll meet here."

"Are we the first to arrive?"

"Actually, you're the last to arrive. Everybody is over at the pizza house around the corner. I'm here to find you and bring you there."

"Well, now that you have found me, let's go."

"I could see you two making your way through the crowd," Roy said as they arrived. "We have our drinks set up at a table in the back. It is nice and quiet. We also put in our orders for the pizza."

"Sounds good, Roy. Are Damian and Shelly here also?"

"No, they're still in Cairo. Shelly's dad commissioned ActSof to upgrade its accounting system. They left a couple of days ago."

"Hmm, I haven't been to Cairo for a long time," said Bob.

"Well, if you were part of our energy team, you could go with us to Cairo. Shelly's dad also wants us to upgrade his facilities for energy efficiency. We're discussing our strategy tonight. Cosmo has been working on it for the last couple of days."

"Things seem to be moving very quickly. Good to see you, Cosmo," Bob said, turning to the other man. "Tell me about your plans for Cairo."

"Yes, Shelly's dad has been blowing up my phone for the last four days. He has several buildings in the Cairo area and all over Europe."

"I have some idea, Cosmo. Remember my wife is also VJ's daughter."

"Oh yes! Of course. So, you have some idea of the magnitude of the job ahead of us."

"Yes, I do. I haven't really been to most of the facilities, but I've heard about them. What is it that you're going to be doing?"

"We're going to start with the three warehouses and VJ's headquarters in Cairo. Each one stores a great variety of items so all of them are equipped with refrigeration, sorting machines, temperature-controlled rooms, and different types of shelving and lighting."

"That sounds like quite a list. Knowing VJ, he will want to upgrade everything," Bob said dryly

"Very true, and there are giant security vaults in each warehouse."

"What do you have to do with the vaults?"

"Nothing, directly. However, the vaults have power feeds and communication hookups we must make sure are not disturbed."

"Oh, I see. So in some cases, something will be in the way and could stop you from doing your work."

"Exactly, we come across this especially in Manhattan. However, the vaults here in Manhattan are well planned and located. The power lines and communication lines are well laid out and clearly marked. The ones at VJ's are not."

"That's a problem. I don't envy you."

"Enough of this talk. Let's finish the pizza and go get some cigars and libation." Roy led the way back to the tobacco house where the gang chose their cigar and brand of alcohol.

"So, Warren. Tell me more about these estates in North New Jersey," Bob said, continuing his fishing expedition when they were settled across the street.

"Early on, some families had very large farms. For generations they would divide up the land to their children. As times changed, later generations sold part or all of their land, becoming suddenly rich. Most of them left the area. Those who stayed often started other businesses.

"In the long run, fewer and fewer people farmed; even if they live on their acreage, they are in other businesses. Some families made big money locally in tech and kept their acreage, others have businesses in Manhattan and keep a private estate."

"So those who grew their businesses and lived on their inherited land could continue to hand the land to their offspring?"

"True, often the name of the owner has changed because the offspring was female, and some of the smaller estates were merged into a larger estate and called a manor. A lot of them can't even be seen from the road, because they have a large, forested property—an ideal place to gain a great deal of privacy."

October 31, 2001
Cairo, Egypt
The Backroom of a Restaurant

"Remember, no shooting unless it is absolutely necessary. We want them all alive so we can question them about their operations." Each of the Cairo police nodded in agreement and quickly entered the back door of the restaurant, rushing into the backroom where the five men were discussing business. No shots were fired and all five were arrested and taken to the nearest police station for interrogation.

"Excellent work!" VJ said as he heard the news. He hung up the phone with a big smile and continued his conversation with Damian.

"Shelly and Pat should be here any minute now," mentioned Damian.

"Good. I would like to get an assessment of how things are progressing," he responded as Shelly and Pat entered his office.

"Pat, VJ would like an update on progress," Damian told him.

"We have been very fortunate. Due to the briefings your man has given your people at the target locations, they are far ahead of where we thought they would be. This is a major labor and time saver.

"There is some needed work to be done on labeling the actual network lines. Rene and his crew are doing that as we speak. The network is sound but the documentation needs to be upgraded."

"I am all too familiar with the phase, 'documentation needs to be upgraded.' It happens on a regular basis in my businesses, I'm sad to say."

"The installment of the new hardware is on schedule and the shadow network is already being checked. By the end of the day, we should have fully exercised the shadow system."

"I am very happy to hear that. This shadow system is the one thing that has bothered me the most. I was concerned that it would cause more problems than it would do good. I really did not truly understand it."

"Most people have no idea either, Dad," said Damian. "And most don't care, as long as they can do what they have always been doing."

"This is all good news. So what risks we are facing?"

"Actually, we don't see any major risk that we haven't accounted for. The biggest was the culture of your employees and what we would have to do to train them to use the shadow system along with the existing systems."

"Good, but I thought you said that there would be something installed with the shadow system so that the employees would not have to input more information than they did in the past."

"That was our original thinking. However, when we started to look at the interfaces in the targeted locations we ran into some trouble. This is when Rene stepped in and told us that he and his crew have been preparing the employees to work with our system."

"Ah, so you don't need this other gadget."

"Not right now, but we will install it as we progress. Rene has given us all the information we need to order the devices and install the hardware. Those devices will be here in ten working days."

"So instead of losing ten working days, you can proceed now?"

"That is right, VJ. Rene has made the difference."

"Thank you, Pat. I think it's time for me to leave you all to work."

Somewhere in Brooklyn, NY

Kachen drove into a parking lot and slowly walked into the restaurant where he was to meet Max. As he opened the door to the back room, he could smell food. "Once again my friend, you have graced me with my favorite meal."

"It is good to see you," said Max. "You have gotten back to me quite quickly. This must be of major importance."

"It is my friend," Kachen replied, smiling. "My people have been very active. Dassault's people have established mineral rights in the abandoned mine outside of Edmonton." Kachen relayed all the news he had received from his people in Cairo, including the "cover" of their ownership by the Canadian government.

"The benefactor will be truly appreciative of this information, Kachen. You have done well. Please enjoy your meal and your entertainment my friend."

Max left the restaurant and immediately called Cisco.

November 1, 2001
Connecticut estate

Cap, Brady, and Cisco waited in the library for the rest of the Power Group to arrive.

"Have we heard from Max?" Red asked as he entered the room.

"Nothing yet. There's some road work that is slowing traffic today, so I'm sure that's what is delaying Max and the rest of the group."

"Yes, I left early this morning and missed most of it. I wonder what they are doing. It seems as if suddenly a group of workers showed up and started rerouting traffic onto a bunch of detours."

"You think something else is happening, not just road repair?"

"Can't say, but it just doesn't have a good feel to it."

"Brady, can you have your people check this out?"

"Already on it, Cisco. I don't remember seeing any notice of future road work," Brady said as he called to his people with directions to investigate the road repair and who had authorized it.

The door swung open and Cyn burst into the library. "Has anybody heard from Max? I'm dying to hear what Katchen has told him. It has to be something big to make Kachen return so quickly to Cairo and then get back to Max immediately."

Once again, the Library door swung open and Cisco preempted the obvious question. "Hello Numbers. Max hasn't arrived as yet."

"Actually, he pulled in right behind me. He should be walking through that door any moment."

"Good to see everybody."

"We're all anxious to hear the latest news."

"Well Cisco, VJ has been even busier than we thought. Dassault's people have established mineral rights in the abandoned mine outside of Edmonton. Both Dassault and VJ are co-owners of the land and all mineral rights."

"It's very unusual in Canada to allow a foreign entity to own the mineral rights. There has to be extenuating circumstances," said Numbers. "Do you know how they are covering their ownership?"

"That information is very sketchy at the moment. The cover is the Canadian government but we don't know what branch or office has the title to the land. We aren't sure of the type of leasing arrangements Dassault has made."

"It takes a long time to set up a lease with the Canadians yet alone have the mineral rights. Something has to have been going on for well over a year to have such an agreement."

"Once again you're right on target. All along I wondered why VJ would go to Dassault. There are other financiers he could have gone to. e needed to stay with Dassault because Dassault has other dealings with the Canadians and is in a better position to obtain the rights."

"Yes, Max. I agree with you. This is a major step for VJ to have accomplished. What is the split between VJ and Dassault?"

"50/50."

"That is even more impressive. Dassault usually gets more than 50% in his deals."

"The word is VJ provided the upfront non-recovery funding for the last four years to the tune of $152 million."

"That is the kind of talk that Dassault wants to hear."

"There's more. The ore deposit is the richest and largest deposit in the world. VJ's insight has paid off handsomely."

"Let me see if I can understand what you are telling us, Max," interjected Cap. "VJ originally sent people to North America to look for this rare ore. Then his people came across one of Dassault's people who lets VJ's people know about an abandoned mine that could possibly have this rare ore. VJ starts investing but instead of establishing a typical operation, he sets up something much slower. Probably with several exit points if the effort proves fruitless. He cleverly hides the money trail. He uses his resources to carry out his exploratory operation and his patience pays off with a large find of this rare ore. All along he had been working with Dassault, whose key role was to establish the deal with the Canadian government to have the mineral rights to this rare ore."

"That's it, Cap."

"If that is truly the case, I doubt that VJ is interested in any other venture, including our Big Kill."

"I agree with you, Cap."

"I don't trust VJ," put in Cyn. "The surveillance equipment in Versailles 80% installed in Margo's villa. We need to finish it and continue our surveillance on VJ, Margo, Shelly and Damian."

"Absolutely, Cyn. We won't let up on that priority. What is our security on them now that they are all in Cairo?"

"I can answer that, Cisco," said Max. "Kachen has set up a crew to maintain surveillance on all of them. In addition, our mole, Pat Sherman, is with them. The Actsoft people are working heavy overtime. There appears to be no special planning on any of their agendas that would involve us."

"You seem very sure of that, Max."

"With the quality of the equipment we're using and the experience of the crew, if they say nothing extra is happening, I believe them, Cisco."

"Once again, that is very good news. Red, where are we with the Big Kill?"

"We've been able to uncover some techniques that Tom Rowe used. Remember, I taught Rowe how to setup a self-destruct if someone was able to break into his coding."

"Yes, I remember that. Another reason why I am terrified of this software world," put in Cap.

"We now understand just how Rowe set that up. If we encounter that method, we'll back off and regroup with a different approach."

"Sounds good but what does it mean?"

"It means we have a far better chance of not destroying the Big Kill than we had when we started to resurrect it."

"Thank you for that plain English, Red. Numbers, what about our misdirection on our money flow, and people and drug movement?"

"Red has set up some identifying routines that tell us if someone is tracking our movements, in particular money flow. The FBI, most likely the DC group that tracks organized crime, is trying to track our money flow."

"Have they found anything?"

"Not yet, but they will. We've already changed it twice since they started tracking our piggyback movements. When they do get a convergence it will be two generations old."

"I like hearing that, Numbers."

"Thank you, Cyn. You may want to tell the group about your people and drug movements."

"We've shared the travel load across a broader base, making it look like minor local traffic."

"How did you do that, Cyn?"

"We restrict anyone from going past their own confined boundaries. Handoffs are made when a runner gets to his boundary. He hands his package to a receiver who assigns it to the next courier to move to the next boundary, reducing the number of electronic messages."

"Great, Cyn," put in Cisco. "What about the heroin movement?"

"That's been a major reroute. We prepared three other routings four years ago. If we seeing anybody snooping, we can easily change to another route."

"As long as we can stay under the radar and keep the Feds off our backs. Any updates from your sources in the NYPD?"

"They're playing this very close to the vest. The only way they communicate is person to person; our feedback is weak at this time. They've also continued their surveillance of the NYC Families' warehouses."

"Do you think that instead of looking for us that maybe they are looking for a new face on the block?"

"We have thought about that. There are other players in Manhattan but nobody rises to the top to warrant special attention."

"Could they be lulling us into a false situation? Have us think they know something when they're just trying to get someone to make a wrong move?" asked Cap.

"I don't think so. They may put up a partial blockade—make the best drop spots look too dangerous so we are forced use a less convenient drop."

"They're doing something, Cyn, and I'd like to know what before they spring their trap!"

"Do you have anything in mind, Cap?"

"Let's back up a little bit, Cyn. How are they watching the warehouses? Are they using surveillance equipment, eyes only, or a mixture? Are they being conspicuous or trying to hide?"

"They're almost right out in the open. They're using a lot of sensors and making all types of recording with video, infrared, and sound. They have rooms across the street, vans down the street, and people on rooftops."

"I need to do some thinking on this, Cyn."

"I am glad to hear that, Cap. We are only guessing what the NYPD and the FBI are planning in Manhattan."

"Having the cooperation between the NYPD and the FBI so tight is part of what is bothering me, Cyn."

"I'm with you on that, Cap, especially since the NYPD is being so secretive about their movements."

Cisco changed the subject. "Max, is there any way we can tap into VJ's Cairo headquarters?"

"What do you have in mind, Cisco?"

"This information that you have about VJ is very good. However, it is from only one source: Kachen. I'd like to have an alternate source confirm what we have gotten from him."

"Red, what about Pat Sherman? He's in Cairo. Can he put some bugs in VJ's office?"

"Yes, Max. The question would be where to put them. From the feedback I've gotten from Pat, VJ's office is almost like a vault. His phone lines are so physically secure that they can't be tapped. His office is swept electronically twice a day, so placing a recording device there would be a dead giveaway."

"What about conference rooms?"

"I can have Pat see if there's someplace we can plant a device and obtain the information in a reasonable timeframe."

"It's worth a shot, Red."

"Consider it done, Cisco!"

"Max, do we have anybody at this mine sight in Canada?"

"I'm assembling a crew that includes a geologist and a mining expert along with some intelligence people to work the local restaurants and bars. They should be in Edmonton by early tomorrow. They'll have cover stories that will get them close to anybody in that abandoned mine area."

"Sounds like a plan, Max. Cyn, when is the drop scheduled?"

"Tomorrow at noon. The area will be very busy at that time."

"Gentlemen, things are going our way. Let us make sure it continues. This meeting is closed."

The group cleared out quickly leaving Cisco, Cap and Brady in the Library who were then joined by Madame and Brady's wife.

"I have some concerns," Cap said, continuing the conversation.

"What concerns are they, dear?" asked Madame

"The FBI is too close. With their tighter ties to the NYPD, I have a bad feeling that they have found something about us and are planning to catch us in the act, and I believe it is in Manhattan."

"So, what do we do about it other than what we've been doing?" asked Cisco.

"I wish I had something specific in mind. First of all, we can't relax. Things are starting to go our way but we saw how fast the applecart can be upset. We need to increase the surveillance on VJ, especially where Dassault is concerned. Brady, you're very quiet. What have you observed?"

"I've been listening—and thinking about the FBI."

"In what way, Brady?"

"If I were they, I'd have had a brain storming session once I got even a tiny sniff that you were in North Jersey. You talk about tracking people, money flow, and drug flow. I image the FBI is doing the same thing to find your place in Jersey. The three of you have been staying here for the last couple of days. Maybe suddenly stopping the activity at your estate isn't a good idea."

"We thought about that, Carl. My sister and her friends are keeping up the activity level."

"Good to hear that, Cisco. You've already changed many of the ways you conduct business. The feedback from my people is that the Colombians have nearly totally lost track of your dealings in Manhattan. They've drawn back because the FBI has them on their watch list. All of this leads me to believe that the FBI is looking for new movement by you as well as watching the NYC Families."

"That's interesting, Brady, and deserves special attention. It would be wise for all of us to do some thinking on this matter."

NYC FBI Headquarters
Hollis' Office

"I met with the cigar team last night," Bob told Cory and John. "Damian and Shelly are in Cairo along with Pat Sherman. They're updating VJ's accounting systems starting with the locations in Cairo then throughout Europe."

"Sounds like a big operation for ActSoft. Is there anything we should know about this, Bob?"

"Not sure, John. It seems to have happened suddenly and that bothers me. Other than that, I know of nothing to be concerned about."

"Didn't VJ say he wanted to do that at Shelly's wedding?"

"Yes, Cory. He also said he wanted the energy people to upgrade all his facilities with energy efficient devices."

"I remember hearing that, also."

"The energy people are right now preparing to send a crew to Cairo."

"Once again, Bob. This is interesting but does it have anything to do with us and the Power Group?"

"Pat Sherman is with Damian and Shelly in Cairo."

"Bob, we haven't found anything that connects Sherman to the Power Group."

"Yes, I know. Even so, my gut tells me that something is stirring."

"Are you more concerned about ActSoft or the energy people?"

"I'm concerned because I know my father-in-law, and he always plans things well in advance. Yet, with seemingly very short notice, he not only has one group in Cairo but also has the second group going there. This is not like him, and that is what is bothering me."

"Do you want us to look into this, Bob?"

"No, Cory. We are too close to moving on the Power Group; we can't afford to throttle back our efforts, especially with you two. I guess I just needed to vent a little."

"Bob, did you talk to Warren about New Jersey?"

"Yes, I did, Cory." Bob explained the information Warren had relayed to him.

"With what Warren said about name changes over the years, do you think maybe that is what has happened with our Power Group? The family name has changed but the sense of the family has a direct link back to the previous owner's name and may even be called a Manor. I'll get with Janet and see what they can do with this new information," said Cory.

Bob's phone rang, and when he hung up he said, "That was Captain Johnson. Word is the drop will take place in sector 24. What's there, John?"

"It's right in the clothing district, one of the busiest areas of the city."

"That makes sense."

"Any timeframe?"

"No." Hollis leaned forward in his chair. "Which of the families have a warehouse in that district, John?"

"Each of them has more than one. We need to talk with Lt. Bonomo."

"Yes, we are going to use Plan C because of the density of the area and the busy activity level."

"I agree. Have you been able to deploy the early observers?"

"Yes, we have redeployed the warehouse observation group to sector 24. The good part about this sector is that it is actually one of the smaller ones. That is another reason why we are using Plan C."

"John and I are with you," said Cory. "With so many possible drop sites it's better to observe the whole area. Has there been any word on the method for delivering the drugs?"

"All of that has been very sketchy. However, we do believe it will all be delivered in one vehicle—with a southern license plate."

"When did you get that update?"

"Just about the same time we converged on sector 24 as the drop area. That's the consensus from the various sources."

"This is big! That gives the early observers a much better chance at identifying the possible drop sites. What about the drop time?"

"That's the real sketchy part of the information. All we know is it will be during busy hours and in daylight. Even so, we'll have the early observers watching around the clock."

"Today is Thursday. It sounds like this will happen soon—Friday, Saturday, or Sunday. To me that means Friday," said John.

"Agreed," said Bob.

"Sounds like Cory and I need to get some sleep and be ready first thing in the morning. I assume the gathering place stays the same."

"Yes—I'll leave in about a half hour. See you in the morning."

November 2, 2001
Cairo, Egypt
VJ's Headquarters

"Hello, this is VJ. Yes, you must follow through quickly with the information gathered from the five men," VJ spoke into the phone at his office. "It must be done now even though we only have partial information. If we do not charge them now, they could easily destroy the information we need. Once we have them, we can conduct a thorough search. Inform me when it is done!"

"Sir, we need you to use your phone while we tap the phone lines so we can mark the distribution lines," VJ's assistant, Rene, told him.

"Please place a call to your warehouse and talk to our man. He's waiting for your call."

As VJ placed the call, Rene left to join the crew at the switchboard, detouring to the main lobby to talk with the receptionist. As he spoke with her Pat Sherman arrived in the lobby.

"The man who was looking for you is over there," the receptionist said, pointing to the waiting area.

Pat approached the rather inconsequential-looking man. "Hello, I'm told you want to talk to me about some devices."

"Yes sir, a Mr. Red and a Mr. Max need you to call them and discuss the devices they told you about earlier."

"Do you have the devices with you?" asked Pat.

The man then pulled a small, cellophane-wrapped package from his briefcase and handed it to Pat.

"Thank you, sir. I'll contact them immediately, but first I need to check these on your scanner." Pat headed outside to the man's van, where he made a phone call to Red and Max.

"Hello, Pat. I assume you have the devices."

"Yes, sir."

"We need you to place them somewhere in VJ's headquarters."

"I think that is a bad idea, sir. He has every room in this building scanned twice a day, the same with his house. Unless these devices can beat that scanning, they will be discovered."

"Are the scans done at the same times every day?"

"Yes, sir."

"Then they can be silent during the scans and operational in between."

"Ok, I'll give your man the scan times as best I know them. He can set up the devices."

As Pat headed back into the office he ran into Rene. "Did you see the man in the lobby?"

"Yes, I did. The devices were older than we need. I checked them on his scanner, and they can't handle the data rates we'll be using."

"Too bad. He seemed like such a nice person."

Manhattan, NYC
Clothing District
7:00 am on November 2, 2001
Lt. Gino Bonomo, looking through binoculars from one of the taller

buildings in the clothing district, watched as Cory and John pulled their car into the parking garage. He was anxious to talk to both of them.

"I didn't expect you two until later but I am glad you are here early," he said when they arrived at his position. "Our sources say that members from three of the NYC families will be here to meet the shipment."

"Wow! That is really big time."

"Yes, it is, Cory, and very unusual. We don't know who the attendees from each family are. They may be lieutenants or lower."

"Hopefully the early observers can recognize them."

"We're currently providing all observers with computer data to recognize all known members of each of the three families."

"When will the traffic pick up here in the clothing district?"

It's pretty heavy right now and will continue to be through most of the morning. It slows down around 10:30, then picks up again at 11:30 when the workers start to break for lunch. It stays pretty even until 3:30 pm when it starts to slacken, then drops about 4 p.m."

"Any guess when the vehicle will arrive?"

"We have been seeing vehicles with Southern license plates all morning, but nobody from any of the families. My guess is midday."

"Part of Plan C is to run some exercises as if we had identified the vehicle," said John.

"That's what I need to talk to you and Cory about. I want to use the partner scheme we devised. Put one of your men with one of mine. They'll get a go ahead from an early observer and track the vehicle to a warehouse in their sub sector."

"Yeah, we talked about the same procedure as we drove in," said Cory.

At 10:30 a.m., John got on the radio. "Well Gino, we've reached the first break in activity."

"Yes, I see, John. Why don't you and Cory take a short break? Have your partners stand in for you."

John and Cory took their break while Gino grabbed sandwiches from the food stash the NYPD had setup.

By 11:30 a.m. activity had picked up. People and vehicles moved in and out of the district, but there was no sign of any of the NYC families until 12:23 p.m. when an early observer spotted a member of the Gambino family being driven by a chauffeur.

"Team 22, a 2001 Black Cadillac, license plates 784W615 has a member from the Gambino family. Track and note."

At 12:37 p.m., a second observer called out. "Team 53, a 2000 silver Lexus, license plates 637W852 has a member from the Bonanno family. Track and Note."

At 12:39 pm a third observer called out. "Team 44, a 2001 Lincoln Town Car, license plate 555W632 has a member from the Luchesse family. Track and note."

A few minutes passed and Bonomo made a broadcast. "All members take note. All three family members have proceeded to the Gambino Warehouse in subsector 2. All members take their assigned positions for subsector 2."

John and Cory quickly joined Bonomo.

"We have some action happening," Cory said.

"Yes we do. All we need now is to somehow identify the vehicle that is making the drop."

"Gino, I think that the family members are high up on the ladder since they have chauffeurs. This drop will have to be made soon."

"I'm with you, John."

"Let's hope that our acoustic sensors can pick up the conversation at the docks. Then we'll know to move on them."

At 12:54 p.m., an 18-foot U-Haul truck with South Carolina license plates drove up to the Gambino Warehouse docks and backed in to unload its cargo. The Gambino family rep appeared on the docks and moved to the truck. The NYPD aimed their acoustic sensors at the U-Haul and started to receive the conversation.

"Hello, how was your trip?"

"It was long. Getting here at midday means less traffic so I made good time. I expected to see my scheduler here. He should have arrived by now."

"He's inside. You can go see him now. I'll tell the workers where to put the cargo."

"Ok, thank you. I'll go and see him."

"Okay men. These first four crates go to the back storage area."

As the workers removed the four crates, three others, with Mideast markings on them were exposed.

"These next three crates go to the staging area. We need to bring two of them back out to be loaded in the two white vans in bays four and five. Each van gets one crate. The last four crates go to the front storage area."

"I think we have the delivery. I also think we may have somebody from the Power Group," said John.

"It sure sounds like it. How long do you want to wait?"

"No more waiting!" Bonomo gave the go-ahead to move. They p stormed the docks, declaring a joint NYPD and FBI operation with a warrant to search the warehouse for illegal merchandise. Each worker was detained and questioned. The second and third waves immediately entered the warehouse and headed for the staging area.

"Everybody step back from these three crates. I am Lt. Bonomo of the NYPD here on a joint operation with the FBI to search for illegal merchandise. This is a warrant allowing us to proceed."

"I can see the warrant," the Gambino man said, "but I don't understand why you think there is any illegal merchandise in the warehouse." Before Bonomo could answer, one of his people rushed up to him and whispered something in his ear. "Really, did they say why they were here?"

"An anonymous tip."

"Tell them we will brief them in about ten minutes." As the man went to inform the media, Bonomo turned to the Gambino family member and asked him to open all three crates.

"As you wish, Lieutenant."

A worker quickly opened all three crates. No drugs. The workers were ordered to take all the items out of the crates and place them on nearby tables.

"Gino, all we've got are Mideastern throw rugs. No drugs at all."

"Yes, I can see that, John," Bonomo said disgustedly.

"Are there any other crates you want us to open, Lieutenant?"

"That won't be necessary. Thank you for your cooperation," Bonomo replied as he turned and motioned for the crew to leave.

As they reached the docks they were mobbed by the media. None of the NYPD nor any of the FBI commented, though the news people continued to hound them.

Finally, one of the reporters turned to his camera and said, "There seems to have been a mix up of some kind since we were given an anonymous tip that the NYPD and the FBI in a joint operation were going to make a large drug bust. Apparently, that has not happened!"

Connecticut estate

"Has the delivery been made," Cisco asked Cyn on the other end of the line.

"All deliveries have been made and all parties are celebrating."

"That is very good news. Have a cigar on me."

Cisco hung up the phone and joined the rest of the group who were watching the news reporter on the afternoon news talk about some mix up with the NYPD and the FBI at a warehouse in the clothing district of Manhattan.

The newscasters seemed to be joking among themselves.

November 3, 2001
Cairo, Egypt

"Andrew, we need to talk about political standing here in Cairo."

It was early morning and VJ was leaving his headquarters, along with Andrew Hollingsworth, Shelly, and Damian.

Suddenly a man jumped in front of the group with a pistol in his hand.

Andrew pushed VJ out of the line of fire as the man pulled the trigger. The bullet missed VJ but hit someone behind him.

Shelly fell to the ground, a bullet in her left shoulder, even as Damian tackled the man and threw him to the ground as VJ's bodyguards wrestled the gun from the man. A police officer, seeing the incident quickly took control. Damian turned and saw Shelly.

"No!" he cried as he ran to her.

"It hurts, but I don't think it's that bad," she said, trying to reassure her husband.

"What happened Shelly?"

VJ joined them and reached out to his daughter. "How bad is it?" he asked.

"I'll be okay," she said again.

VJ gently hugged his daughter as tears ran down his cheeks. "This should never have happened to you, my daughter."

More police arrived and started to cordon off the area, surrounded the small family trio on the ground. A siren sounded, and an ambulance pulled up. The paramedics had made their way to Shelly, gently lifted her onto a stretcher. Damian hopped in the ambulance with her as it headed for the hospital.

VJ turned to Andrew. "Find out who he is and where he comes from."

"I am on it sir!"

I'll talk to the police, VJ said, turning toward them. He pulled aside the officer in charge and had what was obviously a very one-sided conversation. Then turned, summoned a limo, and headed to the hospital.

About the Author

doc mike holds a PhD in physical sciences and engineering. His technical career spans over more than forty years mostly designing and building electromagnetic sensor systems for the Department of Defense. He has been very fortunate to work with some of the great minds in the world. Often, mistakes could not be tolerated. As such, logic and discipline guided his career. However, deep within, he always wanted to write a novel...so one day he began to write. Life got in the way, and he set the novel aside for 15 years. Then he sat down again and wrote, and wrote, and wrote. His first book, *Terrorists and Global Manipulation* is the result. It has only taken him three years to complete the sequel, *Fallout,* and hopes to finish the third book in the series in record time.

One of his great loves in life is the automobile. As a youngster, he knew every make and model of the cars at the time. He studied how each was built and what made them perform. This was his early introduction to technology, which has been guiding his interest ever since.

Living in Pennsylvania, he grew up playing football, basketball and baseball. He and his wife live in Maryland, near their adult children, where he is still a major fan of sports today especially football.